Let Me Go Mad in My Own

Also By Elaine Feeney

Poetry
Where's Katie
The Radio Was Gospel
Rise
All the Good Things You Deserve

Fiction
As You Were
How to Build a Boat

Let Me Go Mad in My Own Way

ELAINE FEENEY

Harvill
Secker

1 3 5 7 9 10 8 6 4 2

Harvill Secker, an imprint of Vintage, is part of the
Penguin Random House group of companies

Vintage, Penguin Random House UK, One Embassy Gardens,
8 Viaduct Gardens, London SW11 7BW

penguin.co.uk/vintage
global.penguinrandomhouse.com

Penguin
Random House
UK

First published in Great Britain by Harvill Secker in 2025

Typeset in 13.5/16pt Garamond MT Std by Jouve (UK), Milton Keynes
Printed and bound in Great Britain by Clays Ltd, Elcograf S.p.A.

The authorised representative in the EEA is Penguin Random House Ireland,
Morrison Chambers, 32 Nassau Street, Dublin DO2 YH68

A CIP catalogue record for this book is available from the British Library

HB ISBN 9781787303478
TPB ISBN 9781787303485

Penguin Random House is committed to a sustainable future
for our business, our readers and our planet. This book is made
from Forest Stewardship Council® certified paper.

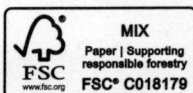

FSC

MIX
Paper | Supporting
responsible forestry
FSC® C018179

For Ray

This can be said about shame: those who experience it feel that anything can happen to them, that the shame will never cease and that it will only be followed by more shame.

Annie Ernaux, *Shame*

Prologue

Tom Morton's sister, Sarah, kept in touch with me in the years after he and I parted company. She called me up on a bright yellow day in late summer, a day that turned cold in the early evening – the kind of day that made me think, reassuringly, of an autumn routine.

'Tom is moving to the West of Ireland.'

I was silent for some time. I could hear sharp rasping noises on her end of the line. 'Are you filing your nails?' I said eventually.

'Just the cat, Claire.'

'Thanks,' I said. 'You know, for the heads-up.'

'You're welcome,' she replied. 'I knew you'd like to know. He's moving into some woman's house – a house-sit I think . . .'

It is likely I mumbled something.

'It's a couple of miles outside of Athenry.'

I imagined a long bungalow – white pebble-dash, green shrubbery and perhaps there was a concrete water feature in the middle of an overgrown lawn. Heather bushes. A small shed. An apple tree or two. Unforgiving leylandii. I imagined the kind of woman who would lend Tom her home to help him write because there were always women encouraging Tom. I assumed she was bright, and perhaps she was scrawny with a thigh gap, smart shoes, minimal jewellery – and before sleep, I wondered, *did he fuck her or just pretend to want to?*

'Claire?'

'Yes?'

'Are you still there?'

'Yes.'

'I want to say that I really do miss you,' she said and it was so out of the blue. Dodododo. I do. I do. The cat was quiet then for some time and now autumn felt somehow far more uncertain.

'And for what it's worth – I'm so very sorry things were bad at the end, Claire. It should never have just ended . . . I mean you were just so,' she paused, 'just so, you know – after your mother passed away.'

She had never mentioned my mother's death to me, not even in the hazy weeks after.

'So . . .?'

'. . . Erratic,' she said.

'Right,' I said.

'Also angry. Yes, angry. I think you were afraid though. Were you afraid? Grief can do that.' Sarah said this all so quickly and then she laughed nervously and it reminded me of Tom's laugh. 'I sensed after you came back to London after your mother, you know, well, you were just never the same.'

'Maybe,' I said. 'I don't know. I find it hard—'

She said that maybe I felt lost without a mother. She'd die without her mother, she said, and then apologised quickly. I said I couldn't tell exactly what had caused me to be less myself.

I considered if there was a difference between grief and fear and loss while Sarah's voice trailed off and the cat started back up clawing. Sarah returned to talking about Tom and Tom's great difficulty in finishing his latest book because it was proving hard for him to find the head space.

'I just don't think he can let it go, Claire – the book, he's like that, you know?'

'Yes,' I said, quietly. 'He is very like that – Tom – very like that, until he isn't.'

'Lately,' Sarah said, ignoring my comment, 'he is madly inspired by this wild Irish guy. Seán – is he an extreme hiker, or is Seán a sailor? I can't quite remember,' she said, and then went on to tell me that Seán once owned a bar in Brooklyn but was back in Galway and was undertaking mad sea voyages to recreate old trips. His wife had given birth to a baby and it stoked a strong desire in him to find the sea or get away and in turn find himself and what he was ultimately capable of. Suffice to say (Sarah's words) her brother was deeply in awe of this man's bravery and for this she was glad he was engaged in a project because he hadn't been himself in some time. Sarah had worried herself to death about him.

'Mental health is everywhere,' she said.

'It is,' I said, imagining it lolling around the laundry detergent aisle in Tesco. I thought about what my base capabilities might be if the respectable parameters of a university job hadn't destroyed my madder impulses. Sarah finished by letting me know that Tom *was* happy. I noted the tense. She added that Tom's move from

London to the West of Ireland had absolutely nothing to do with me and I wasn't to worry. 'I promise you, Claire, I don't even think he realises it's where you live now.'

'I've always lived here,' I said.

'Well, you haven't, *technically*, remember, you were all those years here in London with us and I think Tom saw you as London,' she said. 'You were here for the best part of a decade.'

'He did?' I said. 'I was?'

Her brother's latest obsession with the Irish, Sarah told me then, was beyond her. Although she was content, she said, with his decision to take on a project of this—

I hung up on magnitude.

Tom Morton had always refused to visit my family in Athenry, even in the wild spring of 2019 when I fell apart entirely and eventually returned home for good as they say. And so – his imminent arrival – it felt like a trespass.

I

'She's dead,' Brian said, whispering down the phone line.

'What?' I said.

'Mam . . . Mam – she just died, hello, Claire, hello, are you still there?'

I scanned the kitchen, my mouth was cotton dry but the tap seemed so far.

'Just minutes ago.'

'No,' I said, quietly. 'No, but – she can't. She was fine – just – fine.'

'I can't believe it, Claire.' My younger brother was crying and by the echo of his voice, the way it came in and out of range, I could hear that he was shaking gently like he did when he was a child. I imagined him sat inside the mahogany front door of the bungalow with its yellow glass panes and gaudy indented swirls, his broad shoulders to his ears, a head of brown hair in need of a cut.

An ice-cream van chimed out front of the flat and it revved its engine a few times. I leaned back and the cold of the kitchen wall shocked me, my T-shirt dragged up over my bra, my skin stretching as I hit the floor, hard. It was early in the year for ice creams. I wondered how people died in any peace in London and what were their funeral traditions in a city so vast and anonymous?

'I'm so sorry. I don't mean to be – I dunno, Brian. Fuck.'

'Right,' he said. We were quiet a moment. 'Why are you sorry?'

Was I apologising to my dead mother? Did dying change everything – who was she to me now? I knew she was my mother, but just then, she could have been any-one's mother – she could just as well have been a gentle thin woman on the telly, or a mother down the shops.

'I'm just – it's just, Jesus—'

'Thank you,' Brian said, 'thank you.'

'What?'

'The doctor is leaving. Sorry,' and he muttered thank you again, clipped and followed by a byebyebye, as though the doctor had just installed a Sky Box. 'Claire?'

'Yes?'

'They're saying they have to take her away – to embalm her, what the fuck does that mean exactly – embalm?'

'Is Conor with you?'

'Dad's here and Conor. Máire's on her way over. She was here last night.' He coughed gently and then took a sharp breath. 'Claire—'

'What?'

'She was so . . . distressed.'

'Mother?'

'Máire.'

'They were close,' I said. The flat was quiet now save for the hum of the dryer under the stairs. I couldn't remember when I'd turned it on or what I had put into it. I wished hard for Tom to walk in the door.

'Did Máire say something to you?' I asked.

'No, but, she seemed, I dunno – cross.'

'What?' I said. 'Cross with who? With you?'

'No, no, not me.'

'With who?'

'Mam,' he whispered.

'What?' I asked. 'Why?'

'Claire, she was *so* frail.'

'Máire?'

'Mam. She was so thin. Bone thin. The bones are out through her,' he said, louder. 'Were, were, are, oh fuck – Claire.'

Father's voice sounded in the hollow of the hall. My stomach lurched and I held my breath.

'You didn't see her in months, Claire. She had wasted away.'

'What's himself doing?' I said quietly.

'Muttering into his hands,' Brian said. 'Claire—'

'Yes?'

'She had stopped talking.'

'Mam always stopped talking.'

'But they're saying that she had not spoken in weeks – longer maybe.'

'What?' I said.

'I think you should come soon,' Brian said. 'Please.'

There was no bus to Athenry from the bleak airport terminal at Shannon that was swarming with American troops in faded army combat uniforms and beige sand boots. Joe collected me in his silver Skoda: Máire had insisted. He was waiting at arrivals like a tourist with his agri-business fleece zipped to his chin and he hugged me awkwardly around my neck, then ran ahead out of the terminal in a half-walk, half-skip, pulling my hard case out after him. Out we both went into the wild westerly rain, talking on about the weather and neither of us mentioning the dead except for Joe to say the odd time how terrible things were – terrible – like a global non-specific swoop of the state of the world.

Back home, I was thrown by all the waiting patiently that went on. Waiting for the remains to return to the bungalow. I missed Tom. I had grown used to him helping me through waiting, and keeping my mind off things with his little and often observations. Yet, I was also relieved he wasn't there to watch us, my family, in our own idiosyncrasies, our warm milk in cereal and leaving the shower on in the bathroom, running to the cold hall, shouting: 'I left the shower running for you.' Which also meant, I left some warmth behind. The bungalow was always so cold. The beige squared lino in the kitchen, the red brick around the stove that had blackened over the years, the draughts and winds that came whistling under doors. And then there was the constant cajoling of Father's moods and whims that are easier if not explained at all.

'There's no support in those soft shoes, Conor,' Father said as we waited for the funeral directors to bring the body back.

'Brian.'

'What?'

'I'm Brian not Conor,' Brian said, folding his arms and exaggerating his feet at opposite angles to each other.

'You're fucking flat-footed whichever wan of ye is standing in them,' he said. 'And they must fairly let in the rain.'

'I'm Brian,' Brian said again, assuredly this time and in a tone I knew would anger Father. He hadn't brought his latest boyfriend home for the funeral, things weren't good between them he told me over mugs of tea in the kitchen, the bloated teabag left in, most cups going cold and half-finished. In truth, Brian was never going to introduce Father to a man he loved.

Conor's wife, Lara, was in the living room with some classical music playing on the telly, and Conor, Brian and I waited quietly in the kitchen for her to breast-feed Josh. We stood about in the sea of our childhood objects strewn on the Formica countertops: egg-cups, Tupperware boxes, saucers, tea towels, a defunct SodaStream, the radio. Mother's small sharp knife was just lying there on the draining board. She used it for everything – peeling potatoes, cutting cheese, lemons, twine, her apron strings that time she triple-knotted them at the front.

Soon we were all staring out at the rain that fell hard on the roof of the Old House, there beyond some trees in the back yard. The roof was a rusted bright orange and its colour startled me a little. It was a thatch when I was younger. No one said a word for the time it took the baby to feed, and Brian was crying on and off. Conor seemed lost in another world. He hugged me once or twice in a strong embrace that felt uncharacteristic and mildly threatening.

Máire arrived soon after and tidied everything away, swept up the baby in her arms for a nappy change, dropped me in a white blouse, and brought soup. There was soon more talk of weather as the kitchen filled with neighbours dropping in mass cards and Máire attended to everything they needed. Someone made another pot of tea. Someone mentioned the priest was calling. Someone else said the priest was not able to call as he had to go to Galway to give the last rites on some young people whose Mitsubishi Colt had struck a telephone pole in the early hours of the morning. I googled the accident and it dwarfed the pain I was in.

Mother arrived home in the late afternoon. She was laid out in a dark coffin with brass hardware that she had – the undertakers said – chosen herself. Máire told me we could talk about it all later, but I just walked about looking into rooms of people and slipping away from places Father might be lurking in. The funeral director left the long coffin lid propped up outside the bedroom door and then he turned to me and Conor and said that our mother was a real lady, he had chatted with her and it was all exactly as she had wished. Her name embossed simply on the lid. She wanted no fuss.

Anne O'Connor. RIP.

It was hard, final, to see her name printed so boldly. No date of her birth which panicked me, why was it missing? I didn't know what day she was born on, was it a Monday, or Tuesday. Maybe she was born on a weekend. I knew nothing about the day. Had it rained? Was the sun out? Had her mother been in pain?

They placed the coffin on a single bed with a bloated eiderdown, in the room I had slept in growing up. The wallpaper's border had gnarly and unwelcoming flowers that came undone at the wall's ends and the small corners curled up like wood shavings or copybook ears. The single bed was shoved up against the east wall and there was a narrow wardrobe just inside the door with a mirror that was mock Victorian and wholly out of place, and French louvre doors on the presses that trapped a thin veil of dust.

I leaned in, hinged over her body, my chest on the hard side of the box, my heart banging. I resisted kissing her face, but I pulled the white lace a little from around her neck, and noticed the small x mark on her chin from where she had fallen once and cut it. I tapped her hands with mine and they were so cold to the touch. Her knuckles were huge and purple, one was cut and I wondered how that had happened and how they were so much larger than I remembered. She was wearing no wedding ring and her bare fingers looked longer. Her face was gaunt, fallen in under her eye sockets, and I could see her hair follicles – the individuality of each hair shocked me, where they looked pricked into her scalp. Her mouth was closed softly. In that moment, I so desperately hoped that she had had nothing left she wanted to say. Even though Brian had prepared me – her hip outlines beneath the lace looked like two minuscule bone-horns on a goat. I imagined there was no flesh underneath the yellow dress she wore, just translucent skin taut across a bone frame like it had been pulled tight on a musical instrument. She seemed slightly lopsided in the large box, shoved up against one side of it, as though it didn't fit her tiny shape, and the space left ripples of material like she was a child laying out in the sun on a shoreline waiting for the tide to lift her and take her to the sea, and into its froth where she would dissolve. The more I watched over her, and tried to pray, once or twice among the crying, the more I was full of a kind of disbelief, and then I was a lather of panic. How can you bury your own mother? It seemed so violent.

Candles were littered about the bedroom in red votives, and some had been placed close by her face. Máire kept coming in and out quietly, making Joe fix things, talk to people, she was dividing up prayers and gifts, replacing the candles before they would burn out. When she relit one, she would turn to Mother and bless herself, then rub my shoulders, or catch my hand. Often she fixed the rosary beads into my mother's hands this way and that, and I wouldn't dare do it with her. She started rosaries and would then chat halfway through. I wondered if they had left Mother's shoes on her feet, but I resisted touching them.

The curtains were closed tight as cars came in the back yard, grumbled, deadened for a few moments, and soon started up again and left the yard. Mourners came in to the small room to see her, more just dropped in bottles of whiskey, or food. Dishes belonging to the kitchens of other houses littered the Formica worktops. Father came in with a clutch of mass cards in his large hand and shoved them into her coffin underneath the cheap lace. I wondered if they would cause discomfort to her, but I resisted asking him to be gentle for I would be decades late for such a demand, and he would, like most of our conversations throughout my life, misunderstand my intention.

Eventually I went and took some air outside in the yard. I sat on Mother's windowsill, lit a cigarette and called Tom.

'How is it?' he said.

'What?' I said, irritated by his lack of focus. He took a long in-breath, and let it out, and another one. 'Are you meditating?' I said, my back heavy against the glass. I was finally smoking in front of my mother without fear of reproach.

'No, no,' he said. 'I'm not. Look, I am sure this can't be easy on you. I can't imagine— Oh sugar, Claire, I am— I'm sorry but I have to run, I'm launching Steve's book in five and they're calling me. I'll ring you later. I'm so sorry. Such bad timing.' He paused a moment and cleared his throat, politely. 'I am so very sorry for your loss, Claire.'

We talked on a little and then I lied and said I needed to go inside and make tea, as though it were busy in the house, and I was busy, and he apologised for taking my time. I watched my brothers walking around as if no one had a thing to say to one another. I thought of the Mortons' house on Sundays in London, the constant chat, the weekly updates.

My graduation photo was faded on the wall over her body. I had a head of ringlet curls waterfalling down my back under my mortar board, and everyone was looking awkward and unsure in the university setting. My eyes were closed. Brian had his arm around my back and Father was stood off to the right as though he didn't belong to us, or us to him. Mother's make-up was overdone, which was so out of character, and she was wearing the same dress she was now laid out in – lemon with navy piping, her make-up was a fawn shade, so much darker than her neck, and she didn't look at all like herself.

Late into the small ashen hours of the morning we gathered as a family in the bedroom. Conor stayed close by the door. We said the rosary and when the men slipped out to their beds, I waited on.

I looked about, opened the curtains into the dark yard, a dog barked in the distance. I went close to the photo of us all, and stared. I lifted a gold tube of lipstick from the night table by the bed. I removed the lid and twisted the stick up and out of its shell. It was a dark pink – fuchsia – but darker than I had seen Mother ever wear before and it was moulded to a sharp tip, unlike my lipsticks, which were usually rounded. It struck me how lipsticks take the shape of their owners. Like shoes. I dabbed it on her lower lip, drew it then to define her narrow top lip, staining them. A final statement, even if it was, by now, too late in the day. I leaned in and kissed her forehead.

The next morning we washed in a procession, one after the other running to the small bathroom, and we dressed in rooms alone and quietly with only the dull hum of the radio from the kitchen where Lara fussed and fixed things into the wrong presses and popped her head in and out of the bedroom where I readied myself.

'Claire?'

'Yup,' I said, scraping my hair back into a tie.

'Is there any chance you would have a word with Conor, you know, get him to say goodbye properly, before you—'

I shook my head slowly.

'Please, Claire. He'll regret it.'

'She's gone, Lara. I think it's best just to leave him be, you know, forcing it, well—'

'He's not thinking straight. He's really not accepting it. Sorry. But you know what I mean, Claire – he'll listen to you.'

'Will he?' I said. 'I doubt it.'

Mother's presence in the bungalow was making me hold back because she had held back her whole life with Conor.

'Look, Lara, I love you so please let's just leave it. Not today,' I said, and she nodded, and slipped away. I was glad when she left the room, when she stopped with her habit of pushing for some sort of resolution.

Resolutions are overrated. Lara was a city girl, and the way of family life in the countryside was different. She had given up her job as a postdoc in a Dublin university, researching the effects of ageing on grey matter in the brain, and was obsessed with feeding Conor fish oils.

2

After Mother's burial in a freakish sunshine that was followed by a violent purple hail, Brian and Conor filled in the grave with two long spades. They cast the black earth into the hole. Father watched on. Conor was stoic and threw his black necktie over one shoulder as he set to shovelling spade after spade of earth on top of her, faster now, and faster still, the inky soil spraying down on three white roses. But Mother was gone, taken out to sea like a child, the great folds of material were waves to help her escape.

Lara turned and left the graveside when the rain came down heavy, apologising to everyone that Josh needed feeding. I was relieved she had not exposed a breast in front of the simple-folk mourners. Brian was inconsolable and cramped down on his hunkers. Father grew agitated. He was flickering his eyes in his youngest son's direction, Brian paying himself no attention. It wasn't like him. Father had his hands behind his back, he was bent over slightly which I noted was a new habit and was hard to read. He came close by me and I could feel his damp body brush off me, the mist soaking into my clothes too. His clumsy leather shoes didn't fit him. I wondered if his feet had started to shrink. Mother had all but disappeared.

'Get him up, Claire,' Father said. He moved away and stood fussing under a black umbrella some cousin held above him. I considered how remarkable it was that so many people came to his aid. I did nothing, just waited and again he came by me and he poked a finger into my back: 'Claire, for God's sake get him up, he's soaked through, and does he know where he is? He isn't above in Dublin now.'

I put my hand on Brian's damp shoulders. His knuckles were raw white, all tense and clasped on his knees. He had let the shovel go by the graveside and was shaking hard. I tentatively hugged him from behind: 'Can you stand up?'

'What?' he said, sniffling and staring down into the grave.

'Himself wants you to get up,' I said, again, the rain heavy, my breath on his hot ear.

He nodded.

'Will you both get up to hell,' Father barked.

Brian stood, turned about and looked at Father with a wildness and as though he were young again and sleep-walking as he often did as a child, marching assuredly to the front door, to leave, and go. He walked out of the cemetery and on he went towards the town without looking back. I watched as his long figure disappeared. No one saw him for the rest of the day, and me, I did not – to my shame – see him for some time after.

Father looked blankly as people were coming to him, shaking his hand and pulling out of him in an aggressive kindness. Women waited behind their husband's backs, allowed the men to shake hands with Father first, and they mostly nodded silently in his direction, or muttered: Sorry. Thank you. Very sorry. Thank you. Lovely woman. The salt of the earth. Can I do anything? God is Good. God is Cruel. God is God. It'll be better when summer's long stretch comes, one man said, as though the longer the day, the less grief might be felt. There was a sureness to winter, a certainty that you could take to the bed without causing alarm. Or feeling guilt. Tom texted some heart emojis. White ones. Máire and Joe kissed me before leaving for Glackens's.

Father turned his black suit lapels inward, showing the grey foam linings, and he was now desperately looking about for a toilet.

'You won't find one here,' I whispered in his ear as I slipped my phone back in my pocket. I had texted Conor to go and look for Brian. I texted Lara to turn the car engine on. I texted Brian a white heart. Both my brothers' texts remained on Delivered. Father was turning green-pale now, as a shadow moved across his face and beads of pearl sweat bubbled on his face. It was rare to see him with such a close shave.

'Won't I?' he said back to me.

'No. Come on, let's move on. I'll get you sorted. Are you OK to walk as far as the car?' I said. 'We'll make it then to Glackens.'

'Aye,' he said, turning in the direction of the road by the grey stone wall of the cemetery. A red fox waited on a grave in the distance, and looked down on us. 'Aye,' he said again.

Lara sat in the driver's seat of their dark grey SUV with large sunglasses on her face as we approached. Josh was sleeping and strapped in the back.

'Isn't it great now all the same?' Father said as we happened on the car.

'What?'

'Women,' he said, holding his balls. 'Driving.'

In the back yard of Glackens's loos, the flagstone was damp underfoot. Father had wet himself by the time I got him perched and steady, and I apologised as other men turned and ran from the place upon seeing a woman.

'Ah well, fuck anyway,' he said.

'Don't worry about it, it's dark, the suit, and the material,' I said, 'no one will notice.'

'I'll know,' he said, holding my stare.

'Right then,' I said, 'no one will take any notice.'

'I'll notice,' he said. 'It's me who's damp. I'll know, won't I?'

I nodded.

'It's a rental.'

'What? How do you not own a black suit?' I said, saddened.

'What cause would I have for a black suit, Claire? Tell me,' he said and he spat into the gully.

'No matter. They'll dry-clean them for you,' I said. 'Are you OK? Have you pain?'

'No,' he said, more gently now, and he turned and

looked at me like he didn't know who I was for a moment and he seemed to smile at me, and then his face changed again: 'I'd better head out then because where I'm from you can't just up and leave a bar full of people after a funeral expecting a sandwich, Claire. Can you?' I shook my head and he walked back into the lounge of Glackens's where he went on and regaled the local crowd with a story about a stallion he had once broken after it had smashed its head into two of Father's ribs and finally into his nose, but he hadn't given in, and within days the horse had taken to the saddle. He was immersed in the horse and hadn't stopped to notice his own pain, or slept in days, or so he said. He told the story as though he never had a wife, or a funeral, or a family or a great looming grief.

By the late evening, the dark blue curtains were pulled across the pub windows. He turned to me and said: 'She's gone.'

'She is,' I said.

'She missed you when you were abroad in England, Claire. All the years. Missed you somewhat terrible, you know. It had such a bad effect on her. She had stopped talking to me with the loneliness.'

'You could have visited.'

'You never invited us.'

'You never asked.'

'Plenty of planes coming back, lots returned home now, you could have come home for good – she would have loved that.'

'Don't – please. There was nothing here for me,' I said, resisting the urge to tell him how it would have been impossible for her to fly with him. To board a plane, to pack, to pack correctly, to drive correctly and to predict everything so as he would not fall into a stupor of rage thinking someone or another was mocking him by simply asking to see a passport or a ticket validation, for him to be required by another person he did not trust, to validate himself.

'There's land here, isn't there?' He was playing with me now. 'They're not making any more of it – I'll bet they don't teach you that inside in the universities.'

I wanted to say that none of us wanted his land, full of rock, thistles and furze bushes. That it was a noose. I wanted to say the land was never mine. I knew well enough to know that.

'Will we buy her a drink?' I said.

'We won't,' he said. 'We won't waste money like they might do abroad in England.'

3

'Brian stayed with us last night,' Máire said, turning down the early morning news as she changed up the gears on the way to the airport.

'I guessed,' I said. 'Thanks for the lift.' I was watching the fields go by and the greenness moved faster and I thought each block or green square of field made wounded sounds like delicate whistling. A blanket-grey mist fell over the farms onto the black-wrapped silage bales that littered the countryside. So many of the bungalows had an old cottage close by, like ours, mostly for sheds, some without their roofs.

'Was he OK?' I said. 'Brian?'

She shook her head gently and then she went to say something, but stopped herself and slowed the car. She indicated to come off the road, and pulled over onto a parking verge just outside the town of Gort. She switched the engine off, and started to cry softly. I passed her tissues.

'He was soaked to the skin by the time he arrived in. Jesus, it must have been midnight. Joe stayed up with him the night,' she said, blowing her nose. Then she turned her head to me, dipped it to the side.

'Thanks,' I said. 'It's just – he hasn't returned my texts.'

'Ah, he will, he wasn't thinking straight.'

I nodded.

'Look, I have some things to tell you, Claire.'

'I'd rather you didn't. I'd rather if we just kept on going, Máire.'

'Your father asked me to.'

'No. Máire, I'm deadly serious. Whatever it is, it can wait.'

'Can it, Claire?'

'Yes. Yes, it can.'

'Right,' she said, an air of resignation.

'I'm waiting my whole fucking life. And you want to say things to me to get them off your chest?'

'It's not like that. I think it's better if we just—'

'It can wait for ever if you ask me, whatever he wants to say, all of it, any of it – you're not going to tell me anything I don't know.'

Máire folded over the damp tissue she was playing with in her fingers. We sat for some time watching trucks roll along the motorway. 'Look, Claire,' she said, trying again, 'there's some things being said, there's talk going—'

'Talk?'

'People are talking about the town. I'd rather you heard it from me.'

'People are always talking. Let them fucking talk,' I said.

She stared at me for the longest time and everything in front of me blurred in a wet canvas, greens and greys and the jolts of lorries, and then she turned right to me, coming close, and she pulled strands of hair from my face and took my hand.

'Don't be nice,' I said, 'I can't bear nice.'

'I know,' she said.

'Do you know?' I said, taking my hand back, water pooling in my tear ducts and burning. There was a large neon sign for a fuel depot a way off in the distance. 'Did you know that Lady Gregory gave Yeats bags of presents?'

'What?'

'Yes, she did, so he could have gifts to give to the locals. She helped him to socialise, helped Yeats, because she thought that these gifts would help enamour them to him because he wasn't good with people. And they were suspicious of poets.'

'Who?' Máire asked, puzzled.

'The locals. And she bought them odd things, things they would never need – stupid things like glass paperweights, and fancy shawls, pressed flowers, taxidermy, some bottles of sloe gin. But they didn't like him, they never took to him.'

'Who?' she said again and looked bewildered.

'The locals,' I repeated.

'To who?' Máire said, sounding exasperated.

'The poet.'

We sat looking out through the car window as bright sunlight broke through the grey sky. 'That was his place, in there,' I beckoned wildly about my head. My gesture could have taken in Thoor Ballylee and the whole of Coole Park. It could have been all of the West. 'Yeats and Lady Gregory. It's mad to think about it. Surely you heard of the Seances?'

Máire shook her head.

'Are you mad with me?' I said. She shook her head again. 'Sylvia Plath went there with Ted Hughes too, and I think . . . Or was it the day after. No, definitely the day before and they went into the park. That's right, the day before they went off to Bofin with Richard Murphy. They stole some apples in the orchard.'

'Fucking rebels,' Máire said, drily. Then: 'We don't all have the O'Connor brain.'

'Or their spectacular lack of emotional intelligence,' I said and I stared at Máire's round face. She hadn't changed since I could first remember her as an older girl in my primary school. Full of sense and authority, the same girlish ponytail, same small studs in her red ears like they'd just been pierced for the first time. 'I'm my whole life hoping they'd show me how to live, Máire, you know, and they didn't. But Lady Gregory, she minded him, from everyone.'

Through the car window a blooming ditch of brambles faced us and soon summer would come, unpredictable, alive. I had often yearned for it in London, to hear the birds returning, to see the great buffeting sky of the West of Ireland, the drizzle, the violet-purple hue of the grass before hay was cut. I had been so long gone that I wondered if I was astray with a mad nostalgia. The changing time always brought work to the farm growing up, seasons brought work, and I wanted a refuge from the anonymity of the city. People thinking they knew you, Irish in London.

'Why were they buying them gifts?' Máire said, with sudden interest.

'Because the locals were suspicious of them – of their intentions.'

'I'd be suspicious of anyone who had a big fancy park to roam about in writing poems. Can you blame them? Swanning around doing nothing but writing poems. Were they English?'

'Anglo-Irish,' I said.

'Same, same.'

'Well, technically it's *not* the same, Máire. It really isn't.' I hit her arm playfully.

'Well, *technically*,' Máire said, making a face. She pulled out and changed up gears as she mocked my accent: 'Listen to you gone all English-fancy on us. Ten years, I can't believe it,' she said to me, and began to cry again, dabbing her nose with the sleeve of her jumper with her free hand gripped on the steering wheel.

'I'm not fancy,' I said defensively.

'Oh, you so are,' she said. 'All shy with your emotions. That's fancy. Or maybe it's home that taught you to be shy actually,' she said with consideration.

'This place taught me nothing, Máire.'

'What?'

'Home. Here.'

'Of course it did.'

I shook my head as Tammy Wynette sang softly on the radio. 'I have a good life,' I said, sheepishly. 'Now.'

'And as you deserve,' Máire replied, unconvinced. 'Would you ever come home to live?'

27

'I'm done with this place. Done,' I said, sounding less convincing as I looked out the window. 'I know about Father. I know he's sick. Conor told me.'

'Right,' she said, 'it's just awful. I'm sorry for you all.'

I stared at her. 'I'm not.'

At the Set-Down parking in the airport, we stood out of the car and Máire passed me the handle of my suitcase and hugged me tightly.

'I'll ring you when I get to the flat,' I said.

'Right,' she said, 'right, right, do, please. Even a text will do.' And as I walked to the terminal, she shouted: 'Don't go messing with dead stuff back in London, do you hear me, any of that nonsense, seances and the like – dangerous stuff that kind of thing. Leave the dead be.'

And just for a moment the sun's rays felt hot and my face swelled with tears as some birds flew across my path.

Conor rang me relentlessly in the hours after I left. My phone buzzed as I made my way through the quiet air-port security, and it continued vibrating as I bought a ludicrously expensive perfume in the duty-free.

'Did you have a nice trip?' the cashier asked.

'Grand,' I said.

'The weather though—'

'Yes, the weather was downright nasty,' I said. I thought of Brian soaked to the skin. I turned and grabbed a shoul-der of Jameson. 'Just this also. Thanks.' Her eyes were two different colours – one was a dark forest green and the other a bright blue, and I was just about to remark on it when I stopped myself. She was, no doubt, fielding questions about her eyes for her whole life.

I opened the bottle of Jameson on the Tube somewhere between South Ealing and Hammersmith. When I eventually got out at Waterloo the South Bank was alive with all the promise of springtime. Babies were propped up in snug buggies, and there was a long queue for the London Eye.

I thought of the Christmas market last year, how I was excited in the flat that evening, understanding something of what Tom was up to. He had returned early from work and found me putting cheese into the fridge. He seemed surprised to see me.

'Hi, love,' he said, eyeing my sweatpants. 'I thought you were getting your hair done?'

I was confused. 'Is there something wrong with it?' I said.

He came close to me, and told me as he wrapped his arms around my waist: 'Your hair, like you, is perfect. I just thought you'd be – out.'

He had talked a lot about us in those weeks, about his parents, his sister, Sarah, his friends who had thrown themselves into work without due consideration of the future. There was something about him in the lead-up to that night, the tone in his voice, and his mother had dropped some hints at Sunday lunch. He was nervous when we wrapped up to go out, his hands deep in his pockets, checking a couple of times that he had everything, and rabbiting on about a project and a walk, and he might have mentioned love, and I would have laughed, yes, yes, I am quite certain I laughed.

By the river he said he was terrified of being alone in the future. I said I was terrified of the future.

'Of being alone?' he asked, his hands on my hips now.

'No, of being stuck.'

'A relationship?' he said.

I knew he was thinking of proposing, and at the same time I was filled with fear that perhaps he was considering breaking up with me. I hugged him tightly. 'I'm fine,' I said. 'Just fine.'

'You are,' he said, and we kissed by a stall selling small trinkets. A child dropped an ice cream and her mother finished a mulled wine. A party boat went by with people dancing to Stevie Wonder.

'We are fine,' I said, my hands sweating. 'Just fine as we are.'

And then I told him that marriage – well, marriage fucked up everything. I kissed him again.

I finished off the end dregs of the whiskey and wondered where Mother's wedding ring was now. It hadn't been on her finger in the coffin, her large flat band of twenty-four carat gold, so very yellow with two big claws holding the most impossibly tiny fleck of a diamond in situ like a grain of sugar. It was an unsettling thing, her ring, far too large for the delicacy of her fingers. I remembered looking at my own bulky knuckles in the blue of the market's ice lights that night. I had Father's hands. I would not wear a dainty ring well. He had infiltrated it, the proposal, Father, with his big hard hands, but I couldn't tell Tom that.

Conor rang again and I fucked my mobile into the Thames and threw the empty whiskey bottle in its wake.

4

A cat crossed in front of me as I neared the flat, the tip of its tail white and bloodied. It was dusk and the amber street lights were on. I had walked the South Bank for miles, going backwards and forwards, thinking about Tom – and about how I just went on day-to-day, how taking stock of big events, or planning them, overwhelmed me. I enjoyed my life, my teaching, but I rarely considered it, as one whole piece, a life. It was fragments of me, here and there. I began sobering up as I walked, my throat was dry and my shoulders were heavy with a dull ache from pulling my case. I was still wearing the knickers I wore to the funeral.

The flat's square window was lit.

'Hi,' I said, putting down my keys and seeing Tom sat at the small kitchenette counter. The place was spotless, bar some post on the countertop and one or two affectations of our life together – a photo of us at the Grand Canyon, and a painting of the Duomo in Florence hanging over Tom's head. He looked tired, and I remembered Florence, one of our first holidays together, and we were both so alive with ideas, about writing, and art. We said we might move there for a year or two, we were flexible in our conversation then, but soon the flat in London grew around us, in the way that a place can, and leaving it seemed suddenly out of the question. Until now. I wondered, looking about, if we had outgrown it.

'Claire,' Tom said, rising to meet me. 'I tried calling you.'

'I lost my phone,' I said.

'What?' he said, all a panic. 'Here? Or Ireland?'

'Here,' I said. 'I walked home by the South Bank, it was really wedged. Are there ever no fucking tourists?'

'Shit,' he said. 'Was it nicked?'

'No idea. There was no need to wait up,' I said.

'It's not late. You OK?' he said, softly, and checking about me. It reminded me of Mother interrogating me with her eyes after the pub when I was younger.

'Right,' I said.

His eyes had dark circles underneath, he smiled and came to me with a hug that I resisted.

'Here, here,' he said, coughing gently, 'let me get this.' He pulled the suitcase towards him and retracted the handle. He left it in the corner with a pile of newspapers and some shopping bags. My coat was stuck to me. I wanted a drink.

'You've had a long day by the looks of things, I thought you were on an early flight?'

'I was,' I said, annoyed that he was beginning the evening with the wrong questions. Friction re-entry.

'Right,' he said. 'How was it?'

'The flight?'

'The funeral.'

'Oh, yeah, right,' I said, and shrugged. He came to me

33

again, and put his arms around me. 'It must be so hard. I really am sorry about your mam.' He kissed the side of my face.

'Thanks,' I said. It felt as though we were strangers. Perhaps because I had never introduced him to home, he was, in that moment, a stranger to me. I realised I had always considered myself as an immigrant, that I was living a lie-life that was paused because some day I would have to return to face everything, whatever that looked like, and then I would grow up. Or 'adult', as Brian used to say. 'Watch us adult, Claire.' And we'd roll about laughing. Did you need to own something together to be together-together? Or do the Big Shop weekly? Or have a child? Tom had met my brothers on occasion, but never the place, the farm, my parents. We had never committed like that.

I pressed my face into his chest, looking for some of the excitement I felt in the first years. I inhaled for a long time, but nothing, not even the smell of clothes detergent or aftershave, or wool; nothing but familiarity. I inhaled again and then I cried, softly, and said, 'I'm sorry, Tom, I'm just so tired, I think I'll go up.'

'But I've made food.'

'I'm OK,' I said, 'I'm really not that hungry.' I scanned behind him, looking for clues of food, but there were no pans about the place. He must have it neatly hidden away in the microwave. There was post on the counter, some free flyers for a new takeaway and a delicate Easter card left on the countertop – a yellow chick was emerging from a pastel egg. There were a few speckled eggs beside it. I picked it up and recognised the handwriting and left it down again. I considered my own eggs, clock, time, we had never discussed it.

The card was from Tom's mother, Sharon. She loved Easter, she loved all occasions – they were a chance to show Tom and Sarah how important they were to her, how loved. And Tom was so very loved. Sharon could communicate this with a comfortable directness unlike anyone I knew. Tom seemed so different, like he had dropped from the sky.

'Sorry,' he said, fussing, 'I'll put it away. You know her – always over the top.'

'No, no,' I said, 'I think it's lovely. She's lovely, your mum.' And it was true, and she had tried hard to love me too.

Brown envelopes addressed to me were neatly fanned on the counter. I opened the one from uni, details for the French students we were hosting over the summer. I would teach English through an Irish poetry course. I read the letter like it mattered, as though it were the most important thing in the flat, I read it all blurry-eyed and concentrating hard, like I was going to take it all more seriously. Work. Life. French students learning Irish poetry in London. And then I laughed at the bizarreness of it all. 'I might just head up,' I said.

Tom nodded. 'You really sure? Maybe a drink?' But we both knew I'd had a day of that behind me.

Was he being perfunctory or was I? The place seemed strange, the light duller, it was quieter, and yes, I was likely drunk, yes, but the light definitely felt new, or something was off-kilter. If I asked outright why he never came to Ireland, would I be able for the answer? Was I the reason? Dogs barked again in the terrace alleys as shadows and glimmers from the street lamp flickered on the linoleum. I tore the envelope into tiny pieces and put it in the trash.

'No, no, shit no,' Tom said, quietly, almost under his breath. 'Sorry,' he said again, 'what am I like, it's just—'

'Just?'

'You can't recycle the little plastic window, the little – the raggedy bits of plastic get caught up in the recycling machines.'

'Do they?' I said, wryly. 'Riveting.'

'Sorry,' he said again. 'It's just a habit I've gotten into.'

'Your father owns a car fucking garage,' I said, 'you could start there.'

'I could,' he said.

Then he caught my hand and held it for a moment as though he thought twice about his next move, but proceeded nonetheless to retrieve the tiny window from the bin and stretched it out. I remember it like this. Or did I pull my hand away? Or did he pull away first? Someone flinched. Was this when we broke? Because we did break. One of us moved, as though we couldn't stand to be in the same room together. Was it friction re-entry, had grief made me forget where I was? Who I was? Had I any idea now who I was? Was this grief?

I walked a lot in the coming months. It started soon after the funeral. I had to leave the flat shortly after to replace my phone, and I was so unsettled to have connection with the world again, that I used to turn it off for hours at a time, and walk. And walk. I visited churches – all the great big ones, and all the lost little ones, and I lit candles everywhere I went, mostly for Mother, but sometimes for Conor and Brian. I enjoyed teaching the French students, they seemed to like poetry. There was something magical about poetry in summer, the freshness of the language, and it made me long for home in a way that was new and caught me off-guard. I considered a therapist again, but now in this space and in the great expanse of the city I had loved for years – I knew I didn't belong.

On many evenings of long brightness, the French students and I ended up in Philomena's pub, nearby the classes. My Leaving Cert French came back in awkward waves, usually after carafes of wine, but I liked it – new people who didn't ask about the past, or look as Tom looked, quizzical and unsure, people who did not care for me and took very little interest in me. I liked the sounds I was making, as though, speaking broken French, I became entirely a different person. I could name nouns, and gender them, and it made me feel like I owned them. As though no one would ever know my roots. I didn't have to tell them about lambs to slaughter, or the sting of Father's hand long after it left my cheek or thighs, or the tight grip he often had on my upper arm, teeth gnashing drumming home something, once again, that I had done wrong. I didn't have to explain to them that I used to wet the bed for years, and how it seemed to me that French was far too fine a language to talk of such coarseness, that as a language it could not house the awful vulgarity of my childhood, and there was a freedom in this. I wondered what the French was for sphincter and dry eye and fear and cunt. How I might express that Father was the way he was, or that Mother couldn't care for us in the way a mother should, or did on the telly. I reread Ernaux and wondered how she managed the great distance and perfection in language that I craved. I considered Sharon and the jaunty way she appeared so sure in herself, even when she wasn't – she was – with her bright red-orange lipstick. Sharon who had her hair done once a week, all a-bouffant and bodied, and she said things to me like: 'Oh, my love, you'll fade away if you don't eat,' but then to counter it, and take her own advice, she fed me, big full dinners with no fuss. She took the jibes from Tom's father, Billy, and didn't seem to notice or care. I liked the way she'd come up to Tom, and say, grabbing both sides of his face, 'I think it's younger looking you're getting, Benjamin Button, younger looking you're getting, isn't that right, Billy?' Billy would look up from the paper, the soccer results usually, readers on his nose, and say: 'You're not wrong, Sharon, you are not wrong about him.'

In the short months following the funeral, I called Father in the bungalow more often. Each time it was as though he held the phone upside down or was so nonplussed at the call that he left it on a pillow beside him. He was most often cantankerous at the minutiae of his new existence, the appointments, the help, the carers who didn't listen. He never once mentioned my mother, except something about a marble headstone that he was going to hold off on ordering. He spoke often about the will, the land, and how it was now, to be divided between the three of us if I came home to nurse him. He didn't say nurse. He said came home. I wanted to ask why the sudden change of heart but I didn't bother, because, frankly, I didn't care. Brian was rarely responding to any of us and I left him be, though Lara said Conor visited Father at weekends, and she urged me to return, that things weren't good. Máire rang often, sometimes she was with Father and put him on, and after we'd talk for hours. I'd have a glass or two of wine and we'd settle to a nice chat about things, mostly patients of Máire's that were unruly. We talked in great big stories about people we hardly knew, rarely landing on ourselves, unless it was something pressing, like a tooth filling, or hormonal imbalance.

Tom cooked and cleaned and stayed out of my way and we grew more distant. He kissed my cheek here and there, we went out with friends, never on our own, and his parents continued the habit of Sunday lunch even when I grew more and more dull at the table. He rubbed my back in bed before turning over to sleep. But sex had stopped since Mother's death. Everything about my body upset me. He cycled, long cycles now the days were bright for ever and the summer was glorious. He was in great shape, watching what he ate, cutting back on alcohol.

*

One Saturday in August I went out during the day to the going-away party for the French group, and I got the last Tube home.

Tom was waiting up, his dark outline at the square window. He came out to the street as I staggered along: 'I was worried sick, Claire. You've been out all day. Almost all night. My God, I didn't know where you had got to,' he said.

'Oh, just don't, just please fucking don't,' I said. 'I can make my own way in.'

'Can you?' he said. 'Can you actually stand?' In the kitchen he stood away from me, filled the kettle, put it on, and took something from the press – biscuits or maybe he put down some bread to toast.

I spun into a rage.

I started to shout at him in French – the few insults I knew, that I had learned in a jovial way. But I said them over and over. He smiled. And so I said them louder, and he called me childish, and then he said that I was paralysed. Incapable of growing up. That even simple things eluded me: cleaning, cooking. Looking after myself. I had changed. He calmly told me these were observations and not criticisms, because he cared, and though he loved me dearly, he did say it was unlikely to very unlikely that now he was *in* love with me.

'Fuck off, Tom,' I said.

He never once raised his tone to mine as I followed him about the kitchen, asking him to explain, saying if I was paralysed then so was he. That we were in it together.

'You told me, Claire, and you were quite clear, in the

early days, that you wanted none of it, the house, the kids, that you wanted to write and you didn't want the the, the—'

'Life my mother had? I didn't want that?'

'You didn't say it quite so succinctly,' he said.

'*Succinctly*, who the fuck uses words like succinctly?' I said.

'I do,' he said, and he sounded assured. 'I talk like that because I respect you. I knew you needed space to be yourself.'

'You love space, Tom, don't you?'

'True, but I also didn't want to crowd you.'

'You never came,' I said, crying. 'To my home, to my house. To the funeral.'

'I'm not doing this now,' he said, 'not again, we've been here before. And you're not dragging me into your murky confusion, Claire.'

'Because you can't handle it.'

'No,' he said, 'because you can't.'

He climbed the stairs to bed. Later I danced about in the flat, full of mad energy, and by bedtime, when some talk show with famous American actors was on the TV low, I cried.

He was quiet the next day when I woke up, dry-mouthed and mortified. I was afraid of what I had said and done.

'Morning,' he said softly, dressed for a cycle, when I came into the kitchen. 'You OK?'

I nodded and sat at the table. 'I'm sorry,' I said. 'I was a right sight, just I hadn't, I hadn't eaten . . .'

'Right,' he said. 'You were upset. Do you want to talk about it now? I think we really need to – or we could go for a walk in the park later, or Borough Market maybe?'

My heart was pounding. 'No one was speaking French,' I said, putting on the kettle.

'What?' he said.

'In the pub. It's a language group and I thought we would at least socialise in French.'

'I don't understand.'

'It's a joke,' I said, flatly.

Tom didn't respond for a minute. 'Your behaviour is not at all funny, Claire.'

Was I a child?

Did he see me as a child?

Fuck.

'I'll try, you know – to curtail myself,' I said.

'No,' he said, 'I don't want you to, look, I think you need to see someone – maybe a grief counsellor? It's not about curtailing yourself at all. You need to talk about it. Your behaviour is so . . .'

'So?'

'Erratic.'

This set me back into my rage and I screamed at him. 'For what it's fucking worth, Tom, you never talk about your weird family either.'

'Because they don't make me cry. Or lose it. Or go mad. Or scream in my sleep. I know your father is sick also, it can be a lot. It's a lot. What you're dealing with is huge.'

Tom wasn't angry. He was resigned, and this terrified me.

'You know what,' I said, as he poured my glass full to the brim with apple juice. 'I'm done. With us. I'm done. I can't.' The liquid was steady at the top.

'I was waiting for this,' he said, cautiously. 'For what it's worth, though I was expecting it, I really am so sorry to hear that.' And he turned the tiny green lid on the juice and put the box carefully back into the fridge, closing the door gently. He walked out the front door, unlocked his silver bike, fixed his red helmet onto his head and cycled away.

5

I left London very soon after Tom had moved out and I returned to Athenry. The change in season was special, the oranges and browns, but it brought the kind of cold that cultivated black and furry mildew on the inside of the windows, and this time Father was dying.

For months after we buried himself I rattled around the bungalow, going in and out of his bedroom, placing a cushion here, tidying away shoes and hiding anything that was his under the bed. Eventually I packed everything away into large black bags, and dropped the bags at charity shops around the city. I avoided local ones in case a neighbour or a friend would recognise a coat, or a pair of shoes, or one of his many jigsaws. I dreamed in great big feverish nightmares. In them, I gave birth to girl children and then I missed them with a huge longing when I woke. It grew unbearable. I often dreamed of Father raised on a narrow plinth, high up in the sky, like an electricity pole, or something like that, tarry and wooden, and I couldn't get to him and Mother was telling me to get him down.

After Christmas my hair started greying at the temples, wiry, coarse and unruly hair that I didn't want. Instagram encouraged it, the greying, and soon, by spring, we were all locked in, and I liked it, being shut in. Stuck in the bungalow in the bright spring of 2020, the aloneness of it. The online shopping. Scrolling. I spent days that rolled into months redecorating in the ways that I could, and bingeing Netflix. Working with my hands, painting, re-tiling, and doing things that made my body tired and ache for bed – this pleased me. I dyed my hair brown again. I grew out my fringe, bought some weights, and a desk treadmill that was a waste of time for someone with my balance. A fringe wasn't popular in the West of Ireland, that was a London thing. I wore more make-up, even alone, and I put on weight, but it felt nice, my face felt alive. I gave up drink for a year. I wrote a paper on Boucicault, and enjoyed it.

Brian visited when the restrictions lifted, and seemed back to something of his old self. Not Conor, though we kept in touch on WhatsApp. It seemed I could only ever be in favour with one brother at a time. Conor would get Lara to call me up about big things – if he needed something belonging to Father, a hammer, or a part for a lawnmower, or a charger he had left behind, an old phone card that meant something to him. Conor seemed to have things dotted around the bungalow for me to find, like a Hansel and Gretel trail that made me both laugh and cry.

I found a new job teaching at the university. Máire often called to the front garden wall, we drank wine out the back, distancing, and Joe called to the wall, and university friends broke embargos and came and stayed. I spent a lot of time with familiar objects, looking at them, packing them away, burning bits of things in the stove. Slowly, with purpose, as I unravelled in my own way.

I had still not gone over to the Old House. I had not even opened the door – I had left it shut and bolted as Father had done before he died. It sat there directly behind the bungalow, as if the new house had been spawned from it, its orange roof nestled under large oak and lilac trees that were starting to bud. My grandfather's father, Paddy, had lived and died there with his wife, Lily. They had seven sons, including my grandfather, Jack. On long days of lockdown, alone and lonely, or sorry for myself, I imagined how hard it was for Jack, to live among siblings with short pickings, to live there as the eldest – so he could never leave, not even for a few months. All of his brothers had emigrated to London except one, Thomas, who went to Boston and was never heard from again.

My father, John O'Connor, was Jack's youngest son and it was strange that Jack left the house to him, a youngest son born in the small bedroom.

Inside the Old House you happened straight into the kitchen, with an open fireplace and a settle bed. Piercing light from the small windows, a loft either side, an open fire and a blackened stone floor. All the children that passed through had slept up in the lofts, above the fireplace, which for years had covered over a strimmer, a lawnmower and a garden hoe.

I smoked joints there with Brian when we were teenagers, laid out on hessian sacks that the children had once slept under. Sometimes I hid from Father in the lofts with the stray cats hissing at me, their strong piss all about the hay. Tucked in among the scratchy bales I'd lie, and not take a breath. Once or twice I snuck boys in – but none of them liked the feeling of the place. They said it spooked them.

Jack let Father do his own thing on the farm as soon as his state pension came. They had very little when they left, Jack and my granny, Katie. They rented a small house near the town. Katie was a strong, determined woman and wanted rid of the farm at the earliest opportunity. Father always said she had too much to say. I could feel her energy in the Old House for years after she had left. The choice of paints on the wall. The small parlours with wallpaper. The curtains on the windows with great geraniums. The old outhouse had a modern Shanks Armitage toilet and sink, both of which felt out of place sat in a crumbling wooden box that served as a bathroom. I imagined her often cramped in there on cold nights after giving birth.

Father himself was there in rusty screws in small cardboard boxes, yellowed and mouldy, or glass milk bottles with black rubber teats pulled over them for feeding orphan lambs. There were odd parts of the big horse plough and some wood from an old boxcar, a hulking leather collar with horsehair of many colours still in the crevasses, a red tractor seat, and a few of his old post office uniforms. Mother was about the place in raincoats, some paint cans, her wicker sewing basket still full with tiny spools of coloured thread, needles and measuring tape. I told myself I would tackle it some day. Mother was from the city so the countryside took her breath away. Her naivety about the difficulty of it, she called it *a gift* over and over. The whole place. She was grateful every day of her life for nature, the blackberries, lambs, turf, apple orchards, it all seemed to mesmerise or blind her.

I toyed with paying a company to empty the Old House. For many months I looked out the back patio doors of the bungalow, and I was torn between restoring it and setting it on fire.

Mountain Ellen, Athenry

1920

It was an early summer's evening, just the time when the bees were humming about the elderflower, and a clutch of lavender in the side haggard made fresh scents in the small garden – but not enough to cover the smell of the cow shit in the shed, or the waft of hide coming from the pig tied by the half-door gnawing on a rope. The great oak was alive by the lilac tree and the midges swarmed low about the drains, coming in like spider-webs around the windowsills of the house, where jars with fruit preserve were filled with water and sweetness to trap wasps.

The cottage had a rye and wheat thatched roof that Paddy had laid, and the rough plaster walls of the building were a limestone and daub affair, straw and mud and some branches, and they were nicely covered with thick lime whitewash and looked cleaner than most of the other small dwellings in Mountain Ellen. Lilac flowers hung from a tree overhead the thatch, in full bloom, for it was a time to save the turf and a time to save the hay, and then to take some rest before autumn's harvest. The days to make ends meet were long and hard, ploughing by hand – or in the small field by the haggard making a great haycock with pitchforks, watching for the turn of the wind, or a sudden change in the direction of the clouds. Lily spent hours in the small garden tending the carrots and turnips, potatoes and rhubarb, and hand-weeding the sparse patch, plucking slugs from heads of cabbage. Or she was found standing at the large wooden table in the kitchen of the house, shaking fists of flour and kneading bread cakes to put into the stove and feed her family. The younger boys spent their time with sticks freeing up the shit flowing in the drains by the haggard.

Summer was all about saving for winter's harshness that would rise up in the grasses and in the lands about the homestead, and you would feel it in the land before you felt it in the skies.

The O'Connors were good tenant farmers and had then been given this small handsel of land, a slight acreage of a holding from the Estate in the Land Commission's exchange for compliance. They had, until this, been generations of shepherds. Mostly, too, they were emigrants. A compliant people who believed in God being good and work being eventually rewarded for all eternity.

Paddy and Lily, along with their sons, were plenty busy on their smallholding, but this was the first year in their lives they had two substantial animals, for good fortune had fallen on them. The older boys of the O'Connor family, Jack and Thomas, were just done saving the hay and covering it with some hessian sacks and some large rocks hanging over it from rope like bells that never rang. It would feed the cow and pig all winter. Paddy

O'Connor had been in the bog all day footing turf, and the family, feeling reassurance that was an unfamiliar feeling among them, and caused a little giddiness for they had rarely felt such hope, had taken indoors for nightfall.

'God is good,' Paddy said, but it was untrue, for despite having seven sons, the work was hard and relentless, and one son, Pat, who was lame from birth, took minding as he was sat about the place all day long, and four of the boys were still too young. Pat was particularly kind and yet needy in return.

For now, Paddy had two good strong workers, Jack and Thomas – and he relied heavily on them both.

Lily was protective of her sons. Paddy was soft in this way also, kind of spirit, and he listened to the woman, and took her lead, since she knew, he felt convinced, and rightly so, how to be in the world far better than he did. Which wasn't the way on the small road at Mountain Ellen. Lily knew men who drank too much poitín or brought trouble on their holding with loose lips. She knew some of her neighbour women were beaten often and that husbands could be demanding. But not Paddy, and for this, she was eternally grateful. That said, she was sad of her lot, and had expected a little more in the custom of gathering and storing, and less in the constant panic for foraging that had been their way for many years.

Aye, indeed, and it was true that the man who made work, made plenty of it, Paddy O'Connor would say every morning upon waking up beside his wife in the small bed with its lumpy horsehair mattress in the dark room off the kitchen, and he would empty the chamber pot first and then take down the looking glass from the fireplace in their bedroom, where he would set to shaving with a blade, and fixing his face for the world.

'Who'll see you, Paddy O'Connor?' Lily would jest. 'Is it vain for the pig abroad in the yard you are?'

'Won't you see me?' he would say to his wife.

Though it was June time, and summer, when the sun went down behind the woods in Mountain Ellen, where the great house stood and the O'Connors had never stood inside of, the cold caught the chests of the younger boys who went about after their work was done, chasing cats with long blackthorn sticks. Often causing the boys to cough and cough. It was good fortune, however, that the ground was dry, and there was a little heat to the nights.

Soon the festival season would be upon them – Lughnasa – when, if God was good, which he had been so far this year, indeed he had been great, and Lily had rewarded him with more prayers than ever said before in her life, this year 1920 and he could be very good, then maybe he would bestow further good fortune on a good harvest about the farms and neighbourhood of Mountain Ellen. There would be some carnival atmosphere, with the threshers, and songs, music and poems from spalpeens who came to work for bed and board. There would be plays put on, and some impromptu monologues, mostly they were put on by travelling actors from the islands, these were Lily's favourite. Often long roving ballads, and sometimes there were long verses from Shakespeare, but not recently, and certainly not since the arrival of the blackandtans. Lily liked how the players said out what they wished without fear of reproach from God or Crown, she admired their bravery, and that they had the brave spirit to say, without arms, what the locals could not.

The O'Connors did not need to keep farm labourers all year round, as the house would not hold them, so the strong sons worked like horses and were obedient. But nevertheless they shared, as a family, what they had for a couple of weeks each year with some visiting farmhands, labourers searching for food and board, and allowed anyone to sleep on the settle bed by the fire. They loved to hear the visiting men sing, or some of the more courageous would make comedies for the family and neighbours in the August evenings, just for entertainment. Afterwards the neighbours would talk about it for years. They loved when they did an improvisation of those from the last place they had lain at. Liked it best, when they mocked them, or gave away the gossip of the place. Who was sleeping with who, or worse, who was giving secrets to the Crown. But the O'Connors failed to realise that they likely went on to the next town making play of them. In any case, the travelling groups lifted the spirits of everyone going from house to house, and some of the more fortunate even forgot the hardships they constantly lived under. But most remembered the stories of the Great Hunger, these were sung about in great low laments of close family who left and were never heard of again, and the truth was, little had changed, and though there was no more blight on the potato crop for some time, many were still hungry. Indeed, there was often a night about the low roads, and the boreens, that many went to sleep with their tired bellies bet into their backs, and a mighty gurgle upon them. And some infants did not wake from the sleep.

But for now, the O'Connor family were all inside the small house, and relaxing a little after a long day turning turf at the bog. Lily was excited. Yes, they were neat inside the small house and the prayers were upon them, grateful for the two animals.

6

Tom arrived in Ireland in the autumn of 2022. He texted me soon after and I left him *on read* for days in a blind panic, after so long without contact. Had everything changed since the pandemic, was it acceptable to think everyone was in stasis? And then I started up on Imagined Scenarios: Walking to the shops and bumping into him / Spotting him in the smoking area of Glackens / Cycling past him on the road looking fresh and hoping the rain would stay away / Speed walking for exercise and spotting him on a mile-long stretch and waiting twenty minutes before sharing space with him. I imagined the clothes I might wear. I thought about the food I might stock the fridge with. I shopped the aisles of Tesco in my mind. I went one further, and I took myself on an imaginary trip around a farmer's market. Turnips. Beets. Potatoes. Hake. Monkfish. Steak. Wine. Organic chocolates. Home-made hummus. Scallops. Olives. Bread. Lots of bread. Big soft dough and warm bread that popped when you stuck a finger into it. Mostly, I was surprised at how I felt.

My days had been passing in a blur since we were all back on campus post-pandemic. Home, drinks. Tinder. The odd fuck. Date two. Rarely a third. Uni. Home.

Insta. Netflix. Drinks. Máire's. Joe popping in for tea and pressing me about my life choices.

Would Tom and I forgive each other? What did that mean? Should I be looking for forgiveness? Going back was never a good idea. I might dress myself in a stripy Breton T-shirt, maybe some culottes and chunky boots, a dab of matt red lipstick, just a dab like I had bitten my lip and drawn a minuscule amount of blood.

If Joe caught sight of me cycling about in any of the aforementioned outfits there was no doubt but he'd break his shit laughing and start talking to the cows about *her back from London*. So I figured maybe I'd just wear casual blue jeans and a distressed wax jacket. Notions. But most people look well in a wax jacket. Farmers from here *and* the English. But it is difficult to dress yourself for two worlds. It is more terrifying to think of all the worlds you inhabit, or once inhabited, all being in the one space for ever. I could not imagine what Tom Morton would make of Máire and Joe next door. Joe liked men who were capable of anything but thinking. Máire would be Máire – practical and polite. Tom might even like them. She might mention the price of grocery shopping. The weather. The queue for the local doctor. How everyone was doing; for tea, a sandwich, a hug, a drop of whiskey. The homeless crisis. The earth heating up. An anecdote about me as a child. Joe might talk about the price of a lamb for slaughter. A breed of a cow. Spuds in the ground. Clippings of plants. Porridge oats. Máire's palliative care stories from her work in the hospital reassured Joe there was a God and that God was good and that all suffering was manageable. If I ever tried to argue with him, Máire stood behind him waving her hands at me to stop. Joe had sensitivities.

Tom was a man with the kind of manners that got a person into every room imaginable but he could drift into long chats about himself: his projects, his writer's block, the books he was reading, the theatre he liked, Billy's car business, Sharon's lunches. Answering his text meant my worlds would all collide and I would have brought it on myself.

7

The road out to the house where Tom was staying was reached through the narrow streets of the town – grey Norman streets. I drove by the post office and on past King John's castle and the Dominican friary where Oliver Cromwell stabled his horses when it was a university. On the outskirts of the new motorway there was an enormous glass supermarket where I joined a secondary road, windy and unforgiving, that ran by a large agricultural college where they taught people how to breed cattle, pipe water and apply for EU grants. The land around here was flat, and the roads were twisted and boggy.

The satnav beeped as I turned a sharp bend. Suddenly the house was there and something about its enormity made me consider driving on past, yet I slowed, and in the sun's glare I pulled in by the side of the gable. It was not like the house I had imagined. I deadened the engine and sat waiting like a mother outside her house after a day at work, watching her noisy family through the window. There were no signs of life about the farmer's small bungalow next door except for an idle clothes line stabbed with a few pegs and a turf stack neatly covered with some red tarpaulin that stretched around the peat. Some breeze blocks were hanging from blue rope.

Tom's bike was by the gable of the house and it startled me – the severity of the slim silver frame, his red helmet hanging on a handlebar. I imagined the dogs barking behind our London apartment. Pieces of a broken cement firepit were strewn on the weedy gravel and terracotta pots housed blackened plants that were gnarly and soaked in rainwater, frost had likely taken them like it had taken my olive tree last winter. Someone had entered summer with optimism and checked out by autumn.

When Tom and I first started seeing each other I would have walked right into his apartment and stood in his kitchen and I might have poured myself a large whiskey or filled some wine into a tumbler and turned up the music. I might have taken something from the fridge – some cheese or a fistful of olives. I was always so certain in the beginning that Tom was mine, losing him had never crossed my mind. As I sat outside his house, I texted.

You home?
Y. Come in.

I considered the two full stops. I considered Tom sat inside the house watching me sitting in my car watching him and I had so wanted him to come out to me. Coax me. I walked to the front door along a neat path plonked in the middle of the overgrown garden. Built in the thirties? Some wild summer daisies were holding on but had lost their pride, and the pale yellow roses were alive, though the leaves were traced with angry blackspot. The flowers' bloom panicked me about global warming, they were lasting so well.

Everything was a little off-kilter as though someone had once loved the house. There was no doorbell and I didn't feel like knocking so I stood on the porch, my mood flipping, and I was rather sullen, as though I had been summoned. I waited, but maybe it would have been for the best – just then – to turn and leave the past in peace.

'Hi,' Tom said, smiling widely as he opened the front door. It stuck on the tiles. He had some stubble, a tanned face, and he seemed relaxed.

'Hi,' I said, hands in my back pockets.

'Hi,' he said, again staring straight at me, my eyes, then he flashed a smile and a quick glimpse at my hair: 'You look nice.'

I had braided my hair both sides. We stared at each other and forgetting how long he could hold eye contact for I blurted: 'Long time and all that, Tom Morton,' and just after saying his name I went completely blank and then I talked in mad spurts. En route to the kitchen I checked myself in the mirror by a big lump of a coat stand and prattled on about the farmer next door – his clothes line, his turf stack. I mentioned horses: hunters and then racehorses and how they bring them to the

West to graze them off-season around here, wintering them out.

'Good grass,' I said.

'Right,' he said. 'I have noticed.'

'Yes, luscious grass, small pockets of it.' I stopped myself from saying green.

'Yes, yes,' Tom said, fixing a stack of *Paris Review*s into a perfect pile on a well-worn butcher's block. 'I have wondered why it's so lush, everything west of here is a lot more –' he paused, and flicked through one of the magazines, and then looked back at me – 'barren.'

'Barren?'

'Or broken. Have you noticed – there's stones everywhere?'

I didn't know the why of that – no one looks about their own place, it's too intrusive. I knew it had something to do with limestone and the geographical make-up. But it was shameful to me, the looking back, and so I avoided it. The unpasteurised milk in a large crock on the table. The scrawny lambs. The way birds built their nests and later how they just left. I was focused on getting out for so long. 'I guess it has something to do with rocks,' I said, giving in, 'the lime maybe?'

He offered me some tea, calling out a list of fruity herbals, builder's, black and I said: 'No,' rather bluntly and then coughed to soften the ferocity of my refusal, adding: 'Thank you, Tom. I had some before I drove over here.' His name felt good in my mouth. 'This ornate flooring is unusual for the West,' I said as I tapped on it twice with my shoe.

'It is?' he said. 'How so?' and he raised an eyebrow and smiled cheekily at me.

'More usually found in churches.' I knew this had to do with money.

'Right,' he said.

'Your friend has great taste.'

'Thanks,' he said. 'She does. You still at the university?'

'Still there,' I said, nodding.

'I thought you were meant to be writing? How can you write with all that work?'

'Plans change,' I said. 'Besides, we don't all have rich friends.'

'Please don't,' he said, softly. 'She's not rich.'

'Sorry.'

'You never wanted friends,' he said, finally, and closing the door of the fridge he pulled closer to me, and squeezed my arm, the fat underside and then, he kissed my flushed cheek.

Neither of us should have been writers. First-in-the-family graduates. All that load – the pretence. Me here in this landscape – a (dead) farmer's daughter. Dead mother who had introduced herself rarely to strangers and rarely was it ever asked of her what she did. I was, since returning and not leaving, trying to piece her together about the bungalow – bits of her falling out of presses and wardrobes, the drawers of pills. Serotonin. Beta blockers. Xanax. Unopened food supplement sachets in boxes. St John's wort. But it was likely too late for any resolution.

Tom and I were both playing when we attended literary events. We used to joke about it all but I was happy teaching because it felt the least manipulative option, better than time spent lying about in a house filled with memories that caused me days in bed. Getting out teaching suppressed them. Writing multiplied them.

'So how old is it?' I said, looking up at the stippled ceilings.

'The house?'

I nodded.

'No clue.'

'Really?'

'Yes, really. Why does it matter?'

'Isn't that risky?'

'Risky?' he said, furtively.

'Yes. Don't you normally like to know the specifics of everything?'

'I do?' he said. Tom looked at me a moment and then said: 'Here, here, take a look at this,' and he leaned down and lifted a huge pot by the stove. Inside the pot sat a plant with three hefty, green leaves. He remembered its name, a long and strange name with three syllables. I considered the ease with which he recalled the names of things: wines and poets and trees, and he said again: It's a *such-and-such* plant. 'Isn't it just exquisite? It's such a Johanna thing. Don't you think?'

'How would I know what Johanna likes?'

'Oh yes, apologies. Of course, you don't know Johanna yet,' Tom said. 'I forget, sometimes.'

'Forget what?'

'All the people I've met – since.'

'Since?'

'Us.'

I spoke about the university and he said I seemed tetchy, he thought because I wasn't writing. I said I wasn't tetchy, that nothing made me more tetchy than writing and therefore I hadn't written a word since that story about the couple that got rejected from just about everywhere. It was the last story of mine he had read. The rejections were my fault, we both knew this. I had lost something around that time, caring about them – the stories, myself, him, all while the world had gone full tilt and it was difficult to care about anything. We both set to berating universities instead.

'I'm glad I'm avoiding the radical Gen Z,' he said.

'Oh, they're not that bad,' I said. 'Considering we ruined their world.'

'We have?' he laughed.

'Maybe we have?'

'Boomers,' he said, pulling a face. But we weren't boomers and the categorisation was as arbitrary as taste and as futile as thinking you could effect any change whatsoever on the world.

We were going to the sea. We might have lunch. He might go shopping at the Galway market for tea. He wanted a trout. I would advise him on the best place for fresh trout. He was having a friend for tea later, a friend of Johanna's.

'Who lived here before your friend?' I asked.

'No clue,' he said, tapping my nose with his finger. 'Why all the questions?'

'It's just, I never liked moving into a house where strangers lived before me, that's all,' I said, following him about. 'I'm intrigued.'

'I often wondered about that,' he said.

'Energies, vibes,' I said.

'*Vibes?*'

We both laughed but it was all the left-behind pain of other people in a building that suffocates me.

'It must be hard though being back in your childhood home?'

'It's OK,' I said. Sometimes it can even be reassuring.'

'Really?'

'Yeah, though sometimes it's also hard.' I avoided saying devastating, or explaining why I was trying so desperately to say sorry to a dead woman, and garner an apology from a dead man. 'You know, just going about the day, and for an instance I forget.'

'Forget?'

'Yeah. I might find a pair of my mother's tights in the back of a drawer, or a train ticket down the side of the couch and it . . . derails me.'

'Fuck,' he said on a sharp in-breath.

Johanna's house was filled with books but not in the way my house was. These were colour-coded and neatly stacked. Tokarczuk, and Berlin, Plath, Woolf, and there was Austen or did I imagine Austen? And then I spied Rilke and Waugh, and I lifted one out and I saw there was a second concealed row, more men, all dead.

By the time we got to the sea, the September sun had gone behind great grey clouds.

'Ladies' Beach is best,' he said.

I agreed. Swimming by the diving tower as people leap into the water at Blackrock makes me afraid. Tom wore a black and red wetsuit and two blue swimming caps but we decided against swim shoes and I said that I liked to run into the sea.

'I know,' he said, 'I didn't forget you completely.' He was chasing me, and my ankles were scalded from the cold, the water was icy and for some minutes as it filled my swimsuit I could not breathe and my heart pounded. I then did breaststroke awhile with my head up and out of the water as Tom spieled on about Sarah. When I plunged my head into the sea it stung the bones of my face until they throbbed. We dried off in silence.

We had decided to go to lunch, but I changed my mind. He was packing up, and he shook out his little towel and rolled it neatly and left it on top of his backpack.

'Drink?' he said.

'The trout?'

'Oh, right,' he said, 'yes, the fish. I forgot all about Johanna.'

All of a sudden it was dinner and it was Johanna. There would be fish. There would be Chablis. I rummaged in my backpack for something to tone my skin down and instead I found some red lipstick in the pocket of my puffy coat. The contrast might help but my lips were salty and coarse and my throat was dry. I lifted my phone to check my face and twisted up the lipstick, applying it to the bottom lip first as I ran my tongue over my lips a number of times. I was all brown freckles and dried lines around my eyes, and my lips bright red and flaky. The pandemic had aged the whole world.

'What are you doing?' he said, staring at me. I glared at him and I licked my index finger and fixed my eyebrows, slowly. My braids were still in place and I zipped down my hoody to the tiny flower on the centre of my bra, and said: 'Yes, a drink.'

I chose the pub and sat down by the fire. A few men at the bar were complaining about social media and traffic. Tom returned and left the drinks on a small table.

'Look, fuck it, we – I need to explain – I want to. I was entirely not myself when you – when your mother died.'

'No, don't, please,' I said, fast. 'Let's not go back there. That was a long time ago.'

'I felt I lost you long before I did. And I have things I need to apologise for. There was no talking to you, but I do need to apologise. Look, for what it's worth, I am sorry . . . for what you went through.'

'Tom, I can't – not now, not when we've just come out of the sea.'

'Right,' he said. 'But I feel I owe . . . I don't know—'

'No, no, stop,' I said.

'I can really see that you've – come on.'

I felt like a spring lamb being fattened for Easter. 'Fuck,' I said under my breath.

'But I . . . I only wanted to say I'm happy for you. Takes guts to do what you're doing, facing, well, facing everything.'

We were quiet on the trip into Galway City from Salthill. I pulled up by the fish market. There was no trout left on the stall, it had been a poor catch, but there was some whole monkfish. The fishmonger weighed it and packed its fat body into a plastic bag while chatting with us, and then he double-bagged it. Tom and I walked back to my car with the monkfish swinging off his arm and I said: 'Do you need wine?'

But he drifted away from the dinner and said: 'Is it nice being close to the sea again?'

'Yes.'

'Do you think that's what was wrong, too?'

'How do you mean?' I asked.

'In London, you were just so—'

'So?'

'You were sad.'

Driving out of the city, the lights of a petrol station came on ahead of us.

'Wine?' I said.

'No,' he replied, serious as death. 'Are you OK?'

'No,' I said. 'Not really.'

A girl was seated on a high stool inside the window by the shop's till, engrossed in a book. The red tail lights of the cars blurred and diluted. Tom put his feet down on the bag of fish and it made the bag bloat.

'Don't burst that in my car,' I warned him.

'I won't,' he said, 'don't worry. I have a light touch.'

I glared at him a second, and then I looked ahead and said: 'I always thought, you know, when I was young, that I really wanted one person.'

'Yeah, I often thought this about you, like a trust—' he said, breaking off. 'I'm also—'

'No,' I said, 'please, don't interrupt me. I just, it's trust, yes, you're right, and I haven't had—' I stopped. 'I find it all very hard to talk about. My mam, Mother.' I didn't know what to call her. 'She had it tough, you know, and I'm just – wary.'

'I *don't* know, Claire, I'm trying to, well, to piece you together, because you never actually told me.'

'And now you're back,' I said. 'I'm derailed.'

'One person?'

'It's just that time, on the South Bank, when I knew you were going to propose and I stopped you, I never explained why but I wouldn't have the first clue of it all, marriage. I'm not right for it.'

'You could have said that to me then?'

'Sorry,' I said. 'I thought I did.'

'You could have said anything.' Tom shuffled his feet a few times, on top of the fish, and he let out some gentle sighs. My chest hurt.

'Is this the turn?' I said.

'Have we gone under the train line?' he asked, looking out the passenger window.

'Yes.'

'Then yes.'

I slowed along the boggy road. I remembered this corner. We were quiet.

'I missed you,' he said, interrupting the hum of the engine. 'Miss you.'

'Stop,' I said, as I turned the engine off.

'It's why I'm here.'

'I need to – can I use the loo?' I asked.

He laughed nervously and kissed me on the side of my face: 'See, you did miss me.'

I went upstairs in Johanna's where there were more rows of books, mostly crime, and a bottle of expensive bath oil on a stool by the bath. Two white robes were hanging behind the door like figures waiting up against the whitewashed wood door and they made me angry. I lifted the oil and sat on the edge of the bath, put my feet up on the little wooden stool – it was an old milking stool, rotted with woodworm. I twisted the cap of the heavy glass bottle and I dipped my finger into the oil, then I dabbed it to my salted lips – rosewater. I gathered myself and when I walked out, Tom was standing in the bedroom, his top off. He stood with his muscular back to the door in his blue jeans in his bare feet and I watched as he drew the curtains closed. There may have been a candle alight. His room was dark and inviting and

I waited for a minute but he didn't turn around, and suddenly I started to cry and I crept downstairs and back into the kitchen to find my keys. I heard him in the room above me, the springs of the bed loaded as he lay down on it and called out my name. I licked the rosewater on my lips and took a deep breath. I needed to leave, and went creeping about, unsure, after I'd found my keys, of what door to go through. And then it was there, staring at me, the great big plant, and I kneeled beside it on the cold tiles. I put out my hand and touched it, and I held one of its thick leaves in my palm, tracing my finger along its veins. How long did it take to grow a leaf this magnificent? I grabbed the plant and tore the leaf clean from its stalk. I tore off another – the shiniest and most impressive. I stood up and stuffed the huge leaves into my bra cups, their cool shiny sides against my breasts. The plant looked bald now.

'Claire, Claire wait, don't—'

Outside, two white pillowcases were pegged onto the farmer's clothes line and the flies still buzzing about. I reversed onto the road as Tom ran toward the car, shoeless in his blue jeans. He looked tiny and out of place in the rear-view mirror. Or no, not this – maybe I just think he ran. I wanted him so badly to run to me. If he wanted me badly enough, he wouldn't hurt me, right? In the mirror only the farmer's pillowcases in the dusk now, two mad white balls caught up in the wind.

8

'Do you remember when you could buy ciggies in ones for ten pence?' Máire said, as she tried hard to balance on the high stool and light a cigarette off a candle.

'You're a decade older than me, Máire Grealish, and the world has moved on,' I said. 'Everyone's vaping now, you flute.' We were laughing hard as I steadied myself by the counter in the smoking area of Glackens. We both stared at the image of the Virgin Mary on the wall nearby – a bright red light beneath her illuminated her eyes.

'Is that meant to be ironic?' I said.

'Doubt it,' Máire said, 'they're hardly that smart – the Glackens?'

'There's a new bar in Galway that has an image of Jesus's face in the urinal.'

'That's well out of order,' Máire said.

'I wonder if he's pre- or post-crucifixion?'

'Claire!'

Máire!' I said. 'I've heard there's urinals of women open-mouthed in some bars.'

Máire's face changed. 'Well, actually that's well off,' she said, soberly. 'Well off. How much wine have we had?'

I had not told her yet about Tom's arrival in the West, for I knew she would worry, and ask too many questions.

We were still giggly as she tried, clumsily, to set me up with a bachelor farmer.

'Stop,' I said, 'just leave it. I have zero interest.'

The farmer looked across at us. 'G'wan, Miss Grealish, spill, if you're going to play matchmaker.' His dark eyes shot back to his glass as he swirled the yellowed end of a pint of Guinness about the bottom of it. He folded his arms. He was cute, strong jawline, boxy shoulders, neat shoes.

Máire shook her head and looked down at her drink.

'Ah here, Grealish,' he said to Máire. 'I'm not dating the Brit who couldn't look after her own mother.' He flicked his cigarette ash in our direction.

'What the fuck?' I said.

'You know nothing about her,' Máire said.

'I know plenty about her, all high-and-fucking-mighty. I remember her brother too,' he said. 'Thought he knew it all in school, hear he's a kept man now.'

Máire was all apologies as we moved away to another table and lit two more cigarettes.

'Don't mind him, Claire, I'm so sorry. Lads around here that never get out are only jealous of everyone who gets away.'

I was quiet, wondering what he meant about abandoning my mother.

'Is that what they think of me?' I said. 'Around here? That I didn't mind or look after my mother properly? And what beef has he with Conor?'

'Claire O'Connor – let them think what they bloody well like.'

I nodded.

'Do you hear me?' she said. I nodded again.

'You were with her, Máire? At the end. I didn't know she was so bad – no one told me. I really had no idea,' I said, and the walls spun. My face was hot, and I cried, all drunk and stupid crying. And I wanted so badly to tell her that Tom was back, or here, or new. But I couldn't bring myself to take the telling-off, to face her asking the practical questions she would ask about his intentions.

Instead we drank more and danced on in the smoking area for hours until the bar called Time on the madness and Máire called Joe and he bundled us home in the Skoda.

On Monday my walk through the streets of Galway was wet and miserable. Everyone knew it was pointless using an umbrella with the gusts of wind this city could conjure, and so I zipped my plastic coat to my chin. At the top of Shop Street, I took the curved turn at BT's corner and spotted a bright orange fur gilet looking cosy on a scrawny plastic model in the window. The path out-side Yes Flowers was strewn with all shapes and sizes of pumpkins, white ones with green lines that looked like emaciated watermelons. Women tottered along in Burberry rain macs and high shoes on the way to the courthouse. I carried on into the university grounds along by the Corrib River, rowboats and fishing boats were anchored by the bridge, a few kayaks were strewn by the shed at Macnas, and a new Bicycle Community Shed had attracted a few older people mulling about in hats with bobbles, chatting and smoking dope at nine a.m. I envied them.

A couple of girls walked past me at great speed in matching cream outfits, tanned midriffs bare to the world.

'He is so fucking moronic,' said the one with a glossy ponytail high up on her head. It swept about her bare shoulders as she walked and balanced a puffy jacket somewhere between her back and her hips.

'OMG, don't talk. It's fucking gross – I know all about it, watching him as his mouth moves about and he sweats like a mo-fo in class, what's with all the sweating?'

'Right!?'

'Seems nervous. Like why teach if you can't control your nerves? Like maybe you're in the wrong job. See that blue shirt last Friday? Drenched. I am so fucking done with that class. He is the actual worst lecturer ever fucking created.'

'Not sure lecturers are created, Saoirse.'

'Legit.' They laughed. 'They just crawl fully formed from libraries and start mulling about the place.'

By the large glass library, a clutch of students refilled water bottles at a station and some waited in line.

Inside the concourse, I took the small lift to my office on the third floor.

9

Doll Babić skidded around the corner of the narrow corridor, trying out a wheely chair. She had newly bleached hair, short with flashy pink tips. She turned a one-eighty manoeuvre and screamed when she saw me: 'You frightened the life out of me, Dr O'Connor.'

'Sorry,' I said, apologetically. 'What are you doing out in the corridor? Nice hair.'

'You sure?' she said, quizzing me with a lifted eyebrow. The bar pierced through her eyebrow was making it look angry and inflamed.

'Yes. Love it,' I said, reassuringly.

'Sure, thanks,' she said and grabbed the ends of her hair, and started inspecting them for splits. 'Bleach, it destroys it – punk over perfection.'

'Looks good,' I said. She beckoned at me to come closer: 'They're *in* my office,' she whispered.

'Who?' I said, alarmed.

'The window cleaners,' she said, 'the fit Ukrainians – my ovaries are dead.'

'I thought you were gone off boys?' I said.

'I have rekindled some low-key desire.'

Doll had worked in the English Department since leaving secondary school. At first she wanted a gap year and then a break year. She said she had ADD or ADHD but had never had the funds for a private diagnosis so it was a bit of guesswork with the help of the internet. In any case, she said she had one of those things where you can't concentrate for a long time on any one given task. 'For Real. For Real you're a nice gang,' she said on her first day post-pandemic, when she locked herself out of the office and broke some glasses in the staffroom.

'Indeed we are,' Prof had said walking by her, smiling. 'I give her a month,' she whispered at me in her soft Rhode Island drawl. It had the effect of making her sound both officious and understanding. Wanting to stamp her mark on Organisational Structures, Doll changed the office keyrings from brass tags to little aliens, and one giant ball of rainbow fluff hung on the key to the PhD thesis archive.

'This chair,' she said, trying out a new office chair, 'it's got like, super back support, and watch this – look, are you watching?'

'Yes, yes,' I said.

'So any word from TomTom?' she said, spinning by me. I regretted telling her the whole swim day in detail, but she was easy to confide in, she had a warm and open face.

'Nope,' I said. 'Can't really blame him.'

'Sounds like legit ghosting to me, but can't a girl play hard to get once in a while?' she said in a Mid-Atlantic drawl. 'Though I guess – objectively – you brought this one on yourself, right?' It would be difficult to decipher where Doll was from if you didn't know her mother was from back west in the Gaeltacht, Connemara, and her father was Serbian.

'I think he's being polite,' I said. 'He has that habit.'

'Claire,' she said under her breath and with her hand over her mouth, 'you've known this guy for years – you should know what the games are.'

'How was yours?' I said.

'Huh?' she said, raising the eyebrow again.

'Your weekend?'

'Same, same,' she said and then pulled out her phone. 'Uneventful, but look at this, I have been obsessed with these all summer and I can't stop watching. Here.'

She handed me her phone in an elaborate gesture.

'I went down one long rabbit hole with this one over the weekend, Claire, and it seems I have officially lost my life to these women.' She covered her mouth with her two hands, rings on every finger. I watched the camera pan across a sea of orange pumpkins. A smiling family came into focus. All blonde. All wearing versions of the same outfit – biscuit linen. All barefoot. All smiling. Everyone was carving or painting. Their mother was handing them scissors, felt, carving knives, tying plastic aprons and smiling every so often to the camera, her head bent to one side or another.

'Who has this kind of time?' Doll said, scrolling through. 'Look, look – July the fourth. Wild. Watch. She stitched this flag and then made this insane flag layered cake. Watch, she'll cut through it and the core is full of red and blue bubblegum. How?!'

'Maybe she doesn't work. Here, I gotta move. Any post?'

'Oh ho, ho, HO!' Doll screamed, slapping her thighs. 'Booooomer . . .' and she laughed a great gusty laugh.

'What?'

'Boomer, that's such a boomer response—'

'What is?' I said, bewildered.

'Saying she doesn't work. She has a gazillion kids. You know how much work that is?'

'I didn't say that. Well, not quite like that.'

'You *implied* it, Claire. She has four kids, well, she had five, one's dead. Shit. Imagine having a dead child in your twenties? Heavy.'

'I meant—'

'I know what you meant and frankly, that kind of talk will get you cancelled,' she said, mocking me.

'Do people still do that?' I said.

'Cancelling?'

'Yeah.'

She shrugged.

'Do you have a diamond on your tooth?'

'Sure, I have four – sick, huh?' she said, grinning at me.

'Yeah, they're nice,' I said, adding: 'I'm not a boomer.'

'Right,' she said, inflecting. 'I'll bet.'

'I'm not – I'm Gen X,' I said, rather desperately.

'Gen X, Boomers, listen, lady,' Doll said, 'all the same to Kelly.'

'Kelly?'

'Keep up, keep up, honey. Kelly, Kelly Purchase. Pumpkin mom. Trad wife lady. Phone,' she said, tapping the screen.

'Trad wife?' I said.

'Claire, what's with the faux naivety?'

It wasn't faux.

'Oh, you legit don't know.'

I nodded.

'So here's the spiel. Trad wife subculture is based on advocating for traditional values, and in particular, a traditional view of wives and homemakers.'

'Trump?'

'Likely influential, but not definitively.'

'God?'

'Definitely.'

'Contraception?'

'Never mentioned, but she's in her twenties and five babies, so you do the maths.'

'Right.'

'And they live their lives on the internet?'

'No, they live their lives. They post their lives on the internet.'

'Isn't that the same thing?' I said.

'No.'

I watched a photo reel of their wedding anniversary from behind Doll's shoulder, her husband didn't take his hands off her but was never below the waist.

'Lots of pumpkin carving, and lying back and thinking of whatever country it is you align yourself with. Lots of control,' Doll said.

'Seems wildly out of touch,' I said.

'They *claim* diversity.'

We stared at each other.

'Surely not,' I said.

'Trump? Christianity, capitalism, product placement, lockdown, money, paid partnerships, the work of the devil, picket fences, Walt Whitman, Steinbeck revivalists, who knows, I'm reaching, but she's got a lot of followers. A lot,' Doll said, 'and everyone's been watching that *Yellowstone*, such rot that show. But we have to ask, why the popularity?'

'Never heard of it.'

'*Dallas* for Gen X. But worse, alt-right propaganda and as for the airheads, we can't just dismiss them all as airheads,' she said, as a warning. 'I find that in this place.'

'In here?' I said. '*This* place?'

'So certain of your own perspective on the dead – you fail to see the crisis the living are whipping up.'

'We see it,' I said. 'We just don't know what to do with it.'

The window washers left Doll's office.

'They claim to be heavily influenced by books,' she said.

'Steinbeck?' I said. 'They like Steinbeck?'

'Nah, I was riffing about Steinbeck. More Sheila Hardy.'

'Who?'

'Oh, never mind, but yeah, I see yanno, fan fic, trad roles, but you know this, the naive books that are back in fashion?'

'Back?' I said. 'Did they ever go away?'

'Well, no, but you know, girl meets boy and the life partner thing, and the pretend to be dumb. It's never going away, right?'

I nodded. 'Clever individualism maybe?'

'Right, but not sure there's actually any connection – not sure how many of these women read past recipe books.'

'So are you saying that Trump culture has birthed an online movement of Traditional Women?' I said, perplexed.

'Look – I don't give a fuck about Trump, but why should we blame Trump? Some people seem to love traditional roles. America loves it.'

'America's not a homogenous thing, Doll.'

'Don't tell America.'

The men left the floor as one carried a small ladder, the other had a flask and a large tin tool box by the handle, with a squeegee in his back pocket. Doll returned behind her desk.

'Right,' I said, 'better try and find a correlation between MacNeice and surfing for this class.'

'Huh?'

'Likely as arbitrary as Steinbeck and the Traditional Women.'

'Trad wives even.'

'Indeed,' I said.

'Indeed, indeed, indeed,' Doll said, her thumb flicking as she scrolled, 'there are hundreds of them. These wives, hilarious. A riot. I'll get nothing done today. Look, look at this one, she cooks the dinner in Louboutins. Absolute howl.'

'Sounds like a review,' I called back. 'Doll Babić calls

Trad Wives, a Riot! Five Stars. Absolute must-see madness. A Howl. She blames John Steinbeck and God. But not Trump.'

'Mostly I blame novelists who pretend to be naive,' Doll shouted back.

10

By the time I got home it was dark and the sky was clear. The bungalow was freezing, and I was thinking about Kelly, mostly about the bright blue sky in Dallas and her four children. In the kitchen I turned on the lights and the radio and stuck my head in the fridge. Lisa O'Neill was singing that song about the Irishwoman Violet Gibson who had shot Mussolini. I made a hot whiskey, two shots. Scotch. BenRiach.

In bed I scrolled Insta: Kelly Purchase had 880,000 followers and perfect teeth. Kelly Purchase had a platinum blonde ponytail and tiny pink lips. She had soft sloping shoulders and a long smooth neck with a little chain permanently in situ and a small diamond threaded on it that went this way and that as she moved. She had olive skin, with small fluid hands and small fingernails, impeccable and pink. Twenty-eight. Dallas. TX. Blessed with Four Children. One Angel. Married to Kirk (DH). The DH made me think of Lawrence. Her frilly cheesecloth top was baby pink to match her pink lips and in turn the fat strawberries she was slicing. She mentioned Cottage Core. Every slice she made – of a tomato, or a piece of salami, a mushroom – every time she lifted a pair of scissors, it delivered a noise like a precise slit in Styrofoam. Everything was high-pitched, her voice, the abundance, the exposure. I watched her with Kirk. I watched her as she left a strange kiss on his forehead in a clip where he was having a hard day and she had dressed the children up as office workers to surprise him and he cried and fell to his knees when he re-entered the house.

I texted Tom:

Hi, wondering if you'd like to meet up again sometime?

Sure. Another swim? You owe me a plant

No. Can't. Doctor's orders. [I lied.] I owe you nothing

Land in that case then. Your place or mine? You OK? Anything serious up?

The Barracks. Food place. Opposite the Indian takeaway.

No, just an ear thing. Infection. [I lied again.]

Perfect. Sunday OK?

Great. Lunch?

Let's! Sending love to the ear.

Most of Kelly Purchase's loyal followers were Purchase diehards – some even had her face as their profile picture. They had huge beaming smiles and bouncy hair, usually platinum blonde or a deep chocolate brown with large yellow highlights. They were all living their best lives. Some Dallas cheerleaders followed her and they sometimes commented on her clips: Love this for you, Les. Go Team Purchase!!! LOVE THIS BABY BLUE ON YOU. You should really *be* a cheerleader, Hun. You look amazing. xo Purchase replied to this comment: I can't commit to anything outside my four blessed little ones and Kirk needs me, here, at home, for him. Y'all know the drill. Much love xoxoxoxo

Kirk was thirty-one and wore a suit to work but I couldn't find a photo of a workplace as his account was private. He had forty-four followers and was following forty-five people. I wondered about the missing one. Kelly and Kirk did Gender Reveal parties on bright patios with blue pools and balloons and they did annual miscarriage remembrances with floating candles (same pool). They voted. They had a very busy and noisy barbecue beside a garden pool on July 4. Family. Blessed. Burgers. On weekends they drank out of large red cups and wore matching cream headwear. His shoulders were broad, double the width of her slender waist and large breasts. I was broader than Tom. Sometimes they went House Shopping and they lay down on beds in Walmart and bounced about, giggling. (I wondered where they kept the guns in that store.) They used Safety First equipment with the kids. The kids all had impossibly white hair, with just the softest tint of yellow. Kelly's mother just had veneers for the second time and Kelly filmed it and interviewed the dentist. Kelly also received veneers through paid sponsorship. At Christmas, their Holiday Season, they dressed three Christmas trees. One large white one in the conservatory. One with red and gold swag and one with all the children's decorations in the den. The den is fun, and is allowed a little clutter. On Sunday nights Kelly restocks the larder: school bags, pull-out drawers with snacks. She makes animal-shaped foods for her children's lunchboxes. They are blessed: By Jesus and God and America.

But Purchase also contended with: Didn't fight for voting rights to have you make Swiss rolls all day long and not contribute to the taxes, fuck y'all. Go Fuck Yourself Kelly Purchase and all that sail in you – ahoy. You're actually fat. A woman threw herself under a horse once upon a fine time for you to behave like a sorority slave master – you and your kind disgust me. You! Global Warming much with all the mouths to feed. Leave what you take. Take what you leave. I think this is gross. Trad whores. Whores for Jesus. Lol. Three words for you Purchase: Roe vs Wade. Don't come crying to me when university fees roll around for your whole goddamn soccer team. You're nothing more than a modern Karen on sedatives. Your child is fat, the second girl – put her on a diet. Just die already. I will rape you. I wouldn't fuck you with a bag over your head, Purchase, you should know that. Y'all are all rewinding progress. Not here to hate, but, you OK Hun? Blink twice if he keeps you in the cellar.

The last comment was left by a yoga instructor in Fife called Maud who advocated for Peace, Love and Empathy. I thought of Kurt Cobain holding a Remington Model 11 20-gauge shotgun to his head and pulling the trigger. I had often thought about them, the Twenty-Seven Club – the talented kids that burned out and didn't fade – and I wondered what they would make of the online world, if they would have made it in such a space. I made a rash judgement about Maud the yoga instructor that she was a fader and I didn't know whether Kelly would fade, or burn bright, but she certainly had mettle. Her GPA was 4. Kelly Purchase had a life mantra: I don't do guilt, I do my best.

I scrolled on to the re-emergence of the conflict in Congo. Passed by an image of an orphanage in Pakistan. The Middle East was unstable, again. There was a school shooting in Vermont, a six-year-old had gotten jealous of his classmate's new dog. A woman had come online to show how her husband had knocked out her front teeth and she was looking for anyone to come and help her. DMs open. A video was posted of a homeless man arrested in Cambridge, Mass, for drinking a beer he had assumed was a cola outside Harvard at two a.m. He hadn't the money to appeal his sentence in Rikers. A woman's arse had become infected from a bum lift in Brazil and people were posting solutions. Irish men were seen on Insta returning from Turkey with their bald heads in bandages and they reminded me of watercress I once grew in school in a pair of tights belonging to Mother. A soccer team had had one of its players kidnapped, or was it the player's father? A bright young woman tested urinary incontinence pads that she certainly was not using. Skinny Irish women with too much fake tan were trying out outfits for Christmas because you can never be ready enough, right? Great big swathes of sequinned material on their body. I smiled into the camera to recognise my face and donated twenty euro to

Médecins Sans Frontières. When I fell into a fitful sleep, I dreamed about a large rat stuck in the basement of the Old House, despite the house not having a basement – it gnawed at me, the rat, and I woke sweaty and fretful and afraid and my mind ran images of conflicts, of starving children, images of teeth, images of people sitting in their cars with large Stanley cups talking about their micro-trauma. At four a.m. I went and checked the patio door as the fridge hummed. I stood a while in the cold and looked across the scope of the back yard to the Old House. The two windows stared at me like sleepy hollow eyes as the light of a full moon washed across the landscape.

Mountain Ellen, Athenry

1920

Paddy O'Connor rose up from the settle bed in the thatched house and swatted away some more of the cursed midges that had followed him from the bog, something about the evening was making him feel unsettled. He went about the dirty floor of the kitchen in his bare flat feet, as he liked it – he had inherited a pair of leather work boots from his dead uncle, and these were set by the fire alongside two other slightly more tattered pairs for the oldest sons, Jack and Thomas. Pat had no boots for the problem with his legs, for which, in turn, he was fiercely protected by Lily from hard labour. Paddy walked to the door and shut up the half top, closing it up entirely and bolting it on the inside, for he was cursed with the hot stinging bites all over his skin.

'They're still at me, woman,' he said to his wife. 'I'm being eaten alive. They're coming out of thin air. Christ.'

'Ah, the bog is a quare place for the little buggers,' she said in return, 'and all around were in the bog today and likely followed them home.'

'The bloody heat does no good for the pest, bad cess to them,' he said, as she swatted himself gently about the legs with a large basket that hung about the fire for gathering herbs, or fish, or any fowl that they could eat. Lily was a resourceful and strong woman. He laughed and grabbed her full body in a warm embrace and he was also excited for the days of the festival that would soon be upon them and set to a little dance with his wife. Lily pulled away quickly. She had a secret, and it was difficult to keep the secret if Paddy started rummaging about her clothes in his excitement.

Later, when she would lie with him at night, and they would close the small door of their damp room to the family, she would remove this secret as he set to bed, as they did with their backs to one another, and she would take it and hide it in the flour bin before sleep.

The two small square windows at the front of the house were darkened from the turf fire's smoke. The pig was quiet outside the door, and the cow laid resting, lowing gently in the cowshed by the house. This usually comforted Paddy, but tonight he was unsettled. He assumed it was the midges. It didn't help that the cowshed was a part of the house's building, you could almost feel the breath of the cow, and on cold nights the family would bring the animal in to rest by the fire and the smaller children were most giddy and excitable on those nights and never slept.

The O'Connors were happy and content because they could, for the first year in as many years as Paddy could remember, let the cow out to a bull over at the O'Shaughnessys' soon, and they hoped to calf her, and this would surely be their fortune. The O'Shaughnessys had come into good fortune, and more would come,

Paddy was sure, and perhaps they would bestow a little on the O'Connors, who might then eat for the winter, at the very least they would drink milk and mash it into potatoes, and not have to sup from the river. Nobody dared to ask the O'Shaughnessys a thing about their business. You didn't curse good fortune by talking about it.

Lily was growing a little fretful – she didn't like the long nights of summer any more, since keeping a secret from Paddy for the first time in all their lives, and she said: 'Man dear, but no good comes from all this light, it drives the men mad for rebellion.'

'No shortage of rebellion at the moment,' Paddy said in return as he walked back to the settle bed, the doors bolted.

'We might all regret it yet. Most are too hungry for rebellion.'

'And isn't that just the way they'd like us,' Paddy whispered. 'Starving by the ditches.'

Lily said nothing, she knew her husband was right. However, he was a passive man, and there was no use in rising a temper in a man who was as passive as Paddy O'Connor, for no good would come of it.

The young men of the house had no notion why the O'Shaughnessys had taken such a Christian turn with the family. Thomas and Jack had spoken about it, and it filled them with a sense of dread, for they were not a family to be given gifts. They had only one relative in America, and he was never heard of since he took a ship some time ago.

But Lily knew. Lily knew her secret, and her favourite son, Pat – he also knew, because he was there when she made the promise to the O'Shaughnessys, he was always there about his mother because he could never take leave, and he was getting far too heavy for the woman to lift. He was the quietest of her sons, but full of wit, a thickset boy with two tiny eyes, and big soft hands, and he helped her knead cakes and bread, and he could sing like a blackbird she told him.

'You're soft on that boy, woman,' Paddy would say.

'I am,' she said in return, 'and what of it, amn't I soft on you too? And don't ye both deserve it?'

But in the shadows of her own life, she worried herself to death about Pat for he wasn't made for work, and nor was he made for books, and heaven forbid if he should ever take to the road with the limp, for he certainly wasn't made for the road neither.

But the truth of the matter was that the O'Shaughnessys had only promised the bull for the cow if Lily kept a gun on her person for them and handed it to the older son of the O'Shaughnessys on the evenings he called before their nightly raids. So she did this, and never opened her mouth to one about it. They met in the haggard when he whistled. Lily had kept her side of the bargain as did her neighbours. It was for good reward, which was more than most women were getting, delivering letters in the dark of night, and hiding guns for no return whatsoever. She had done it for some months in secret, ever since the blackandtans had arrived in their village, burning houses and holdings, stringing people up for hanging, and doing unimaginable things to the women, things that the women spoke only to other women about and tried to keep from their men. Lily O'Connor did her best to keep her boys from harm, and told them to keep their heads down in the cabbage patches, working, should the buggers arrive to upset their peace, or to lay low in the potato garden, do not breathe, or say a word, hide out in the bog holes. And run if they came to you, and never stop running should they take a set against you.

'If they come, Pat O Connor, you must get into the flour bin and hide. Do you hear me?' she said, realising there were scant places to hide for a boy of his size, and as he couldn't run, she was determined to have a plan. But she regretted saying it, for he was too clumsy and slow to get to it and she had filled him with worry. But they practised it the odd time, and sometimes it was a success.

'But why would they take a set against us, Mother?' Pat asked on one such occasion.

'Because they can do what they bloody well like, Patrick O'Connor, that's why, because they think they own all the land in all the world, and worse, they think they own us and all we have, but they can never own your thoughts. No one can.'

'Do they?'

'They certainly do not – do you hear me,' she said, her face wet with tears of fear for a boy like him about the world. 'You listen to me – no one owns you, Pat O'

95

Connor, not one bit of you, not even me or your father, you're your own man, and never let wan tell you otherwise. Do you hear me?'

'I do, Mother.'

'Promise me.'

'I promise you.'

'But let them think they do if they ever catch you and mind your manners.'

'I will, Mother. I will.'

The rest of her sons were hardier for the world, some would even court trouble, and fall into it, long, long after she was gone and buried. But Lily had told them each in turn that they were not to bring trouble to her house. Paddy hadn't the heart for violence. They obliged. Her husband was an unusually mild and philosophical man. He learned to read from an uncle who was a Franciscan, and one of the few men of letters in the town of Athenry, and he had loaned him old Bibles, and writings by Plato, and he liked to read poetry and Shakespeare. Paddy didn't play music and did not seem to belong on a farm holding, but such was the way the inheritance fell, and so he was grateful. He was a man unable to be cruel to an animal, or a woman, which was much to Lily's great fortune, for men about the place often treated their women like dogs, but no, he could not swat a spider, he was a man that made do with his load, like all men about him.

Unlike the men about him, rebellion was not in his nature, and he cursed the English to his wife at night, but never to his sons, for he knew how the anger could rise a giddy young man's temper, and who could blame them?

On this one balmy night, the O'Shaughnessys had not called or whistled about the haggard to retrieve the gun, and everything seemed settled. Lily held it on herself until sundown, in case she would see one of the older men stirring and looking for her out beyond the haggard. When darkness fell, she too could sleep – as was the deal.

The blackandtans – their noses in everyone's business and named for the motley clothes they wore and a tassel on a beret – went about the fields and in and out of outhouses, like they owned all belonging to the town, and they went searching rivers and streams and bog for men with guns, and women who they all believed, rightly, were hiding guns for their men in intimate places in their bodies, in their bodices – the most unholy thing a woman could wear.

No one around was to be trusted for they had the ways of talk on them, and the blackandtans knew the women were mouthy, or so they claimed, and could hide things that would put the whole town in danger and they had developed ways to get them to talk. Where the guns were, where the men were, where the danger lay, in settle beds and outhouses and under the skirts, in meal bins and flour bins, and that's right, the women were not to be trusted for the rebellion worked only with them and their fair faces going about on bicycles and delivering messages from door to door, as though they were going in to keen and wail over a dead body, or to say goodbye to another young soul off from the West to America, to escape England and the hungry hole in his belly.

Oh yes, the O'Connors were once always hungry, starving, as were their people before them, and those before them, but the pig had arrived and the cow and so maybe, God willing, a few of the sons would get out and never return and make a life somewhere in the world, maybe America. Lily and Paddy could leave the place to Pat, and the souls in heaven of his sisters would mind him when they departed the world.

Tonight Lily was busy putting the children up in the loft to bed, while Paddy laughed at her vain effort and tried to drag her around the kitchen for a waltz, and she said: 'Bad cess to you and your dancing, Paddy O'Connor, we need to put these boys to bed.'

'They're grown men, woman, you know it,' he said. 'Fine strong men.'

She had birthed all of her children in the small house, but the few girls had died in infancy, one as a toddler had choked on some berries she had picked up in the fields one day when they were making cocks of hay. Lily stood a little still, and shook, and Paddy knew that she was thinking on the little girls' faces, and he remembered them laid out in the small parlour, one small girl after the other, all laid out in the same dress, that they took off the body before swaddling it for the earth in a hessian sack, and the neighbours had come and paid their respects to the girls and Lily cried but she said to all from around: 'Tis no world for a girl, God was good to take them from pain, and haven't I my strong boys – sure, no world at all for a girl and all we put them through.' The neighbours had always come with generous gifts of food and drink, and keened loudly over the little bodies, one after the other, and everyone agreed that indeed the world was far too harsh for any little girl.

Lily, upon remembering the dead girls, well, she fell on her knees again as she often did, pulling away from Paddy trying to dance with her, and when grief came over her, he knew to be silent. The younger boys all scurried up the other side of the house to the far loft, having had enough prayers for a week said, and they were used to their mother taking a fit of grief, and they laid down quiet under the hessian sacks on the wooden pallets that made a bed for four, quiet to let her pray. They lay still as anything when they slept, out of a habit of not disturbing each other, and Jack and Thomas were downstairs, the two oldest boys kneeling to pray with Lily, and Pat was beside his father who propped him up a little by holding him about the waist. They kneeled down on the flagstone and prayed and prayed for the repose of the souls of their sisters, for they were not christened for the most part, and Lily feared that they were being held in limbo, so she prayed furiously for the release of their small souls to God. Paddy sat on the settle bed with his head in his hands, his son in the crook of his arm, warm and praying too, as Paddy was not as inclined to prayer as his wife, and murmured the response with Pat.

But now there was the rosary – yes, yes, the rosary was called out and the oldest boy, Jack, set some kindling to the fire, he was young, about nineteen, and down in age Thomas nearby him was eighteen, and Pat was fifteen for two sisters were lost in between and they prayed for all the girls, gone. And Jack was so young, and it's a quare thing to imagine him as a grandfather, and he was small and everything was huge then – the huge kettle, and everything was so huge.

    Lily hung the kettle over Jack's low fire . . .

and then

Twowindowsatthefrontofthesmallhouse
A garden
Asmallgardenandflowerstherewereflowersgoingupthe-
    gardenpath
There were flowers
no more
And they went up the garden path
Tantantansthetansandthewaytheywouldfrightenyou
Tothedoortothedoor

    Knock
    Knock

Knock
Knock
Knock

Let us in let in by the hair of your chin, you must let us in.

11

Through the front window of the living room I watched a skinny brown hare bound about the green end of the garden and leap over the drystone wall. Mother seemed very about the place, a strong smell of cooking hung in the kitchen, a Sunday roast, or perhaps it was just the early morning rise.

There was, despite the sun, a distinct chill in the air, and so I dressed and took the keys from inside the back door, and I went quickly, before I could change my mind, out to the Old House. The key jammed a little in the rusty lock, but with some force, it crumbled into two pieces in my hands. Inside there was the strong smell of oil and petrol, it was dark and dusty, some birds had roosted in the rafters and they woke and began fluttering wildly about the place looking for the light. One flew close over my head, and another swiftly out by me, to the open doors and the sun. A stack of old turf was covered in a corner, together with some kindling, drying for years. I filled up some firewood for the afternoon as though it were the most mundane thing in the world, as the past kept coming at me. Underneath the old logs I came across a roll of wallpaper and as I unfurled it, I remembered Mother had used this pattern on their bedroom walls when we were children. It smelled musty and damp, and looking at it filled me with a longing just to speak to her, one last time, though I was unsure of what I would say, and so I said nothing.

Back inside, I lit the stove in the living room and burned the wallpaper in small sheets, cross-legged in front of the stove, tearing apart little batches of it, the flowers darkening and burning round the edges and the mould catching in my throat. The great bird pattern taking fire at the edges, smouldering and then catching flame.

Máire and Joe's black Labrador was howling and barking mad next door. The moaning grew closer and so I went to the window and there he stood, looking in at me, his great pink tongue hanging out of his mouth, panting, and his woven collar all about his head as though he had caught himself in the brambles. A tuft of black hair was dragged behind his ear, where the skin looked cut. I went outside with some biscuits.

'Claire, hi, come in, come in,' Máire said, eyeing their dog, as she stood in the hallway of her house in bulky socks, her wax jacket zipped to the chin. 'You again?' she said to him. 'I swear to God, Claire – he's like a baby. Getting lost and over-excited. Jesus, he's obsessed with that Old House of yours lately. If he isn't running towards it, he's howling at it or running away from it. Lucky it's your place he's taken a fondness for, not many around here with much patience. Come in, come in.'

'Thanks,' I said as I followed her into the house.

'Have you time for tea or are you back to the job?' she said.

Máire was always going back. Back to town. Back to the woods. Back to the road. Back to work. Back to a diet. Back to the gym.

'I'd love a cup,' I said.

'Great,' she said, and lifted the kettle to the tap to fill it. Her house had a large range, a fire of turf was lit in it and a pot on the stove, she always had something heating.

'How's the hospital?' I said.

She rolled her eyes. 'Don't mention the war.' She placed the kettle on the stovetop. 'Any word from the lads? I haven't seen them in the longest time.'

I shook my head: 'No, no, WhatsApp mostly.'

'They all OK?'

'They are,' I said.

'And how're you?' she asked, her head in the fridge.

'I'm OK, good.'

'Good?' Máire said. She shut the fridge door and arched her eyebrows at me.

'Look. Just so you know. I'm seeing Tom again, just a little bit, just for dinner tomorrow, lunch I mean, nothing official,' I blurted out.

'Seeing?' she said, poker straight now.

'Here and there.'

'*Here and there?*' she asked and looked confused.

'It's just a catch-up, don't overthink it.'

'What? But why? Just because he's close by? I don't know, he'll break your heart – again.'

I shrugged. 'I don't think he actually *broke* my heart.'

'He most certainly did. You didn't get out of bed for weeks.'

'That was because of Father.' I shook my head in the direction of the bungalow.

'Don't be ridiculous, Claire – we both know it was an ease to you all and look—' She stopped mid-sentence. 'Sorry. I've overstepped. God rest his soul.'

'You're full of contradictions, Máire.' But I knew she was right.

She looked at me kindly. 'Well, whatever it was, love-sick or a breakdown, it was very scary, and I worried a lot about you. We don't want you going back there.'

I was embarrassed at her saying breakdown. I looked out the window, hoping she might stop and leave it.

'How do you know you'll manage to mind yourself? These things are far from simple. And what does he want coming here?'

I shrugged.

'Have you slept with him?'

I shook my head. 'Not since . . . London.'

'That's something. Look, and I mean this in the most kind way I can say it, do you think you have lost your mind a little . . . again?' she said, and she said it so softly that I knew she meant it.

'No, no, least not like that,' I said. I had begun to go a little astray with copying Kelly. I knew this, but I was taking the good advice from her, and filtering the rest.

'Like what?' Máire said, pulling an ugly face as she threw teabags in a ceramic pot that had sponge-painted poppies on it. 'You know how you can get very hung up on things, Claire.'

'Like –' I paused – 'just like, well, you know.'

'So you *are* fucking him,' she said. 'Jesus, Claire, why can you never just come out with it?'

'MÁIRE,' I said, unnerved by her language, 'I haven't had sex with him – I mean, not since he's come here. I just want to talk to him, I need to figure out about— I missed him.'

'Figure out, *figure out what*, Claire?'

'I wasn't easy to be with, Máire,' I said. 'I was – I don't

know, absent. You're never objective about these things, least not with me.'

She thought about this. 'Claire, I remember you shot out the door of the Skoda at Shannon like the American troops go through the place. I couldn't even—' She stopped dead. 'Sorry. I shouldn't have said that.'

'It's fine,' I said, as we set to drinking more tea. 'I did. Knowing it would make me have to face it. Father's dying. I just couldn't bear to think. It was all becoming too real, and I knew in those moments that I'd have to mind him.'

'I know. I felt for you, I really did, like it's a disgrace how often for us, that's our lot.'

'But why should it be?' I said. 'It is so unfair. Maybe we women are the problem, maybe we allow it to be?'

'There's no answer to that. But look, Claire, you did it, you came and looked after him and he didn't suffer and it was a great kind thing you did, you know that and I know that and John knew it.'

'But I did it for the wrong person,' I said. 'We both know that too.' Máire's face darkened, as it did before she delivered bad news. She put her cup down, and looked out the back window for a moment.

'Remember your obsession with crochet,' she said, deciding to change the mood, 'you went all in with that.'

We both burst out laughing.

'And after that? What was it? Rocks or crystals? Or remember the jars of jam. Dozens of them.'

'The blackberries were everywhere,' I said, 'it was a shame to waste them.'

'No one could eat that much jam in a lifetime,' she said, laughing again.

'Stop it, you're making me out to be fully astray in the head. I won't get obsessed, not this time, I promise. I will keep it casual.'

She mock scowled. 'So where's the big date?'

'The Barracks Restaurant.'

'For actual fuck sake, Claire. I thought you'd be meeting him inside in Galway at the very least, and hide yourself from the local gawkers.'

I grinned.

'It's not funny. You'd be as well to keep him out of this town.'

'But he lives here now, and I had nothing to do with it – besides, I can't be dealing with Tinder!' I said.

'Red flag, Claire, that he just arrives and expects you to—'

'No, no, it's not like that, he's finishing a book. Or starting it. He's here to write a book, it has nothing to do with me.'

'Oh, he is, is he?' she said and grimaced. 'Meddling like that Yeats, and will you buy gifts for me and Joe, little trinkets to make us like him. Because I won't—'

'Won't what?'

'Like him,' she said. 'Where's he staying?'

'He's in Johanna Moore's house,' I said. 'Over by the agricultural college.'

'Tom Morton is staying in that trollop Johanna Moore's house,' she said and I couldn't read her expression. 'Shit. What will you wear?'

I laughed at her sudden new focus. 'Dunno.'

'I wish you would just tell him to fuck off home. And look good when you do it.'

'Máire, you can't say things like that, like go home, it's not 1920 – no one has to *go* home.'

'Oh, you know I don't mean that. And don't come all moralising on me. He and Johanna-the-Posh-Trollop are not our kind of people.'

'*Our kind of people*?' I said. 'I think you need to get out more.'

'You know what I mean. That's what university did to you—'

'What?'

'Posh friends.'

'You went to university too,' I said.

'I went to learn how to save lives and burst bed sores,' she said, and set to clearing away the plates, throwing an eye out the window again for Joe who was down in the sheds opening a round bale. She checked her phone.

'Don't be mad,' I said, and rubbed her hand as she went to turn to the sink.

'Nurses see the worst of life – we're realists,' she said. 'Look, I'm just protecting you. Wear that blue dress you wore to our summer barbecue, the A-line one. Do you remember it? I think Joe might have burned it with a cigarette though. Wear something like that – it was flattering.'

'I remember it,' I said, and stood up to leave. 'Now, I'd better move myself. Thanks for the tea, and I'll pop in next week, for a debrief.'

'Or a whine and wine,' she said, smiling, and rose to see me out the front door. 'But don't come here crying because he's suddenly upped and married Miss Johanna and moved to fucking Paris.'

'Don't,' I said. 'Please.'

She placed her cup on the table, shifting it this way and that as though organising her thoughts. 'I do admire you, Claire.'

'You're gone soft,' I said, in a flurry of shame.

'No, I do, but. I worry about you with men.'

'Tom is a good man,' I said.

'Whatever you say,' she said, letting me out the front door. Then she called after me: 'You're a ride, Claire O'Connor!'

'No, you're a ride,' I said as I laughed back.

The air was full of optimism as I walked out into the October light. The ditches were a beautiful tangle of shades. They would be bare soon.

'Claire!'

'What?'

'Don't dress up too much.'

The O'Connors' Black Mare and the Queen of England

I

And so the rumours went about the town that the Queen of England was sending some horsemen to Athenry and its surrounds during the summer months of 1990, just as Thatcher was on the way out. The Queen's men, or so they were named locally, would talk with the farmers around the town about their plans for developing the breed of the Household Cavalry, and it was rumoured that they were looking in the area for suitable equines. It was, of course, more likely that these were equestrian officers to the Royal Family, and not actually the Queen herself, but this didn't quell the excitement or anxiety that news like this dug up in the place. Never mind the facts of the thing, all summer long the town was giddy with talk of the Queen of England and her men coming, this time, not to take, but to do business. Some said that she might arrive in the cover of night, others said she would make an official visit to put to rest some of the hate, such was her love of a horse, and who knew what kind of madness that might bring with it. It was rumoured she knew much about a horse, and liked to approve those for breeding in person.

The Queen's men, it was said, would be willing to speak with anyone who had a horse – preferably a black horse, or a very dark bay, and it must be over sixteen hands and two, at a minimum. They would be content to speak with anyone who might have news of a horse, bred a horse, kept a horse, knew of a horse – and so upon their arrival they met with all kinds of men: men that worked two jobs to keep roofs, men whose fathers had owned small scraps of land and had a horse wintered out, men who had fought in the War of Independence, and men who had received land from the estate, mostly it was noticed that they met with men who were men of men who had never bowed or scraped for the Crown – and everything about this new venture felt very uneasy about the town. They didn't meet with many women – given the Irish had long ago adopted the custom around these parts of primogeniture and women were rarely gifted farms, or held in any position of manager of a farm, and this spread to most other areas of life also, including not owning land, or animals, which they rarely did.

It was also rumoured that the Queen's men had had an unsuccessful and rather traumatic trip to the North of Ireland on a quest for such horses, and that the small entourage had been sniped at on the Armagh border – this, again, was only whispered at and never made the news cycles or was confirmed. But it was deemed that Connacht might be more suitable to search about for new breeds – and safer areas to do their bidding, even if they had never successfully planted it, or according to Cromwell, wanted to plant it.

Informative posters went up in a handful of places, with elaborate text superimposed on the large head of a black horse. Posters were spotted in the butcher's shop and the vet's, one in the co-op but that was defaced, the poster placers, whether they were locals or not, apparently didn't set foot inside the creamery for the manager had a hurley at the gate and was in a fit of rage when they arrived, and swung it about the Range Rover they had, it was rumoured, been escorted in. It was also rumoured that the vehicle was bulletproofed. Two posters remained intact on the noticeboard of the garden centre, and one or two in the mart were torn down, thrown in an empty half-barrel and set on fire. Most bars and pubs around the town refused to carry the poster, but for a finish, the Queen's men were meeting anyone who wished to do business, and they would be gathering in a humble pub by the Norman Arch in the town. The Norman Arch, known as the North Gate, was once the only way in and out of the town of Athenry, and rumours were that it would collapse when the most handsome man in Ireland walked under it.

People started to baulk, some out of a moral obligation to the dead, but others were getting nervous about the revenue commissioners finding out that they kept a horse or two on the side, that this might only alert the powers that be to the farming tax evasion that went on, and so only the brave of heart, or the dead of heart, made it to the event for any semblance of serious business. Many of course were there to show interest only in the lives of their neighbours.

The dimly lit pub was packed to its mahogany rafters with sweaty bodies, mostly men smoking and drinking pints of porter with chasers of whiskey and black rum. There were three men seated by the toilets, dressed like outrageous gentry and sipping on mugs of tea. They all stood up together and a hush came over the place as they explained the kind of nag that would keep Her Majesty happy. They spoke in formal tones, but added some anecdotes about the Queen, which seemed to get the hostile crowd on side a little. They were full of praise for the breeding of horses in Ireland, and how the Irish knew their horses as well as any country they had ever traded with.

Before sunset on that evening in late summer 1990, John O'Connor walked up and down the streets of the town, trying to make a decision, eventually dipping into the bar, and standing alone at the end of it, a sign that denoted a willingness to do business, should such business arise.

They first began to talk about cross-breeds, shouting over each other as local rivalries started to emerge, and then turned to Connemara ponies – which while being hardy and beautiful, ran too many lines of white and grey to suit the dark outfit of the Queen's Guard and would not be considered in any case due to size. Everyone agreed about this. Even people who came out from the city for a look, and who worked in the factories and had never sat on a horse, agreed. The visitors bought some rounds and everyone relaxed a little when the local cobbler, who lived right next door to the bar, and considered himself a townie and not at all versed in the way of a horse whatsoever (nor did he want to be), wagered every man present to walk under the arch. They all poured out of the pub and set to competing all in jest, even the Queen's men and one carrying a pint of stout and laughing for the first time since he arrived. Then someone started to whistle the air to 'Danny Boy'. But no matter the gait or the speed of the walk, or the swagger of the fool walking under it, the arch, of course, stayed standing.

It must be said that most people in the pub that evening didn't make enough money to ever take a holiday, or buy anything outrageous, and many had not had the phone installed, and did not own a dishwasher or microwave. Some of the punters didn't have central heating. Modernisation was slow in these parts and so the farmers were excited, as everyone knew if you sold a horse to the Queen and opened up that channel of sales (someone early in the night had spoken about the *channel of sales* and it was a phrase that was bandied about the town since). It was likely she, or most likely her entourage, would return for more if it all went well. It was also rumoured that if she liked what they bought upon her inspection of the Household Cavalry at the Trooping of the Colour, then she herself would visit on private business – for she liked nothing more than horses, whiskey and men who knew about horses and dogs. Racehorses, hunters, jumpers, those set to the trap, much like the farmers, the Queen and the locals might have something in common after all and selling would change a life, and the fortune of a family.

But others were certainly uncertain. Some didn't take the free round at the bar, others walked out, indignant, and stood about, one man spat viciously outside the pub and another smashed a glass against the arch in honour of his grandfather who was hung upside down by the Black and Tans and his throat slit so he died a long and slow death.

'No one worth their heritage could dream of selling to the Crown,' he shouted as men left the bar.

'Ah, g'wan out of it, Pat-Jo O'Dowd,' John O'Connor said, 'we're a long time past the Black and Tans now. Haven't you made the canon above in the parochial house your king in any case, bowing and scraping to him like a fucking blackguard.'

'Your people would turn in their hungry graves, O'Connor. Well you know it.'

'Plenty round here more than happy to serve a God of their own making, O'Dowd. You'll answer to someone yet, your kind always do. We're a long time past the Crown now—'

'We are if you tell us we are, O'Connor,' O'Dowd shouted back as he leaned forward and put his hand on the stone of the arch and began pissing up against it. The spray came back on him.

'Sure all yours are abroad in Digital inside in the city

taking the American dollar. Fuck-all difference if you ask me.'

'Better than taking the Queen's shilling,' O'Dowd said, zipping up his fly.

'Tell that to the Vietnamese,' John said and made haste for his jeep.

But John O'Connor knew selling to the Queen would be the worst tainting on the name of his family since the time some of the locals had taken the soup during a famine that slaughtered the countryside.

John had a knack to break any horse to saddle, and knew about leg winds and weaving, he was good on their bone structure, health, fitness and came into contact with many of the horses in the area. Mostly, he knew about breeding, and they needed black horses for the Guards. Pure black or dark bay. A white blaze down the forehead was OK, but mostly, they were to be clean of markings.

The men returned later that autumn as promised. It was a Monday afternoon and the O'Connors' dog had taken sick. Claire O'Connor and her brothers had just come home from school when the three men pulled up in a black Range Rover. Two of the men had raspberry pants on, one had mad forest green, and all three had their felt hats with feathers, and spats over brogues, wax coats and serious faces. Claire felt embarrassed for their ignorance. It was not good to be flashy about these parts. All of them wore little silk cravats tied in ornate knots on their necks. Their faces were well coloured from the healthy outdoor life, none of them looked as weathered as the Irish souls that they made trot their horses up and down narrow boreens.

'Turn him again,' they said to John who ran up and down the road, leading a young colt he was breaking. 'And again. That'll do, thank you, sir.' They often spoke in unison as they stood on a steep ditch out on the road watching him lead horses. 'Good man. Many thanks. If you wouldn't mind, we'll put a stick on him.'

John tipped his cap. They measured the colt at the withers.

'And again, trot on now and turn him back, once again, please.' They squatted down to look at the horse's legs and asked to lunge one or two in the field by the Old House, and John obliged.

When he brought the mare out, the mood changed, and the one in green trousers asked to saddle her and rode her about for a while. 'Lovely mouth on her,' he said, down to the other men.

Their vowels were flat and nasal and came out slowly. They spoke with a great command and could tell a wind or a twist of a horse at a great distance. Or so they said, yet John O'Connor wasn't convinced they knew much more than the colour of the horse's coat. Truthfully, the men were wholly out of place, and unwelcome. Claire watched the spectacle as her father complied, and it made her uneasy. It was difficult to know who was more afraid or suspicious of whom. The men told him about the manners of the kind of horse that might suit the Queen of England, and that they would go to see this horse they had their eye on, in tomorrow's hunt, and after that, they would take the great big animal back to Buckingham Palace providing that it passed a vet's report, and that it would be entirely well behaved. Claire had never seen John as polite and softly spoken her whole life and she was relieved when they left the back yard of the bungalow and got back into the black Range Rover. One let his window down: 'We'll come tomorrow, to the hunt, bring the last mare you showed us, we'd like to see her in action.'

It was John's own mare. He always hunted her, trusted her as far as he could trust anything, and liked her, more than he liked any living thing, and he knew she was good and capable. He had kept the best horse until last and had not trotted or primed or shone any of the other horses he was breaking for locals, to the same degree. John owned two: the mare, and a young yearling, rumoured to be spoiled. John had raised the mare since she was a foal. A man from the city had left her with him in return for some livery he could not pay. When the man had died no one had ever come for her return.

'If she can jump these drystone walls and clear them, we'll take her,' the other man called out as he hopped into the Range Rover nodding at the walls all about the place, which seemed to John very extravagant for an Englishman well versed in polite manners to become excited and to give away his business like this. He watched him wave a hand out of the passenger window as the Range Rover headed to Mrs Hynes's lodgings in the town.

*

The children were back inside the bungalow and just finished their tea and homework as John O'Connor stayed out late on the farm, nervous for Tuesday's hunt. He went rattling and tinkering about the yard, in and out of the Old House for bits of leather straps and feed, and he groomed the mare for some hours. Rain lashed hard against the side window of the bungalow and their old sheepdog lay in front of the tired fire until the last sods of turf burned through.

Anne O'Connor came into the living room and lifted the remote control from one of the armchairs, turned to the portable television to mute it. The children, accustomed to her action, knelt to prayer. Claire was down first on her bony knees, the carpet stinging her, followed by Conor, then Anne. Finally, Brian perched in a half kneel-half sit, wiggling about the floor and unable to hold still as the four souls prayed a decade of the rosary together. Anne was the call, and the children, the response. Their old dog was shook and fallen in at the hind leg where the pink of the stretched skin looked dehydrated. He whimpered by the last low flames as Anne muttered Hail Marys and finished the night's praying with a Confiteor.

'Shep is looking very shook,' she said, suddenly, after they had finished the prayer. She always noticed the flesh of anything about her, often in a battle with her own weight. She ate many of the hens' eggs – existing on a diet of protein with some spoonfuls of cold peas. She boiled a clutch of eggs every few days and shelled them when they cooled by the square tin sink in the kitchen and left them rolling about in a glass bowl in the fridge. She also plucked big heads of cabbage from the vegetable garden, rinsing the curly leaves that were often full of holes from slugs lying in the damp clay about the old farm. She boiled the cabbage in a large pot on the hob and drained the liquid to drink seasoned with pepper and salt. She allowed herself a square of chocolate now and then, but usually apologised after eating it. Treats were only purchased on Sundays in the newsagent's by the church after mass when the children would have a weekly bar of chocolate.

'Maybe it's the smell of cabbage that's making Shep sick?' Conor said. No one answered.

Claire was eleven and her life was an eternal worry about turning twelve. She watched girls in the next class grow breasts like soft saucers under their thin maroon gym slips. She didn't like how age took away the aerobic figures like the one she still had in common with her brothers. Worse, she didn't like how these new figures seemed to draw everyone's attention. Boys were lucky, they just stretched up, got some spots, a deeper voice, and some facial hair. Girls who were older looked different from their brothers, and therefore, on farms around Claire's place, they were treated differently. For now, Claire, Conor and Brian shared clothes and vests, toys, crayons, and ran about the fields with sticks, and raced on wild ponies. But like every certain thing, this was about to change.

'We'll say one last prayer for a special intention,' Anne said.

'What's the intention?' Brian asked.

'It wouldn't be special if we named it,' Anne said.

'What? That we sell the mare to the Queen of England?' Conor said, eyeballing his mother. She dipped her head. 'Because we're broke, and we need the Queen's help,' he said.

'Do we really?' Brian asked simply and inquisitively. Claire stayed quiet.

'Stop,' Anne said. 'Such talk of money is crass, and you'll bring nothing but bad luck on this house with that kind of mood about you.'

'I don't think it'll have anything to do with me,' Conor said, 'our bad luck, so let us all pray for the Queen of fucking England to not starve any more Irish people.'

'Stop it,' Anne said, again. 'Conor. Stop. Never ever swear. You know this. It's a sin.'

A curse rarely went unpunished, but Anne knew not to raise her husband's temper when he was agitated, so this time she would not tattle on her oldest son.

'I'll stop,' Conor said smartly. 'Sure I have prayers to say, God save the Queen prayers. Should we sing it? I'm certain there's an air to it.' Claire remained kneeling a little longer, closed her eyes and prayed hard, splitting another rosary between saving the starving children in Africa from drought, and three last prayers for her own body – that it stayed lean. She hoped, if she was to grow breasts, that they would be paltry and unnoticeable, like hailstones. Or fried eggs. She also prayed that the Queen buy the mare and it might help her mother have some peace from her father for a while. After prayers, Anne did not tell her children to go to bed as she usually would have, instead she got up and went to the kitchen to prepare the morning's breakfast, soaking porridge oats and fussing about a table setting.

The children then took to laying down and sprawled about the threadbare carpet hugging close beside the old sheepdog with the telly still muted. They all agreed that no one liked noise when they were sick.

Brian added: 'Or sad. No one likes to watch telly when they're sad.'

'Is he dead now?' Conor asked flatly of his mother as she came back into the room on the balls of her feet so as not to disturb them.

'No, no, he's not, love, don't be silly, he's just exhausted. And sure aren't we all?' she replied, yawning. She was attempting to excuse her husband's behaviour with this pre-warning, should the need arise, and not to lose face in front of the other children. She leaned over her taller son and bent down to kiss the top of his head. His dark hair was greasy because he was nearly thirteen and this was a time that required a lot of attention to personal hygiene. Anne often mentioned personal hygiene to the children. She also spoke often about those in the town who were sick and suffering for she was a gentle and sensitive woman who spent a lot of time encouraging her young family to be grateful for the meal they had just eaten, to be grateful for the school books that lay dog-eared in their schoolbags, grateful for food, for love, to pray hard for children in Africa and mostly for more vocations to the Church. Conor swatted her and pulled away. He was beginning to think all her sensitivity was a waste of time. And worse, could endanger them.

With the volume on the telly risen once again, the children shouted out answers to a quiz show they liked. Spain. Dublin. Lamb. May the road rise to meet you. Thirteen. Knock. An oak tree. The Black and Tans.

'Pricks,' said Conor out of earshot of his mother. Claire resisted correcting her brother, though he annoyed her.

Then Brian shouted: '*Die Hard*,' loudly and enthusiastically, and they all forgot about the sick dog and the Queen's men for a few blissful moments. Brian excelled at film, and Conor at the history and geography of Ireland and Europe, despite having never left the country. Claire knew everything about books, something that bored her brothers, and even though she owned no books aside from her school books, and the use, every week, of the local library. After the quiz, the mood flattened and the children stayed quiet and demure when the nine o'clock news started up as they knew that no child was ever allowed up past the nine o'clock news.

'*Will* he die?' Conor asked his mother bluntly. Anne stared back at him caught by a moment of surprise, or fear. She lifted her slim hand to his face, and on instinct he thought that she wanted to strike him, but the movement was too slow. She knew her oldest son well enough to know that he was hurting, and when he was hurting, he was angry. Besides, Anne never struck her children. Even so, now that their relationship was changing, she flinched and everyone held their breath a moment – except Conor, he seemed hardened. Anne, sensing his recoil, gently allowed her hand to hang back by her side. Claire's eyes filled up and she bit her bottom lip down hard, fixed her nightdress about her ankles and looked deep into the fire.

'Be nice,' Brian said to Conor, simply.

'I am always nice,' Conor said and thumped his younger brother hard on the back of the head.

'No, you're not,' Brian said, rubbing his head. But he passed no notice, which was the way he had always responded to Conor's temper.

'We are so nice we are going to sell a horse to the Queen of England. Aren't we mighty?'

'Stop it, Conor, I won't warn you again,' Anne said, pleading with her son. Brian leaned hard in against his mother, nervous at the newness of the situation, his thumb stuck in his mouth as she hunkered down beside them, his big blue eyes staring at her like honest moons. She didn't tell him to stop sucking because his mouth would get full up of warts like she usually did before his father would slap his hand out of his mouth.

Anne had been considering the dog, and was unsure what to do. She was past lies with the children, and Conor especially punished her for concealing truths. Though she was unsure of any other way to live her life. 'I don't know if he will die,' she said, to Conor's earlier question. 'But I don't think so, maybe he just ate some-thing strange. Chocolate maybe. Maybe he was nibbling on some. He'll be right as rain soon. Just you watch. He's a fighter that one, just like you.' But all the children knew eating any chocolate was impossible for the dog. Chocolate was a treat on Sundays only – except during the long forty days of Lent.

'Should we ring the vet?' Brian asked. But the family knew that John O'Connor called the vet for bigger animals only and ones that were of value. Anne took a long inhale, letting it out slowly through her pursed lips. All eyes stared at the woman in the dark room with the dead fire, hopeful but helpless as children are. 'We won't, Shep will rally,' she said as she rose slowly.

Claire and Brian said one last prayer, and were more hopeful in God. Conor thought God was a load of nonsense because he had spent a full month praying for snow one winter and it never arrived. Spring came, and they all continued to pray despite the proof that their prayers were failing. Conor went through the motions out of habit. That February, Claire burst her thumb out on the farm when a stone from a wall came down on it as she was climbing into the apple orchard. She received nine ragged stitches at the doctor's, and a tetanus shot in her bottom that stung hard, after which their mother took them all to the local grotto to pray to Mary the Virgin Mother of God for fast healing. And when Claire's stitches were removed, the scar was all but invisible to the naked eye.

Claire had no interest in the news lately, watching the grey uninspiring faces of men in suits that were arguing over Charlie Haughey. Claire thought Haughey was an odd and ugly man, with a smile that sent shivers down her back. She nervously watched Conor watching his mother, as she sighed hard again and looked at her hands, up and down of them, as though they held the answer to the dog's sickness. These were not her rules and the children knew that Anne had a slightly more senior position in the home to the children, she certainly had in law and in custom, but barely in the eyes of her husband, and she had, like her own mother, and her mother before that, very little in the way of any financial freedom, which included many decisions on a day-to-day basis. Everything needed considering, calling a doctor or a dentist for one of the children, filling the outside plastic tank with heating oil, new shoes, or the authority to call a vet for an animal that was of little monetary value. Anne had, in effect, very little permission to do anything, so they spent long days in churches or libraries, or anywhere with no entry charge when the work on the farm and the schooling was over.

Brian felt vulnerable in the care of such a powerless adult and started crying in great big gusts, his tears falling on the cracked granite flagstone of the fire. Anne gently tapped his young shoulder and handed him a tissue from up her jumper sleeve, and, in a moment of indescribable guilt, he thrust his short arms around her wiry neck again, leaned his round head like a large hazelnut into the crook in her arm and cried out for nothing specific. Pausing for a moment, he looked at the tissue in his hand and grimaced. 'It's dry, go on,' she said as she began unravelling from his thin body.

'My teacher says when you're too hot and you're a dog

it's hard to tell anyone, so you should leave out a drink for them all the time, because they can't ask for themselves,' Brian said, between sobs.

'He's not too hot,' Anne said, looking from the dog to the miserable fire and back again, and tapping him gently, 'but no harm in getting him a drink just to be on the safe side.'

Anne was always willing the safe side. They had prayers to keep the family safe, and holy water drops flicked onto them every so often to keep them all safe, again. They had to pray for the souls of the dead, pray for the souls of the living and pray for all the ailments of the living. They were encouraged at school and at home to listen for the cries of the dead in limbo – for babies of unmarried mothers or those stuck unbaptised in purgatory and everyone who had sinned out of fear, that might take the right path in the future and that God would protect everyone – from threats that loomed large outside the house, things they were to fear but were never told about.

Whatever was outside their front door and away from the farm and the safety of the bungalow, was, the children were always reminded, very dangerous. Anne kept extra money in a fireproof tin and this reminded Claire of the mother played by Brenda Fricker in the film *My Left Foot* that they had all watched recently, it had stayed with her, the scene when the mother almost burned herself alive going up the chimney for the money for Christy's wheelchair. Claire learned from this that women needed to save money and hide the saved money, and that was one way of helping ward off the danger. Claire watched her mother's face as thread-like red spider veins burst bright against her white skin and ebony hair.

'Are you OK, Mam?' Brian asked. It was the children's favourite way to see her, her face free of make-up, bare. Anne only wore make-up if she went to Glackens's in the town on Saturday night with John. It looked harsh on her, the paint, the orange hue that was different from her neck and ears, and it deadened all the emotions she portrayed that could signpost the day, and help them to navigate.

Claire loved her mother best when she was fresh-faced in a ratty jumper and lying about with them. With John away up the fields she was allowed the freedom of reading to them, or laughing without caution.

'Yes, yes,' she said. 'Yes,' she said again, and looked at Brian, kindly at first, and then she nodded, and appeared flustered and rose to a light squat, where she bounced gently awhile. 'That's enough now, how about we get Shep a drink, and see if maybe he is overheating.'

Anne lifted a poker to the grate and prodded the last of the fire, unsettling the grey powder and the few bright embers. Then she wiped some ash from her pants with the leather knee patches, and pushed her feet back into house slippers – furry things with rubber soles. When she walked out of the living room and into the dull kitchen, Conor stuck his tongue out at Brian, and then poked his brother hard in the shoulder, before digging his bitten nails and hands deep into the pile of the dog. He looked at the dog's eye a moment, then began to stroke him hard from his tail to his head and back. The other children knew he was hurting him but neither of them could stop him knowing they might be next.

'Right, you lot,' Anne said, coming back into the room with a bowl of water. 'Claire has a very big day tomorrow. Now let's hope this water works, and then it's bedtime for you all.'

'The mare has all the work to do, not Claire,' Conor said. 'Not sure what Claire can do to help.'

'That's a big idea for a small brain,' Claire said.

'Stop it, both of you,' Anne said, as she left a plastic bowl of water by the dog, and after Claire coaxed him to drink a little. Conor did not retaliate against his sister, who got up, threw a blanket over the dog and went to her bed. Inside the dark room was a little cot bed, too short for her growing body, with a puffy eiderdown. Beyond the light curtains you could see across the yard to the Old House where the yard was still lit dimly with a flood light. She listened to the mare whinny for her feed. She lay down under the navy sheets and the heavy scratchy blanket that poked through – everything felt cold – and rocking herself back and over in the bed, she eventually fell into a fitful sleep.

II

Claire woke early the next morning. The rain had stopped pouring outside her window and everything was silent but for a muffled sound like she was under-water. Her head was banging and she was freezing, her legs were leaden and when she tried to get up from the bed to pull open the curtains to see the day, to check on Shep's progress through the night, she could barely lift her head from the flat blue pillow. It felt bloated like a pig's bladder full of sludge. She wondered for a moment if she had been punched in the face, but she hadn't. She tried but had no recollection of any row with her father. She hadn't run into a fist or the heel of his foot. She went back over the previous night in her head – yes, they all sat to tea, liver and mash with green beans and brown sauce. She hated liver, could it be the liver? A reaction? Then they set about helping the dog – yes, Shep, she remembered Shep was sick and after they all set to helping the poor runt, she remembered going to bed. The cold sheets. She was overcome with a fear that the dog would die in his sleep. Prayers. Yes. They had said prayers. And then, alone in her bed, she had said more of them, over and over, many decades of the rosary.

*

Tuesday was Hunt Day. From autumn through spring John joined with clutches of horseback riders about the Galway countryside saddled on bays and chestnuts, greys and pie-balds, with eager hounds at their hocks, as they flooded about the square fields, roads and streets of the county. The hunt started at eleven in the morning, and – depending on the fox's cunning and level of exhaustion, or if they had young cubs buried in foxholes, and also depending on the ambition and age of the hounds that chased the scent like hungry maulers – it could end as abruptly as it started. Or sometimes it could carry on until last light.

It was far from being a sport of kings around these parts, for even the poorest farmer in the area had a horse. There was the legacy and the thirst for blood sports from old families with double-barrelled names and huge, crumbling estates who came along full of their own importance, the women with wizened faces and men with booming voices, their riding style slightly at odds with the locals. They shoved more of the foot into the stirrup, and rammed their feet forward, rode big quiet horses with large bits in their mouths. The locals knew that the cull of foxes was an important consideration for their livestock and so mostly everyone got along together, understanding their rank and station.

The poorer farmers farmed a dry mix: some sheep, cattle, a pig, a brood of hens, some farms didn't even have their fields fully plumbed with water, so bringing fodder and water around to fields and animals took up most of the day's work.

*

John O'Connor was more ambitious for the farm than his father, Jack. Jack had given the place to his son when he was in his mid-sixties and moved on into the town, where he lived on an inadequate pension and very little else but his wife, Katie's, insufficient takings from a cottage knitting business she had going. They had both washed their hands abruptly of the land, and Jack of his son – though he maintained a civility, they rarely saw each other despite the short distance between their houses there was a long gap between their lives. Then Jack had died, bare months after his wife, he was reading some prose by the window on a sunny day, some book by a new Japanese writer he had taken to. Only Conor was old enough to almost remember him. Jack was a man far more educated than his son in words and worlds, he was always surprised that John could deliver the mail to the right houses, considering the difficulty he had in learning to read when he started school. But John had plumbed the fields and pumped water in places of rock and hard clay where his father had failed, and even had failed to try. He had done it against his father's advice, and he had managed it quite well. He had built a few new stables behind the Old House, and had tried his best at a mild form of modernisation.

John spent much of his time on the farm working with young horses – lunging them, settling them, breaking them in to the saddle for the rich and upwardly mobile about the countryside. He had identified a niche in the area, and broke the horses for the busy folk, though none of the profit ever seemed to make its way down to the family, unless for essential items – clothes and food and school books. Never a holiday. Or an expensive toy. Or treats. Or, indeed, a pony of their own, though they used to ride many of the more spirited horses, and help break them in, the children sitting on young horses from the age of nine or ten.

The more settled horses out on the hunt often belonged to the old gentry, who were clinging on to big kitchens with bells. John broke horses for the new rich that had moved in, doctors, school principals, people who had jobs that involved travelling to the US, a few managers from the companies in the new industrial estates, one of which had recently given all the local staff a turkey and ham for Christmas as a bonus. The turkeys did not fit into most people's ovens, so on Christmas morning birds were hacked into two parts and roasted on two days. No one complained because investment was rare in the West of Ireland and people did not want to bite the hand that fed them, even if it fed them what they didn't need. And no one dared to say that geese were the custom in these parts. No one wanted to say they liked those things just as they were.

The daily news was filled with car bombings and deaths and Gerry Adams's voice was dubbed over. This was everything and nothing to Claire's family and families like Claire's, but it did mean that those from landed estates of old, who hunted alongside the farmers, were differ-ent, and everyone knew it and no one dared to ask why. They sipped their whiskey, brandy or sloe gin. Classes mixed when they were chasing a fox, they all needed the hounds to pick up a scent, and this was hard on wet days, harder on icy days, when the risk of a horse breaking a leg was high.

Claire's school peers were growing environmentally conscious. They had grown to hate her for her father's complicity in the hunting scene, not from a post-colonial perspective – most of them didn't quite understand that – but because of the cruelty of ripping a young fox apart in a field. Nevertheless Claire did it without complaining. Horses were big and mad, with a whole head to themselves, and they rarely shared what went on in it with humans. She had hunted measly ponies once or twice and found them terrifying. The idea of jumping stone walls with a young pony out of control was a strange thing to a shy young girl who hated making small talk. Out on the hunt was much talk about animals and breeding them, the confounding parts of horse trucks, old engines, carburettors, windows, ramps, wheel braces that were letting them down. Conversations were always about before. Everything was better before, before, before they said. Before Thatcher and women's lib, and as bad as Thatcher was for the Irish, she was good for the hunt so there was confusion about Thatcher amongst the farmers – she wasn't their class of a person, or was she? Besides, the farmers convinced each other that they needed the hunt for the cull of foxes, and John had done a good job in convincing his children of the same. They needed the lambs to kill for Easter. They needed the rich punters at the races. They needed they needed they needed. They were owed, they were owed, oh, but they were owed. The women – well, no one sought to consider them much at the time. While Thatcher had starved the Northern prisoners, to the smallhold farmers of the West of Ireland, the North felt very far away, something they didn't discuss except that they were sympathetic to the cause. Neil Kinnock, who was perhaps more of the thinking-man's man, seemed to be no improvement on Thatcher. He had notions about what he could do with land, was keen on banning fox hunting in England which would have repercussions in Ireland's horse industry, and the Irish of the West had had enough of being told what to do with their land. If they banned the hunting, everyone was in trouble.

But still, it was confusing to Claire. Her teacher Michael, who she held in high regard, and had made a change from being taught by a nun, loved Neil Kinnock, loved Labour, and he had been to university, which seemed like an exclusive place that no one in the hunt ever talked about – not even the English, or the Anglo-Irish, or those with hairnets who spoke down through their nose. Some of them hadn't been to school at all.

'Just like the fucking royals,' her father used to say. 'Inbred and full of it.'

Out on the hunts, people chatted about hunt balls and who did what to whom – and how the English never really hated the Irish in the way the Irish thought they did. Many of the farmhands about the place had slept with the daughter or granddaughter of some Lady, or

Lord. No one picked their shiny pennies up off the ground as they had done a few decades previously. But despite all of the relationships, it was unheard of, for the most part, for the Lord or Lady of anywhere to marry the farmhands. Neither of them would ever dream of marriage. People were wild and wilful – but they were not stupid with the family silver.

Anne O'Connor sat on the edge of their bed and pulled a bra around her waist clipping it in front of her under her breasts, and then dragging the cups into place. She was careful not to wake John too early and usually changed her underwear under the bed sheets for modesty. She washed her face in the bathroom. Her black hair around her forehead was damp and starting to curl as she dressed in the same pants as the night before, with the patches on the knees and a white jumper with a thorny rose bush embroidered across it.

Anne got up and began her morning jobs, mooching about the hall. She switched the immersion on in the hot-press and got some towels ready to go about her morning fuss. She then went into the kitchen and out to the scullery to attend to the dog, always up and about and alive in the morning, always behaving as if the day before had not happened at all. Seize the day before it seizes you.

A sharp blast of air came in underneath Claire's door and the cold startled the girl and she started to cry. Anne heard it and went to her daughter. 'Claire, love,' she said as she came into the room, 'did I hear you crying?'

Claire didn't respond.

Anne went to open Claire's pale primrose curtains but stopped short of her destination and gently squeezed her daughter's toes. 'Oh my,' she said, and then she sat by her and put her cold hand on her forehead. 'You're boiling up, love.' She leaned in and touched Claire with her lips: 'Yes – definitely boiling, you are running quite a temperature, lie back, good girl, gentle now. I'll get you some water,' she said as she moved to the kitchen. 'Damn it,' she said to herself. 'Damn it.' It was difficult to have a child home on a busy day for John O'Connor. No woman needed a husband and a child about them for the morning when there was housework to be done. Anne rattled about the kitchen, opened out the window, and as she took a tumbler down from the glass press its rusty hinges squeaked as they always did. 'Good, good. Well, Shep,' Anne said, leaning down to the dog, 'and aren't you looking a lot brighter this morning?' Shep's tail tapped off the hollow pine door by the scullery. 'You've only gone and given it to Claire though, haven't you?' Anne said. There was a calm kindness to her voice, a brightness and trust that she saved for talking to the animals. Shep's tail went over and back again and Claire shivered but relaxed into her wet pillow in the next room, reassured by the knowledge that the dog, at least, was OK.

After rinsing a facecloth under running water, Anne wrung it, left it neatly folded and set to pulling open a drawer that had come off its runner, rattling icing nozzles, whisks, a steel potato masher and then the squeak of the tin opener as she said, 'No, no, down, down, boy, look how our prayers worked.' She left the dog's bowl on the floor and then she did the strangest thing – she clapped her hands as she went back into Claire's room and fussed about, helping her to sit up to drink some water. She handed Claire a small white Disprin tablet while she told her of the dog's great improvement, and that the tablet would take down the heat of the child's body. Finally, she left the cold facecloth neatly folded on her daughter's warm forehead.

Claire tried to swallow the tablet, but it was huge and her throat was narrowing and soon closed tightly to her swallow. The pill lodged, where it fizzled about stuck in a swollen crevice. It should have been dissolved in water, but Anne never read the packet of anything. Instructions were simultaneously above and beneath her – speed in the bungalow was always of the essence, even if no one had anywhere particularly important to go to.

Anne had married John in haste, after ten weeks of courting each other. They were both nineteen. 'No point in putting off the inevitable,' Anne said to Margaret on the morning of her wedding. Margaret agreed, but some years later the sisters, who were always close throughout their childhoods, lost contact.

Anne, anxious for her daughter, returned to the room, and brought some more pain relief balanced on a spoon. It went down better than the Disprin, and Claire took another spoonful. 'Fine girl like you,' Anne said, 'you could drink the bottle. We need to get you better. You have an important day.'

Claire had tried to forget it, the day, all the work that lay ahead of her. 'I'm not pretending,' she said to her mother.

'I know you're not, love, but your father needs you.'

'Can't he bring one of the boys?' Claire said. 'Please.' Claire didn't like to beg her father for anything as she knew through experience that the outcome was usually unfavourable.

'He won't manage without you, Claire love, I'm sorry, but you know it has to be you – you'll impress them with your cleverness.' Anne smiled and lifted her tone.

Claire groaned softly.

'That medicine will soon start to work, and look, I'll get Conor to do the morning feed. You can lie on for a little while, but not too long, Claire. Claire, do you hear me?'

'Yes,' Claire said turning away from her mother. Her throat was alive with swelling as the last fragments of the white pill sizzled in her tonsil and disappeared. And for this small mercy, Claire was grateful.

III

'Claire, pull some decent clothes on yourself,' John said. 'Something smart,' he went on as he stood outside her door. He used the word decent when he was bringing his children out in public: face and decorum were important in front of others. Today he was coiled tight and Claire felt it. He would be quiet, respectful to all at the hunt, he had decided, he would brag little but was certain he was going to come away with a new start for his family, and this might take some pressure off.

Claire groaned.

'Oh, come now, quit your complaining, we've a fine sight of work to do to make today a success. Hup, put some smart clothes on, you'll follow the hunt on foot. That'll improve you.'

'OK,' she said back out to him.

Noting the lack of enthusiasm in her voice, he walked in, looked about the small bedroom: 'Don't you know how lucky are you, not having to go to school like your brothers?' Claire knew she was being brought because she never argued back, or contradicted her father in front of others like Conor had taken to doing lately. Brian, her mother often said, was one of life's dreamers.

Claire lay still and watched her father go about her

room. He picked up a hairbrush, inspected it and left it gingerly back in its place. He was about to take his leave again, when he stopped by a photograph in a mother-of-pearl frame hanging next to the light switch. He straightened it with his ruddy thumb and index finger before clasping his hands behind his back and peering into the picture. It was a colour photo of her with her two brothers at the zoo. He stared at the picture for another few moments, tapping a foot gently, then he left the room.

Claire got up out of bed slowly, pulled a bundle of clothes from drawers. Her skin was sensitive to touch and her head throbbed, and she walked along the short hallway to the dark bathroom where she brushed her teeth and gargled her throat with salt water. It stung. Her face was red in the reflection of the mirror, she looked swollen. She filled the blue plastic basin used for sick children at night and sat awkwardly on the closed seat of the toilet, dipping her feet in to wash them, but it was too hot, even when she added cold water it stung. She felt so unwell that a shower was out of the question. She dried her feet off with a hardened towel and hung her head between her legs. It felt a little better to stay like this a while until John rapped on the bathroom door and interrupted her peace: 'Claire, Claire, come on, get a move on.'

'Coming,' she said, quietly, and her belly ached, and she was sure she would be sick from the pressure. Waves of disappointment washed over her. She slowly stood upright and brushed out her long hair, tying it in a neat low ponytail, taking care with the strands, gripping the unruly ones behind her ears. She pulled her shirt over her white bralette and buttoned it to her wiry neck. Next she unfolded a soft blue pullover that always made her happy – perhaps it was the soft material or the muted tone – and finally dragged some dark slacks up her legs and fastened them. John didn't approve of denim. He waited nervously outside the bathroom while she left the room in a pirouette to creep fast under his arm and walked to the kitchen where she refused all food that her mother offered. John arrived some time after, having shaved, cursing loudly a nick that he made on his cheek as Claire drank some tea. She eyed the red bull's eye dot on his face. He was wearing yellowed jodhpurs, a white shirt, with a cravat around his neck, and a gold-plated horse pin through it. He pulled on a quilted green sleeveless gilet, and took his seat at the table.

'Christ, I don't know if I'm able to eat a morsel,' he said, looking about him to locate his wife for reassurance that food might help. The boys were, by now, gone to school. Anne knew John's statement to be rhetorical, and so she set to, picking out sausages and rashers from the greasy frying pan off the stove. He sat and taped the bottom of the jodhpurs to his legs, round and round he wound the tape as Claire watched him, hoping he'd notice her fever, and her general malaise.

'Two black puddings I said,' he told his wife, and he stabbed the steel fork into a piece of the white pudding that was on the plate in front of him, his hand in a fist like a child might hold their cutlery. 'I won't eat this,' he said lifting it up. 'It repeats on me – an awful piece of food a white pudding is.' Then he put his fork down on the table and stared at his daughter.

'You not eating?' he said.

'I'm not hungry,' she said.

'Not hungry?' he said, puzzled. 'But you haven't eaten since yesterday.'

Claire nodded.

'What's the matter, cat got your tongue? You need to eat breakfast, that's the point of the first meal of the day, you won't keep up with us, you can't go out with your belly bet on your back. You won't manage a whole busy day with hunger upon you.'

Anne busied herself at the sink swapping the white pudding for black and making John content. She knew Claire wouldn't keep up anyway, no one could, it was an impossible task to do so. Claire shook her head as her mother put a sausage on a little plate in front of the girl, and said: 'Try a little,' and Claire dutifully lifted her fork and gently pierced the sausage skin and it hissed. She cut a narrow slice and brought it to her mouth, John watching, his arms bent at the elbows and a fork in one fist and a butter knife in the other.

'Eat it,' he said. 'Go on, you can't stay all day on your feet if you don't eat.'

'I was thinking, maybe she could come back, I could go and fetch her on the bike, you know after you set off,' Anne said.

'Were you?' John said. 'That won't be happening, I need the girl for the whole day. Only way to get better, is get up and get out.'

'I'm not sure she's up to following about the hunt on foot,' Anne said, persisting. 'She's not herself, she has a fever.'

'She'll do as she's told,' he said, and both Claire and her mother nodded in agreement and apology. 'Can't be always getting out of work we don't want to do, the world doesn't work that way. But maybe no one has told ye that, so I'm telling ye.' They nodded again. Claire's eyes watered and her throat was dry and though she tried to swallow hard, not to stoke his temper, she gagged involuntarily and spat the food back out. Anne rushed to her daughter's mouth with a tissue. 'For fuck's sake – that's good food that is, Claire, your mother is cooking all morning to set you off in good fettle. Don't get all moody today, I am warning you. Today is a big day, might even buy you a pony if you keep up.'

Claire took a drink and said: 'I won't mess up. I promise.'

'Good girl,' he replied, softening a little. He needed her more than she needed him today, and this was unusual he thought, as he began scooping grease from his plate up to his mouth with a slice of white loaf. He stuck the top of a sausage into a yolk, popping it, and the bright orange poured out and made Claire fainter.

Claire was a good daughter, reading her father, trying to predict his moods, his laughter, if he had drink taken, read his silence, reading the road ahead of him – the day, the weather. She had become much like her mother for trying to make everything fall into place for the family. The boys didn't seem to feel the same pressure, and Conor actively appeared to rail against his father lately.

John soon dabbed the corners of his mouth with the corner of the tablecloth, and went out to give the mare some grain. Claire went into the front room to fill his hip flask with spirits from the cabinet. Whiskey. She then lifted the bonnet of the jeep and filled the water, put a hay net in the back, a first aid box, an old feed bucket, a drum of water, leather saddle covered with a sheet to stop it scuffing, a heavy horse blanket, rubber boots for the mare's feet, bridle, numnah, and a change of bit, martingale, and finally, John's whip and spurs and helmet.

She used to get excited when she was younger and her father said he'd buy her a pony, usually after drink, and mostly if there were a crowd around him. Along with her brothers they would talk endlessly about their favourite kind, they'd dream for months about winning a local gymkhana, or competing in the Olympics, dream that maybe he'd buy a bay one with a blaze, or a steel grey – Claire's favourite. But she knew now, on the cusp of womanhood, a time that was terrifying to her, that this motivational talk was lies. He would never spend money on them. Only ever for basics and a wedding, he had once said, if the time should arrive and only for his daughter's wedding, and only if she married the right sort – a request he never elaborated on and he didn't need to, Claire understood exactly what this meant: no one above John's own station.

The Queen's men were standing at the foot of a small hillock just outside the town when Claire and John arrived.

'Fuck,' he said, panicking as he drove by, 'I didn't think they'd be here already. They're early.' He drove on about a half-mile. Claire knew not to respond. 'I'll pull up here, and hack back, I don't want them to see this rig-out.' The mare was loaded in his old horsebox attached to the rusty jeep and John was ashamed of it. Some way out they brushed her down and Claire shined her off with a dry rag, took the plait from her tail and brushed it out like a great black fan, and fixed four boots on her legs.

'Good girl,' she said quietly to the mare whose ears flicked about on edge and excitable. 'You'll do good,' Claire said to him as she tied the girth, checked it again by running her hands between it and the mare's warm and pulsing belly. She checked the stirrup length was to her father's leg, and took an old feed bucket from the jeep, turned it upside down and held the mare at her head to allow her father to mount. She passed him his whip as he lifted his leg in silence, and she tightened his girth again.

'Hurry now, lock up, and be close by. Do you hear me?'
'Yes,' she said. 'I do, I hear you.'

John trotted the mare up the narrow road, quickly now, and there was no way Claire's legs could keep pace. He didn't look back. She cursed herself for not loading a bicycle. Feeling faint, she sat back in the jeep. Claire knew today's hunt would be slow and predicted they'd all parade in front of the men to begin the day. It had started to rain and a wind had whipped up again: the fox's scent would be poor. She shivered. When her father was out of earshot, she switched the jeep's engine on and revved gently to warm the heaters, and in turn, her hands. Then she warmed her gloves for later. Anne had slipped two Disprin into her pocket alongside a bar of chocolate. She opened her water flask and dropped in the pills, watching them fizz about excitedly in the silver body, she could swear as they zigzagged that they were trying to escape. She twisted the plastic lid back on, shook it, and after finishing it all down quickly, she felt a little better. She turned up the volume on the sea forecast on the radio. It was wonderfully hypnotic; listening about places she had never been and she would have liked to lie there all day and throw the horse blanket over her and sleep. But soon she got up, locked the doors carefully checking each one in turn, swept out the horse shit from the ramp, and took off to walk the half-mile or so back on foot to the field where the hunt had gathered, in the drizzle.

There was a fine gathering of horses by the time Claire arrived. Riders were mounted in black, red and green coats, some children darted about on small ponies with colourful anoraks – which were not strictly permitted, but it was difficult to tell the son or daughter of a landowner, no matter how inconsiderable the acreage they held, to change their apparel as they could block access to their land from the hunt. Claire spotted the black Range Rover abandoned on a green ditch. It was spotless, shiny and out of place. She walked close by the men. Claire thought about her aunts huddled once in a small kitchen, waiting on the post, on news, hoping to be given Donnelly visas and get away to Boston for ever. Some were working at the time in sweet shops, one was working three jobs to raise the fare to go, and others were on the line in the factories in the city. America was the dream – a dream where, much like the lottery, you had to rely on someone picking your name out for this new start. Selling a horse to the Queen was not a matter of luck. It meant you had a good eye for an animal, you knew what you were about – and mostly, it meant that if the horse was good enough for the Queen, so were you, perhaps.

John's mare trotted about the soft grass on the hill and he was going boldly up and down passing the men. Mares were worth more in this transaction for they could be bred after service, for the black cavalry, ninety-eight per cent of which was Irish bred. John looked serious and he was holding his hands high as he rode. Everything felt forced.

The men nodded and John nodded in return.

The horn sounded and the hounds, tails high, noses on the ground, set off sniffing and running across the green field. The gate of the field was open out onto the road, but the crowd who gathered to hunt and show their horses off decided to jump the wall by the gate.

The first rider – the huntsman – leaned back on his horse in great exaggeration as he cleared the wall ungraciously. Mid-jump, he roared out: 'Wire!' – and 'Wire!' they all shouted back to each other in panicked unison. Some riders waited to show the men what their horses could do, many looked nervous and pale, others cared less and chatted away as they jumped. The rest trotted neatly through the gate and out onto the road where the traffic was stopped. One woman sat on the horn of her car, late with her children for school, and this drove the younger horses wild and a palomino pony took off through the field and up over the hill at a high gallop where it flung itself against the trunk of a tree, blindly, and parted company with its startled young rider.

John O'Connor waited back on the mare and decided he would jump somewhere in the middle of the field of riders. The mare was growing impatient as she blew out hard, and pawed the grass. One of the men lifted his camera, took off his hat and clicked some photos of her as John trotted the horse to the wall, cantered for two strides, and cleared it with air.

The hunt disappeared out of sight, pounding through the next field at speed. The men jumped into their Range Rover and took off with optimism that they could keep up. Claire was certain they wouldn't catch the field of riders, and knowing this she walked back to John's jeep, slowly, where she lay under the horse blanket listening to the radio. She tuned into a current affairs show talking about Gorbachev and the Cold War. After some time she switched it off for fear that she would burn out the engine's battery, and shivered herself to sleep.

Some hours after, she heard the hoot of an owl and it woke her — and then the lone clip-clop of the mare's hooves up the narrow road.

IV

Claire's stomach cramped hard and she was bent over by the side of the jeep when some men arrived with her father. They spoke out of the sides of their mouths smoking cigarettes with their hands cuffed around and smoke was blowing back into Claire's face.

'You'll be a rich man tonight, John O'Connor.'

'Go on about your business,' John said, dismounting.

When the men had gone, Claire unbuckled the girth and lifted down the heavy saddle from the mare's steaming withers. She was soaked wet from rain. Claire dried the mare and then the leather with an old sheet and felt a great deal of sympathy for the horse. John stood quietly holding the bridle as Claire bent down and untied the wet and mucky boots from her warm legs. She was doubled in pain.

'Did you catch anything?' Claire asked. She brought the heavy horse blanket. She was too light of frame to thrust it up and over the mare by herself.

'We'll leave it for now, Claire, we'll put it on her at home. Let's load up.'

Claire sat in the front, her arms and legs hot and aching now. She turned on the radio – risky – but she was feeling brave after all the help she had given over the course of the day. Suddenly the jeep swerved on the road, as John drove the nose of the vehicle towards the ditch.

'Well, there he is, the beady little bollox,' John said. A lean red fox stood up in the high ditch, sniffing about the grass. His tail was huge, he looked smug as foxes tend to, something about the slyness of their eyes.

'Don't, please, don't,' Claire said, full knowing her father's next move. She was alarmed at his irrationality, and she started begging as he chased towards the fox with the heavy load he had on, accelerating. She thought of what would happen to the mare if her father hit the ditch at speed. His emotions were running high, she knew this, that by cavorting with the men to sell the mare, he was himself running with the fox and hunting with the hounds. John had convinced himself that this way lay survival, but he was having second thoughts.

'Right, I won't kill it then, if you don't want me to. But pray it doesn't head off to kill a flock of lambs tonight then, or it's on you, missy.'

Claire stayed silent in case he'd change his mind and charge the front grille at the animal. They listened to the news coming in on the radio. Something about Iraq. She wished she hadn't turned it on, this was souring his mood also. He leaned forward and ground up the gears.

'I don't know in the cursed Christ what they do be doing abroad in those countries, they aren't half right. Treat their women like dogs, I heard.'

Claire didn't answer.

'Did I tell you that the fox went into the back of Brenda Walsh's kitchen, and the stupid bitch screamed in fright? You'd have heard her above in the town. I don't know how Paddy Walsh manages her.' He whistled for a while, then rolled down the window of the driver's seat. 'They're taking her, they are taking the mare,' he said all of a sudden, looking at Claire. 'She's off all the way to London town – imagine that.'

John had never been to London, much less Claire. John's uncles, all bar Thomas in Boston, who left and was never heard of again, had come home over the years. They drank whiskey and played cards, and talked about racehorses, McAlpine's, and the Irish cliché of posting a fiver on payday Friday to have on Monday in Cricklewood. They had never resorted to it, posting themselves cash, but it was done, and done often. Most of the Irish in England, according to the uncles, seemed to work for Irish, who it seemed took them for all they had in their lonely bones.

'So we'll give her a good looking-after when we get back, the mare, and we'll sort her bed well and nice, and throw down some new sawdust, right?'

'Right,' she said, watching as two crows fought over a piece of a plastic bottle. The bigger one picked the lid and flew away, content with its lot. She longed to be a crow. They never looked sick or dull or unable to fight.

Father reversed the box in by the side of the bungalow.

'Should I turn on some floodlights?' Claire asked.

'No, no,' John said, 'do not, you'll bring in the dark.'

'Right,' she said.

'Hop into the side of the box, Claire, slip the knot, and you unload her, I'll do the ramp. Easy letting her back, now.'

Claire panicked. She was never tasked with unloading the horses. She had problems with releasing the knots, and she didn't know how she would keep a horse this size straight as it came down off the ramp. She had never been shown. Her stomach burned.

'Fast, fast now, come on, good girl, they could be here any minute, want to be ahead of them. I wonder where they'll get cash tonight. I won't take no cheque,' John said, muttering to himself as he set about the jobs. 'I told them that though, Claire, I did, I'm sure they have ways. I told them I will only take cash. And sure I can wait for it until the morning. I won't release the horse until then. It's a lord's sum, Claire. Right you be, that's a plan,' he said, talking on to himself again. 'Don't release the mare until you have the money.'

Claire lifted the two latches at the little wooden side door of the horsebox and crept in under the mare's nose. She seemed brighter now, as though she could tell that plans were afoot for her. She pawed the floor with her hoof in big high lunges as Claire tackled the rope, clumsy and awkward with the quick-release knot. Eventually it loosened, and she pulled it out through the box rings, until it slipped fully through her shaking hands.

'Right, Claire, gently back with her now,' John said loudly. 'That's it, aisy now, aisy,' he said, as he lowered the ramp to the ground.

Suddenly the mare flashed her eye, pawed high and pulled hard on the rope. Claire let it go, the jerk was too powerful for her young body to hold her, and in the fright, she bent over quickly, gripping her stomach. John had unhooked the chain at the horse's rump and in that same moment he swished the chain in a clumsy move that startled the mare underneath her belly, where she was sensitive. She reared back in a half-dance half-thud, flashing the whites of her eyes, snorting, followed by a long and desperate groan, and she pulled away, fast backwards she went bounding and dancing in high lunges, crashing out of the box, and fell off the side of the ramp, where she waited, shaking by the front window of the Old House. John stood up straight in shock. Claire could see him looking in at her. His eyes wild in his head. She watched for the mare, and in the shadows of dusk that could play tricks on your eyes, Claire saw a long rope-like vein fall out of the side of the mare's neck – her flesh was slit wide open, long and perfect, like the silver flash of the blade of a sword, or how you might open an envelope with a knife.

'Oh, my fucking God,' John roared. 'Oh fuck,' he said again, breaking the heavy silence, and he ran this way and that about the dim yard, holding his head. Claire bolted down the ramp, and to the mare. She gathered the rope-like gut that pulsed as she lifted it so gently and pressed it back into the neck with the soft palms of both her hands. She waited, then, the pulse of her palms against the pulsing neck of the animal. The mare's head pushed into Claire's warmth.

'Oh, Christ,' Father yelled at his daughter, his own neck bursting underneath his cravat. He screamed to the sky, and in a remarkable move, he ran to the horsebox to see what had caused the injury. It was a nail, and as he stared at it, he lifted his index finger and stroked it back and over, and seemed to laugh a little, bargaining under his breath – something about this for that, and give and take, as he pulled some small tufts of the horse's coat free from the nail, hair that was caught up in a piece of flesh and on seeing this, he howled at his daughter, and then he laughed a moment again, engaged in a full ramble with himself, saying: *who did you think you were, man dear? and sure we're all fucked anyway, a nail, a nail, a fucking nail*, and then in a moment of terror, he looked Claire straight in the eye as she pushed hard against the neck of the horse and said: 'No, no, it's you, and your sickness – you fucking did this, you frightened her, you did, it was you, Claire. I could see all day you didn't want any of it.'

Claire stood silent and still with her hands pressed to the mare's neck. She knew from school that pressure was needed on a wound like this, but she had no idea for how much longer she could hold her hands in place. She was beginning to panic that the horse would die unless someone took some action. It was impossible to read her father now. Any move could end everything.

'Is it bad?' he said, eventually.

'It's very bad,' she whispered.

'They'll never want her now, fuck, sure they won't, they'll never take her from me now. Who wants a ruined mare? Can't show a horse off in Buckingham fucking Palace with its throat slit.'

Claire didn't respond.

John spoke louder, and it attracted attention from the house, something Claire feared deeply.

Anne O'Connor came to the back door of the bungalow, and asked if everything was all right. Claire's head spun as her father took off roaring and Anne shot across the yard as he chased after her. It was what the man needed to release his temper. Anne started to run, fast now, away from him across the yard and Claire watched her mother's narrow shoulders disappearing from sight as she slipped into the Old House, where a single bulb was lit. John followed her. The roaring grew louder like rolling thunder, until nothing.

Claire desperately wanted to go to her mother. She couldn't let the horse free to tangle herself on her insides. She looped the mare's lead rope around the tarred fence with her bloodied free hand, dragged her soft blue pullover with one arm over and off her body. It took time, but when it came free, she lassoed it around the mare's neck and pulled the two sleeves until they held like a neckerchief. On both sides of her tight knot in her soft jumper a great bulging could be seen.

Claire ran and opened the doors to the Old House gently without making a sound. Holding her breath, she carefully let the lever come up slowly and back in its place. She was shaking all over as she pushed the doors in, her left hand leaving a trail of sticky blood on the handle and the old wood. From behind Claire the mare's shadow loomed on the ground and she could make out the shadow of her mother, Anne, caught up in the scene, moving into it and out of it, swaying. Was she dancing? Who had lifted her? Claire couldn't make it out. She gripped her stomach and groaned, and she said: 'Please,' or a 'Please no,' and 'No,' again, then she said: 'Stop,' and this came from her guts, and again, she said it, on and on, and again, and then she looked to the ground, into the dark shadows, where black drops were dripping from between her own legs onto the dark slate of the stone floor.

13

I woke at seven on Sunday morning, and resisting the urge to check in on Kelly, I watched a soft crime drama about a man who had stolen everything from his son by swindling him in a joint business endeavour. The son was destitute and living on the streets of Toronto.

I showered in lukewarm water, washed my hair quickly, towel-dried it and fixed it into some spongy rollers. My bra and knickers matched: turquoise with giant print slices of blood oranges. I lathered body cream all over, focusing on my elbows and knees. I avoided my tummy, for the softness of it irritated me, the lack of bones – of muscle structure.

It was some weeks since Tom and I had gone on the swim, the seasons had changed. I felt giddy. Was I nervous?

I cleaned my bedroom through the climax of the Canadian drama, changed the bed sheets and chose a white crisp set that I enjoyed the feel of. I took a narrow jar of cut flowers from the kitchen and left them by my bedroom television. Tom did not approve of screens in the bedroom but there were those long days during lockdown when I had stayed put in bed. I placed fresh towels and some Italian lemon soaps in the bathroom. I changed the head on my electric toothbrush.

I dressed sharply at first in a grey pinstriped suit, formal and well-structured, but then felt like I was in work mode and switched for jeans with a blazer, looked in the mirror and pulled the whole fussy affair off. I hung it neatly back in my wardrobe – a first. I chose a dress that was flattering on my hips, with a subtle plunge line, and finished with some light foundation, pink cheeks, and a shade of lipstick that was – according to Kelly – the correct shade for every woman, two shades darker than the natural pink of their lips.

I looked about: the bedroom was inviting. I sprayed perfume into the air. Grabbing keys and my coat in the kitchen, I imagined what Tom might be doing. A short shave, shower, jocks, shirt, trousers, socks. I considered a beta blocker – but decided against it.

The restaurant had flower baskets spilling on the windowsills: mulberries and mauves in lavenders and tawny pansies. I passed the glass counter of meringues and pies, pastries with intricate toppings. A coffee machine spat steam.

I was shown to my seat by a young waiter with angry beard rash and a tight waistcoat.

'Something to drink?'

'I'll wait. Thank you.'

'Sure, no problem. Take your time,' he said and left a large steel jug of water and two glasses on the table by a yellow carnation in a small vase.

I scrolled: Something about Myanmar. Fall Aesthetics

2022. Get the We Heart It App. A drunk man on a flight from Ibiza hit a woman on the bridge of her nose, breaking it, before the flight made an emergency landing.

'Hey there,' Tom said, pulling up to the table.

'Hi.'

He stretched over and kissed me on my neck. 'You look really lovely,' he said. 'I hope you've not been waiting too long.' He picked up the menu and left it right on his lap which was the correct position so as to maintain eye contact.

I pulled at my dress to cross it over my breasts.

'Just in the door ahead of you,' I said.

We chatted about the change in season and the damp cold and the isolation of the place which Tom seemed to really like – and this pleased me. He asked about my teaching and we talked about the why of poetry – this we agreed on, right now, it was a very difficult question to answer. Was there a point? Was the world fucked? The world was fucked. Was there a point to punctuation? We spent time on punctuation and laughed about it. Then war. Then war poetry. Was there a point to war poetry? We talked about the strange feeling of complicity we both had – in wars – in greed, and how nihilistic it was to talk about it, and then, how nihilistic it was not to talk about it.

'You OK?' he said and took my hand.

'Yes, yes, all good. I'm OK,' I said.

The young waiter had been watching us. He came back to the table, smiled at us both, lifted his pencil and I ordered first and fast. A burger.

Tom ordered a fancy salad, 'but hold the pickles, and tomato'.

I was fit to order a glass of wine, but Tom called an espresso, so I made do with the water jug.

'Were you out last night?' I said.

'No, I watched a film.'

I considered him on a couch with Johanna, what she would wear. How she sat, how or if they sat beside each other. 'What film?'

'*Another Round.*'

'Any good?'

'Fascinating. You should watch it. How about you?'

'College reading,' I said, lying.

I had watched Kelly. I had waxed my legs. I did some moronic face yoga like Kelly. I put mayonnaise in the tips of my hair overnight, like Kelly. I used a home-made honey and salt scrub, like Kelly. I used an eye mask, yes, yes, like Kelly. I did not go braless like Kelly.

When the food arrived, the burger seemed unsteady and I regretted my decision. Maybe I could use cutlery? I picked at some sweet potato chips. I ate in front of Tom for years in the flat, but this all felt new – as though it were the first time, as though he were someone I desperately wanted to impress. I looked across at Tom's neatly placed leaves of rocket, a shaving of chicken, a cherry tomato and some froths of lemon on the tines of his fork.

'Oh, wait – there's tomato,' I said.

'It's OK,' he said, as he chewed. 'I'm trying to be more adventurous.' He tore the top off a pipe of sugar, nimbly, and tipped it onto a tiny spoon before plunging it quickly into the espresso, and set to spinning the black liquid with the tiny spoon. He let it settle a minute.

'A brandy?' I suggested after we finished at 1.30 p.m.

'Can't,' he said, 'sorry,' gently dapping his face with the serviette. 'I'm driving.'

'So am I,' I said. 'One won't kill us.'

'I'd rather not,' he said, looking down at his little cup. 'I'm working tomorrow.'

'Never stopped us before,' I said, and he smiled in return.

'Dessert then?' he said.

'Great. You choose.' I was conscious at this juncture of all the left-unsaid. Me running from his house. Johanna's house. The sea. Me. Him. 'How's the writing going?' I asked.

'Going well,' he said.

'Good, good. When will you be finished?'

'Hoping I'll have a decent first draft in March. But you know these things.' I nodded at him as the waiter made his way back to the table.

'A lemon meringue tartlet, please, cream – no, wait, ice cream,' he said, looking at the young boy, the white shirt too large on his narrow frame. 'Oh, and two spoons.'

'Always,' the waiter replied.

Tom leaned in across the table. 'I'm at a crucial scene where this Sherpa has gone to urinate and seems to have gone missing, one of the team is considering his frost-bitten toe stuck in ice, if he could just go for it and pull it off, and by now no one can find the Sherpa, he seems to have abandoned the whole team.'

I winced. 'I thought it was a guy in a boat?'

'Oh, right, no no – it's many guys. A dozen in fact. All taking an extreme journey, or returned from one. All of them have met a crucial stumbling block in life, and picked themselves up. To date I've interviewed a sailor, a Grand National jockey, an extreme hiker, a deep-cave swimmer from the North.'

'That sounds intense,' I said.

'It's not a major toe.'

'Major toe?' I asked. 'I meant the project.'

'Oh right. But you know, the frostbite – a balance toe, one you'd need for balance.'

'Oh right,' I said. 'I'm sure it would be necessary to have your major toe, like how climbing Everest was so necessary in the first place. How'd he get the toe stuck?'

'Right, so –' Tom said, missing my sarcasm. 'Thing is, he was changing his socks because his feet had gotten wet and it's so important to keep your feet dry on these expeditions. Anyway someone called out to him, and he clenched to get up, forgetting he was sock-less. Instinct, survival, most likely. Stabbed it into the ice, and it was a soft patch so it sank, and then froze over.'

'Right. Fuck. Ouch.'

'Fascinating how some people just pack up and leave their lives in search of adventure?' he said, making the crease between his brows thick and deep. I longed to kiss it.

'Is that what you've done?' I asked, suddenly.

His face turned a little, his mouth down, brows creased: 'No,' he said soberly. 'You?'

The lemon dessert arrived – a tiny affair with burned meringue topping beside a quenelle of ice-cream.

'Voila!' the waiter said, noting that the table's energy had turned. The two dessert spoons were crossed like swords. Picking one up, Tom went on: 'I've been following that Galway guy coming from New York on a boat. You been watching that? I'd love to write about him next. Do you know of it?'

'It's difficult to avoid him online. Strange algorithms lately. Every time I open my phone it's him and his beard. It's either boat-boy crossing the Atlantic or fertility sticks.'

I didn't complicate things by bringing up trad wives.

'Fertility sticks?' he said, thrown. 'You OK?'

'Yeah, of course I'm OK.'

'So this boat guy, as you called him –' Tom said. 'Lost his mate too on the journey and he ended up going it alone, like it must take guts to do that, out in the mad ocean. Must be lonely.'

'Guts?' I said. 'Mad ocean? It's the Atlantic. He's not in bloody space. We just swam in it a few weeks ago.'

'Well, we didn't *swim*-swim, did we? And besides, it's a totally different thing. This man is out in the middle of the swell with his small rowboat capsizing night after night. Imagine that,' he said. 'But I'm glad you brought it up.' He stared at me now. 'Our swim. I wanted to talk to you about it, I didn't expect – I mean, that all went a bit—'

I pictured him in the wetsuit – was I turned on or turned off by it now? Could I tell the difference? Did I know any more? I could get horny to Jeremy Allen White in *The Bear*. Instagram kept sending these oddly shaped men forward in stories, and I had begun to find these unorthodox face shapes and brows and jawlines rather sexy in a feral way. Maybe it's biological feedback: these men will be available. But not Allen, every woman I knew wanted to fuck Allen. No one wanted perfection in men any more, just some oddity, or some need, something to fix, but maybe that was always the way. Perfection was only expected in women. Gender essentialism was back with a bang – for women. Had it ever gone away? It seemed more than capable of reimagining itself every season. Tom, though, was conventional in his attractiveness, he had a Helly Hansen charm that was exciting and neat and assuring when I first met him – the very opposite of Father. He smelled good and was desirable. Other women flirted with him and this always excited me.

'Yes, takes guts facing that loneliness,' he said, quietly, as though it were a secret. 'Must have been wild, facing your own mortality alone every night.'

'Everyone faces their mortality alone at night – every night.'

'True – but can you imagine the loneliness?'

'He's lonely because he chose to be. He made him-self lonely. I have zero sympathy for people who make themselves lonely.' I was getting angry. 'He's a gobshite if you ask me. He's putting himself into the way of risk. What about those who have no choice but to live in risk all the time? His wife has a harder job.'

'Wife?'

'Yeah, his wife, at home alone with the baby. He has a young baby, I think he's gone to escape his duties.'

'Claire,' he whispered, 'we don't have a clue what his wife feels about this. Maybe she's delighted he's gone off to sea for a couple of months, and allows her, I dunno – some bonding time.'

'Well, if she's delighted he's gone away, then he's the problem, right?'

He paused and put his cup down. 'Each to their own, no?'

'They're not fourteen,' I argued. 'They are full-grown ass men.'

'Right, but everything doesn't always have to be – adventurous,' he said. He took the little cup up again for the last time and sucked it rather than drank from it. I laughed and he turned a bright red colour.

'Each to their own,' I said, softer now.

'Sorry,' he said, 'it's just, I don't think that you under-stand that they might think differently to you.'

'Who?'

'Men.'

'Of course I do,' I said. 'Don't be absurd.'

'Well, sometimes, sometimes I think you can be a little bit – well, frankly, reductive.'

It stung.

'Reductive, how?'

'Just saying this about these guys and their wives. The relationships are personal.'

'I know that,' I said. 'But sometimes it looks like someone gets their own way and someone else comes along for the ride.'

'But that's just it, it doesn't have to be like that. And so what if it is? Maybe, like I said, that works for them.'

I waited for a minute: 'Why are you here, Tom? To annoy me?'

'What?'

'Here, in my town. Why?'

'To write.'

'There's a whole fucking world out there to write in. Go anywhere,' I said. I wanted to say something aggressive, something maddening. But I said: 'Sorry. It's just, I mean, I don't know quite what's happening here.'

'Here?'

'*Us.*'

Tom looked at me: 'I'm trying to figure it all out, make some kind of amends. I want to try—'

'How do you mean?'

'With *us*. I mean, I think I want to, maybe try.'

He said it. Just like that. Simple.

I froze.

'So it's not for the book?'

He didn't answer.

'What I'm asking is – if Johanna had a house in Kerry, would you be there?'

'What? No,' he said, with a certain urgency that I believed. 'But you were impossible. I loved you, love, but you were . . . it was impossible to be with you after your mother died.'

'I am sorry for my grief.'

'Are you?'

'What?' I stared at him. 'No, of course I'm not sorry for my grief.'

'It's good to hear you say grief,' he said. 'You have never said you were grieving.'

'Did I need to wear black all day?'

'No,' he said, quietly, and rubbed my hand, 'of course not, I don't know, but you were so . . .'

'So?'

'Out of control.'

'Out of control?'

'The way you criticised yourself. Constantly. Drinking. Staying out all night. No contact. The way you criticised *me* all the time.' Then he put his head into his hands.

I wanted to shout something ferocious at this, to tell him this was my town, I could do what the fuck I wanted. Maybe he should go home. But his face was soft and his eyes were lowered to the table, and he dabbed his napkin on the sides of his mouth, which was strong and angular and made me feel sad for him for some reason.

'Sorry,' I said again. 'I can't imagine what it was like. I was just, unravelling. It was a lot. It was too much.'

'It's OK,' Tom said, and leaned over and took my

hands in his. 'I wasn't perfect. But you never spoke about her, ever, and I just couldn't figure it out. Brian said to be patient. But I was done with it. I wanted to—'

'What?'

'Hurt you.'

Kelly Purchase said that angry women are ugly women. They make ugly faces. I relaxed my jaw and dropped my shoulders. I was crying and so I got up in silence, walked the long corridor, avoiding catching my reflection in the mirrors, and tapped my half of the bill and walked out without looking back or saying goodbye. I was crying as I stepped out into a beautiful October afternoon, the leaves drying out, the smell of food in the air. I watched couples stroll by as I crossed over the road to my car, children ran about, still in light T-shirts, which was unusual for the time of year. People were calling it abnormal and strange – an Indian summer. And indeed, everything was strange.

I drove home fast. I presumed Tom had set off to Johanna's house and for all I knew, Johanna was back for the weekend from wherever it was she spent her time and was back in his bed doing everything for him that I used to do, and that I eventually resented and I resented her doing it in equal measure. Máire's dog was barking as I locked the car and went inside. I poured a large cold glass of Soave and I took my clothes off and left them strewn across the floor. I wiped my make-up off, slowly.

*

Kelly Purchase had uploaded a Sunday morning story: Her mother had taken the four children for a sneaky *them*-time afternoon. Kelly waved them off and then she climbed back into a large white SUV where she pranked Kirk on the way to a restaurant with a special mixtape she had made for him. The music was awful. The Eagles. Air Supply. Taylor Swift. He cried and then they took a stroll in a park full of yellow flowers. In one memorable moment, she thought she saw a bear, but it was only the bark of a large tree that had fallen over in a recent gale. Then something else startled her, and Kirk consoled her by putting his great big arms around her thin frame and holding her close to him moments before they shared a meal of goat's cheese lasagne and a bottle of orange wine from Austria. The orange wine threw me – I was sure Kelly was far less sophisticated than an orange wine, but she noticed notes of apricot and oak. Fuck, Kelly. Who knew? Piano music sounded as she traced her socked foot up along his leg in the restaurant. Had she given the phone to the waiter to record her promise? Kirk ate most of the food, while Kelly played coyly with the cutlery and batted her eyelids. Every date was a first date, she said. Every day was a new day to discover something wonderful about her husband, she said. Every day was a surprise. 'Be in the moment,' she said, finally, just to me.

I lay down on the couch and picked up a book, some debut fiction by a man finding out his mother was an MI5 spy. I tried to sleep, but tossed about. I replayed the conversation with Tom. I turned on the telly, turned it off. I opened the book again but couldn't remember any of the characters. I dozed off, got up, had a second shower to pass the time and when I returned from the bathroom, I texted Tom.

> I'm sorry for running
> Call over. x
> OK x

I dressed quickly, left my hair down, the roads went by in a haze.

'Hi,' I said.

'Hi,' he said, closing the front door gently behind me. Tom didn't turn to walk into the kitchen and I grabbed him by the waist, kissed him hard on his lips. Upstairs, his room neat, some book pages about the floor, I opened his zip, pulled his green sweater over his head, it caught on his stubble.

I shut my eyes and imagined Kelly and Kirk on the corner of their huge bed, her lips glossy, her glossy pussy, neat bottom, his stubble, and his large arms around her, how perhaps he might smell on the evening of a date, somewhere between Ralph Lauren and a petrol breeze from Manchester-by-the-Sea.

Tom moved into me, slowly at first, harder now. I kissed him some more, looked at his face, his eyelids were gently closed, he was familiar and yet older – grey hairs about his temples, strong jawline. Tom's rhythm took over as I arched to him.

Afterwards, we lay in bed, silent for some time, the charcoal curtains askew. Outside: the rain coming down, down.

Evening came and Tom brought us some food on a tray and we chatted. We talked about his book again, and he said that he had met so many Irish men, and they were driven, something determined about them, but yet they all craved solitude, long, long periods of solitude, and that, so far, was what he had uncovered.

'Freud said you can't psychoanalyse an Irish man, and I want to see is that true.'

'Wasn't that Scorsese? Freud said you wanted to fuck your mothers.'

'Maybe we do,' he said, laughing.

I slept until Monday morning and for the first time in my new job, I rang in sick, and we went back to the sea.

14

Before work on Tuesday morning I put on a wash, unloaded all the green laundry pods into a nice green glass jar in the scullery and cleaned the shower door. I folded towels. I felt pleased with myself as I ran from the house pulling keys and chargers in my wake. I would pick up some tie wraps and sort out the lead issue next weekend.

The light was warm, the clouds were hoary, great and alive, and the sun appeared here and there as the first leaves were falling. I walked fast through the town, stopping to purchase a coffee in the new little coffee shop on Shop Street.

'Morning,' Doll said, throwing an eye on her Apple watch. 'Whoa, you're late, Dr, not like you. And also, a day off. You never take days off. You know if you take a Monday you should also take a Tuesday too – it's the law of manners.' One of her tooth diamonds had come undone and was stuck in the gap of her teeth.

'The law of manners?' I said. 'Is this also new?'

'Also new?'

'I'm only coming to terms with trad wives and we've the law of manners.'

'Manners are as old as you, Claire, and in fact, far older.'

I grinned. 'Doll, your diamond, it's falling off.'

'Here, let me help, don't move,' Prof said, coming into the office. She picked between Doll's two impossibly white front teeth. They locked eyes.

There was an awkward silence, then a seagull on the top of the building cawed and broke it.

'There, all done,' Prof said, still holding Doll's jaw.

'Are they real?' I asked.

'They are, like anything, Claire, real if you believe.'

'Need help?' I asked as I followed Prof back to her office.

'Do I ever?' she said, splitting an armful of heavy tote bags with me. 'Never seems to end, does it?'

'Sure doesn't,' I said.

'How was your weekend?' she asked, placing a tote of scripts on her desk.

'Grand,' I said, looking about her office, which was full of clutter.

'Always busy,' she said, responding to my watching, as was her habit.

The desk was covered in papers, coffee cup lids, some manuscripts and a bobble-head Jesus. 'I'm waiting to recycle them,' she said, nodding to the lids. 'All. Of. Them. Doll said I need to clean up!'

'Did she now?' I said.

'She did now.'

'I'm not judging.'

'The hell you're not,' she said smiling as she sat back on her swivel chair and looked up in earnest from behind her black fringe.

I fixed my shirt into my new trousers.

'Nice pants, very sartorial, and you look . . . I don't know, were you sick yesterday?'

'Mental health day.'

'Right,' she said, 'good for you because you look fresh.'

'Thanks.'

'Welcome.'

Doll arrived in with a reef of paper. 'Now spill.'

'Spill?' I said, and they both just sank their eyes into me.

'You can't escape with head shakes and umms, you're not an undergrad,' Prof said.

'The date,' Doll said.

We laughed.

'Oh, it was fine.'

'Fine!' they both declared. 'Monday off?! Spill. And *fine*. After all this time . . . listening about Tom this that and the other, *fine*.'

'It was – well, it was – it was nice. Nice night,' I said finally and I smiled, and turned to leave.

'We'll want more than *nice*, Claire, I won't rest,' Prof said laughing. 'You know I won't.'

'Good morning,' I said to my class. The room was freezing. It was a protected building and would have to fall to the ground before anyone could interfere with its great postmodern structure – and for this reason it was always cold. 'Good morning,' I said again. A couple of young people stopped talking, turned about and looked at me.

One pulled his hood down and another removed an earbud from his ear, but left the other in place.

'Hi, Sam,' I said to a student who had been missing since August, 'nice to see you too, have you been ill?'

'No,' they said, and turned and began chatting to the girl in the seat behind with make-up like Ziggy Stardust and cat tattoos on her hands. The make-up was impressive, the incredibly steady line of the eyeliner. 'Well, how about you turn around then?' They did, slowly and with the grace of a deer.

We began the workshop.

Poems about colour.

Pair-work discussion of a Billy Collins poem they all agreed, contrary to my opinion, was Mid. Those that spoke and committed to workshopping had chosen some shade of blue for their own poems. Cyan. Navy. Royal. Sea. Tranquil. Hockney. Bayern. Admiral. Denim. The last to read was Job, a boy from Barna, a pretty town outside Galway and on the coast. He had chosen to write about the colour pink.

'I've had enough of blue,' he said, quietly. He had been soaked in it in his boys' school, in his clothes as a kid, and in the loos in the college, so he decided to look inside, to what mattered, he was tired about writing about what doesn't matter. 'It's exhausting,' he said, playing with long green and purple plaits in his hair.

'How so?' I asked.

'I think,' he said, unsure, 'I was going through the motions, and this Collins poem told me what I don't want to do when I write.'

'And what's that?'

'Nothing.'

I was confused.

'What's the point in nothing?' he said.

'True,' I said. 'Nothing can come from nothing. I paraphrase.'

He nodded, approving my plagiarism. 'The point of poetry should be to move something somewhere,' he said.

Mia interrupted: 'There is no point to poetry, Job.'

'Flippant,' he said. We all laughed.

'No, no, that's the point. I am not being flippant. But there cannot be any point to it. Poetry is around a long time, and the world is—'

'Fucked,' Pedro said.

'Fair,' Job said to the room in general.

'But if it is pointless, it must be about nothing,' Pedro added. A kid in the back row took out his phone and put in his second earbud. Job said when he investigated his impulse on Sunday afternoon he wrote the poem in one sweep with a bad hangover, and he wanted to explore his dad because he had been watching him out in the garden pruning back rose trees. He wanted to explore everything that his dad had in common with him and everything through the shade of pink.

'I love the extended metaphor,' I said, after he read. His next poem compared his dad to a blow-up flamingo. 'So, he's playing, yanno, he's sitting in the conservatory, and there's like, there's like a whole pane of glass in the conservatory that's cracked right through. He's just spent a few hours trying to cut some plastic to seal it up as there's a breeze, right, and I'm watching him and he takes up the guitar. Anyhoo, he's just like sitting on the sofa, or like one of those wicker things, faded now, it's been there for years. I think it was my nan's before Dad cleared her house out, and we got all this shit we didn't need—'

Some students laughed.

'Yeah, well, Dad, yanno, he just moves his hands up and down the fretboard, like he doesn't even play a chord, not for ages, and then he does and he's strumming. He looks so bloated and I hadn't noticed before. He's fit, right. Or at least I thought he was. Like I always thought he was, I guess – immortal. Like he sails and swims in the sea and stuff, but he's so pink in his face and I had never noticed it before. It reminded me of a time we bought a plastic flamingo on holidays, sorry, I know, it's not cool, plastics and all. But my dad . . .'

'Sweet – Paul Mescal vibes,' Sam said, referring to the film *Aftersun*.

'Mam was with us,' he said to Sam. Everyone laughed. 'And my sisters – the twins.' But he explained how shame and guilt stuck out. About buying plastics and then about not noticing his dad, and how he tried to link them in some way in a poem. The class agreed that they were filled with shame and guilt, a lot of guilt about plastics and one girl was in a deathly shame spiral about something she'd rather not talk about.

'My mam moved out some years ago,' he said and then he read:

Everything seems alive. The sun. The water is blue, and
Jade and Jess are laughing. Mam is packing, and the sea
is coming and going. I can't breathe.
Maybe, I will write lines about hope, or maybe the fat of
the pink flamingo in a blue sky is the last thing that
childhood brings, the body, deflated, and there is something
about the smell of plastic that makes me feel alive.
At Shannon airport the American Army is coming through
in dull green uniforms as we land in the grey rain. And you
carry Jade and Jess as I carry the deflated flamingo all the way
home
where it sits, out of place among the greenness and the rocks.
And now, You in this glass box, shattered, your guitar,
I remember you on the escalator, and
   here, in this moment,
   you have blown up fully.
   I should try to speak.

15

I intended doing my mid-term marking when I arrived back to the office after lectures but I was distracted by a cherry picker outside the window, blowing back and over like a tree branch with leftover fairy lights. And Job. Job's poem and his quest for beauty and love – or something close – had thrown me. Perhaps his love for his father. I stood at the vast window watching students bushing from paper bags under the bridge by the river and they seemed so free in themselves, passing around vapes and bottles, jumping up and down to act an impulsive scene or a moment from a past time together. It made me long for Tom. I packed my bag, pulled on my rain mac and flicked through Shakespeare's sonnets, his head on the cover.

> *And every fair from fair sometime declines,*
> *By chance or nature's changing course untrimm'd;*
> *But thy eternal summer shall not fade . . .*

Some men really know how to love, or at the very least talk about it. I switched off my lamp and locked the door, catching sight of Marina Abramović's reflection on Prof's door as I passed. Prof was still in her office.

'Goodnight, Dr O'Connor,' she shouted out and

I stopped for a moment and waited by her door, and before walking out into the dark, I considered Abramović's body performances in *Rhythm O*. I tried to remember some of the objects she laid out on the table for the audience, recalled: a hairbrush, mirror, comb, red lipstick. She also left an axe, chain, knives and a loaded pistol. I thought of how the audience glared. Was she afraid? I considered how ferociously they pulled off her clothes, and cut her. Did anyone feel regret? Did her crying make it more exciting? Did anyone want to mind her, but were afraid to speak out? Who wanted to fuck her? And then I thought if perhaps night changes everything? Are we destined to relearn in every generation? Did the objects give them permission? Did they feed her cake? Or stuff her mouth full of it just to watch her gag and choke? I couldn't remember precisely and I was angry with myself that I could not recall the scene in more detail – it seemed suddenly so important. Why cotton wool balls? Why the loaded pistol?

Prof lifted her narrow face up from the paper she was correcting. She looked pale and tired, and her hair seemed a different colour under her green desk lamp.

'You OK?' she said, looking at me with concern.

'You up for a chat?'

'Always.'

'Notice they're all bushing down by the river?' I asked as I looked out of her window at the students drinking under the bridge.

'Bushing?' she asked.

'Drinking, al fresco.'

We laughed. 'Oh, to be young again,' she said.

'Wouldn't wish it on my worst enemy,' I replied.

'Really?'

'Really.'

'I'd love to go back,' Prof said. 'Minus the misogyny.'

'Go back, maybe,' I said. 'But to be young now – they're so unsure.'

'Unsure?' she said. 'We are all unsure. We were the most unsure generation. Everyone's unsure. Most are just pretending they're not. Right?'

'Yeah. Perhaps. Confused then.'

'Huh. Maybe,' Prof said, 'I was always confused.'

'I doubt that very much,' I said.

She pushed back her chair, got up and walked to the window, it was darker now, and the rain had stopped.

'I guess,' she said, her arms folded as she peered down under the bridge. 'Ever see them when they swim in the river? I think it's a dare, or a bet or something. Must be freezing with the cold, but they do, they seem to dare each other and they jump in and swim to the other bank.'

'I'm surprised it hasn't taken anyone.'

'Killed them?'

'Right.'

'You Irish and your euphemisms, makes this whole course a nightmare to teach.' She waved her class notes at me. 'Why do they need to get so drunk though?'

'They're just having fun,' I said. 'Or maybe it quenches something, of how to be . . .'

'How to *be*?' Prof said.

'Yeah – a way to be in the world.'

'It's not very imaginative. They are *in* the world. In fact, I'd hasten to add, they *are* the world. They see themselves as the world, this is their world, and we should move along. We broke their ground, or ceilings, or whatever it was for them, just for them to go and preoccupy themselves with men. Fuck, it's all so relentless,' she said on another inhale.

'Who's preoccupied with men?'

'All of these essays,' she said, shaking a paper at me. 'They seem to be asking for nothing but security.'

'Security?'

'Life partners. Love.'

'In academic papers?'

'Yup,' she said and yawned. 'Where are the revolutions?'

'So they are in a quest to understand love?'

'Exactly, but here I do text analysis, this isn't personal.'

'Revolution is always personal,' I said, 'as is love, so if you expect them to change, maybe you need to engage.'

'With this one –' she waved a paper – 'the end of the novel was a delight. They got fucking married.' She never cursed. I thought of Mother who left school at thirteen. Of Abramović's bare breast. 'It's just the, well –' and she lifted the paper and rolled it into a baton – 'the constant hyperbole about women's fiction, and women characters, and the expectation they put on them, to be likeable. They don't like this one or that one, because they had an affair or left their children, it's always the same argument, made poorly. I wonder, is this all they want? They are asking for nothing else. As though a partner, or someone else's partner, is a revolutionary act.'

'Maybe it is all they want,' I said. 'Maybe that's enough? Maybe managing to keep a partner *is* a revolutionary act.'

Prof raised an eyebrow. She was against all forms of relationship institutions, especially marriage. 'It's an academic course, Claire. And I have a pile of these bizarre love stories to get through before I leave, and I'm on the bike, so I'd better get some done before it's too late. May the Lord have patience with me, and may I have it with them.'

I wasn't sure of what it was too late for. Cycling. Rain, the dark, though it was already dark now, or perhaps the lights in the college made it appear darker than it was outside.

'Oh, wait,' she said. Then: 'Did you want to talk?'

'We just did,' I said.

'Right,' she said, 'glad I could help – I think.'

Walking on out of the tower, I pinged the lift and thought about Prof's desk light and how it reminded me of a lawyer on a show I watched as a teenager. I couldn't for the life of me remember the name of it. This bugged me as I went out onto the concourse. I was getting less able to recall specifics, my ease had gone.

I crossed over the Salmon Weir Bridge and watched a couple kissing by the ruins of an old house. Two winos sang on Eyre Square, loudly, a rebel song, and one put her two hands up to the other's face. She was wearing red lace gloves. I stopped in at a shop by the station, noting that it still stacked its magazine racks like it was 1999 and I loved them for it. I picked up an Argentinian Malbec, the *New Yorker*, some chocolate almonds and a huge chocolate muffin that sweated inside plastic.

At the station in Athenry I jumped into my car, which was cold, and the windscreen was fogged over. I threw the wine on the front seat and squeezed the muffin so hard it popped its little bag. I drove out under the bridge, and I felt myself getting giddy as the car bumped along the bog road, on right now to the big grey house. I would call to Tom. I would not announce the visit.

16

'Oh, hi,' Tom said, and though we had just spent the night together, he seemed surprised to see me as he waited awkwardly by the jamb of the door. 'Did I miss a text?'

'No, no,' I said. 'No missed text, I just thought I'd surprise you.'

'Right,' he said and closed a copper button up on his blue denim shirt with one hand. I loved him in blue. 'It's just, I wasn't expecting you. But lovely to see you, you look great.'

'I look bloody damp,' I said and smiled. 'I'm like something the cat would drag in. Whole county is damp.' I looked up at the black sky, something about Tom seemed nervous, or fretful. 'Does it ever give up?' I asked.

Tom smiled, and then folded his arms. 'I heard the Irish weather is like its women. Relentless.' Was Tom flirting? He never flirted. Was he going to let me in? No one flirts any more, I thought.

I felt myself blush and heat up under the damp veil of mist. 'Jeez, Tom. Are you playing hard to get?'

'Shit, sorry,' he said, 'come in, come in.'

The hob fan in the kitchen whirred loudly as I followed him along the hall, he must be cooking. A dog barked in the distance, loud and wrathful. Tom was wearing ivy green woolly socks and lounge pants, corduroy. I followed him through the hall and glimpsed fast into the front room where a gathering of cream candles were set on a square of mirror and glowed on the coffee table. The stove was also alight, tangerine flames came off some burning logs. Tom had added a sheepskin rug to the parquet floor. Everywhere seemed neat, well put together, and a lamp was lighting the hall, the base flocked with great painted kingfishers swooping about. How had I not noticed it before? Fuck. Same parquet. Same plant. Same, same.

'Oh, shit, I've interrupted your supper,' I said, smelling food. Fish perhaps, but sweet. 'I'm so sorry, I'll just . . .' I said.

'Supper?' he said. 'That's new! Since when do we have *supper*, Claire O'Connor?' he added, quickly flashing back to me, grinning.

We. Ah.

'Hi, I'm Johanna, hi, hi, so lovely to meet you, Clara,' she said, licking a wooden spoon as she stood by a great range in the kitchen.

'Claire,' I said. 'I'm sorry, I didn't mean to – interrupt. I didn't know that Tom had visitors.'

'Would we call the homeowner a visitor?' she said smartly, as she smiled brightly at me and extended her free thin hand, a loose gold watch slunk on her wrist. I worried for her impossibly tight white jeans and the dripping spoon.

I shook her hand: 'Oh, yes, yes, I apologise. Of course

it's your house.' I said: 'It's a beautiful house.' I left the bottle of Malbec down on the kitchen table.

'Yes, it was my great-grandfather's,' she said, waving the spoon about. 'He was a vet, same as my grandfather, and father.'

I wondered what her mother did. If it mattered.

'Right,' I said. I resisted the urge to pick up a *Paris Review*. I resisted the urge to run. I resisted the urge to say: I have a house too.

'Thanks for this,' Tom said lifting the bottle of wine from the table. Johanna and I both stared at him as he flicked his eyes at us both in turn, and then again, her first, then me.

'I am so glad you've met now – now you both know each other. Finally.'

'Might be pushing it,' I said.

'Now, now,' Tom said. 'Play nice,' he whispered as he leaned over me and took some wine glasses from a cupboard.

'Oh, none for me, thanks,' I said, as he sliced the foil from around the bottle's neck and dug into the cork with an opener. I watched as the silver arms of the thing dragged upwards like a child waiting for a parent to remove a jumper.

'You sure?' he said, furrowing his brow. 'Just one?'

I shook my head.

'How nice of you – look, Tom, don't these look decadent,' Johanna said, as she tore open the packet of chocolate almonds I handed her and poured them into a tiny bowl. She popped one into her mouth and I could swear she never chewed at all, not once, just sucked it, because I was focusing on her long slender neck, the line of her clavicle and how her shirt seemed to match Tom's. Could it? I was struck by how she seemed to match Tom: olive skin, her thin wrists, her manners.

'You from around here?' she said.

'Yes, yes, Mountain Ellen,' I said, waving my hand in the general direction of nowhere in particular.

'Strange,' she said.

'How so?'

'Just all so flat around here, is there even a mountain?'

'True,' Tom said. 'Is there even a mountain in the town?' he parroted.

'No,' I said, quite certainly. 'Mountain can mean rough grazing, possibly from the word sliabh.'

'What?' Johanna said.

'Irish,' Tom replied, and Johanna pulled a face.

'Much like a moor,' I said.

'Of course,' she said.

'Did you grow up here?' I asked.

'Lord no, we just summered here. You couldn't actually *live*-live here. Could you?'

Summered. A verb. Cunt.

I was embarrassed and instead of talking about what had happened to the names of places in the translation from Gaeilge to English, to explain the mountain, I said that there was once a little village on the road where I live. A little village of one hundred and twenty or so before the Famine. I told them how after 1847 records show that no one lived there, all of the people had gone, some to the town, and most had emigrated or died. I explained that if you travel two miles from my house along the northern railway line that's mostly obsolete, you will come to a large mound of stones and rock, and underneath there are bones, mostly cattle, also dogs and old wolves, rats and the like, animals that had ravaged the place eating those who had fallen foul of the Famine. There were human bones too, skulls of children and long thigh bones, teeth, fingers, and if you dug deep enough, as I did with my brothers when we were children, you could find any kind of bone you wanted. I said this all of a gush, and then I stopped saying bones. I stopped short of saying genocide. Then, breezily, I said that's where I thought the mountain had come from: 'It's a mountain of our dead,' I said.

'Intriguing,' she said. 'And so, so sad.'

Tom stared at me and finished his wine.

'What are you cooking?' I asked, changing the subject and running my hand along the countertop. I would regret my long monologue later, and re-run it in my head, unsure of the impetus. It was cold, the countertop. Stone? I placed both palms on it and it snapped me out of my panic a little. But my heart still pounded as I watched Johanna turn to the stove again, her lush dark chestnut hair falling in waves down her slender back, a little greying at the temples, baby blue shirt draped down at one shoulder where the heavy collar pulled at it and revealed a glimpse of her tanned back. A navy ink tattoo ran from her neck along her spine for as far as I could see. I wondered how far it reached? There was an arrowhead drawn at the nape of her neck, delicate, and a little map to the left.

'Just some fish. Just fish . . . Did they ever actually try to fish?' Johanna asked me. 'The people in the village?'

'Where? In the rain puddles?' I said, bluntly. 'We're a little distance from the sea here. Hard to walk twenty miles when you're starving to death.'

'Sure, sure, sorry,' she said, cupping her hand to her mouth. 'Of course.'

'That's OK,' I said. 'It's not your fault.'

There was a long silence while Johanna carefully stirred the contents of the pot. 'Well, in any case, it is nice to finally meet you, Claire,' she said. 'Tom mentions you so often, don't you, Tom?' She added salt to the broth. This disappointed me. 'I'm serving a lobster bisque,' she said, 'you're very welcome to some.' Two bright pink carcasses lay hollowed out by the stovetop, boiled now, and puny. Tom was watching me watching the delicate husks, and suddenly he grabbed one and then the other and approached Johanna with them making a childish noise and he pinched her nose. 'Stop it, Toooooom,' she said in a long, nasally whine. 'You know I hate when you do that. You're such a child. Isn't he such a *boy*, Claire?'

'I guess,' I said. 'Who dropped them into the boiling water?'

Johanna looked confused.

'The lobsters? Who boiled them?'

'That would be me,' she said, playfully. 'I have no heart. But Tom has already told you that, no doubt.' She laughed madly now. 'Tom here couldn't bear to hear them prattle about the pot and had to cover his sad little ears.'

'No,' I said. 'Tom hasn't said much. He mentioned you owned the house. Sure. Tom, you have lovely ears,' I said suddenly defensive of him.

'Sure I have,' Tom said lifting a brush from behind the fridge and sweeping lobster shell from the floor.

'It was mainly Sarah, she filled me in,' I said.

'Sarah?' Johanna said tapping his hand gently with the wooden spoon.

'His sister.'   'My sister.'

We said together.

It took her aback and I watched her wince slightly.

'Mad,' Johanna said.

'That I have a sister?' Tom said. 'You met her!'

'I did?' Johanna said. 'I can't remember it. No, mad that Claire here wouldn't be able to boil the lobsters.'

'I wouldn't *like* to boil them,' I said. 'But I would be able to.'

'Yes,' she said, 'of course you would.'

I reddened. It had been a long day. I was certain I smelled bad. Or was it Johanna's onions?

Johanna turned back to stir the bisque.

'They have no feelings,' she said, elegantly. 'You know, Claire, they're much like men, lobsters – gluttons for punishment.'

'Ha,' Tom said, slowly, 'funny,' and then he leaned forward and kissed my nose and I kissed his lips hard and he didn't resist.

'Get a bloody room,' Johanna said, scooping the

bisque into elaborate white bowls. 'Please stay, Claire, there's lots. Fleshy little pricks this pair.'

'No, no, you're good thanks,' I said. 'I have to head. Marking.'

'Oh busy, busy,' Johanna said, and seemed annoyed all of a sudden, turning her back to me, her perfect shoulders olive and taut. 'Well, it was very lovely to meet you.'

'Likewise,' I said, skittering to the hallway.

'But your wine—' Tom said as he followed me.

'You guys drink it.'

'But,' Tom said, 'are you sure? Please wait, stay a while. There's loads.'

'No, I'm sure,' I said, as I made my way to the front door. 'I have marking, I'll let myself out.'

'Claire,' he said, calling to me as I walked out the garden path.

'Yes.'

'I'll call you.'

'Great,' I said back.

'You OK, no?'

'I'm fine,' I muttered to myself, minding my step.

What the fuck does 'no?' mean at the end of a sentence? It's an infuriating affectation. As I drove away, Johanna had come to the door and was right by him, her hand on his shoulder now, her socked feet, their shirts both open to their sternum that I could make out even in the fucking dark, or did I imagine it? And she waved as though she owned the place.

Which she did.

17

The next day I was agitated, raging with jealousy. I was on the train when Tom texted:

Morning, I'm free tonight. Would you like to meet after work?

I didn't reply.

After work, back at the bungalow, I pulled off my shoes and left my jewellery in a little bowl by the porch, like my mother always did. Head in the fridge, there were many kinds of tomatoes, so I fixed myself a tomato salad. I had purchased tomatoes of every colour at the farmer's market on Saturday, he said it was the very end of his crop. I drizzled balsamic vinegar and olive oil about the plate, set the table, and lit a candle in the centre of it. I didn't turn on the television. I tugged large chunks of mozzarella from a soft ball, added some dried basil as the fresh plant had wilted and there were holes in the leaves, and some sea salt. I sat in to the table, properly, on the seat I had always sat on as a child. Father to the top, Mother opposite me and Conor and Brian either side of him, that way Father could direct conversation at the two boys, and Mother and I could engage in our own, as he said, 'small talk'. I wished I could say something to her now.

When I'd finished, I rinsed the plate under the tap

and I sat down to work. I wrote up my notes for Monday's lecture on Louis MacNeice's 'Valediction' and afterwards I danced about to Abba. I knew I needed to figure out about Tom. Why was I so reticent, and then so impulsive? I was trying to catch my thoughts here and observe them in the moment, rather than have them sneak up on me in some undignified ache or undiagnosed virus that was only pain coming to flush itself out. Truthfully, I was afraid of being hurt again. Or of giving Tom any control in the world that I was building, or rebuilding, that I was trying to, in some foolish way, turn over a new leaf. Reset. I was growing reassured that everything was where I put it, and within easy reach for me. Objects mostly. Everything except love, or companionship.

Online again: I read the news.
I read tomorrow's weather.
I read some more news.
Then: Hi Y'all. Today I want to show you some table dressing. I watched as Kelly wrestled a bush and tied chequered bows around bunches of it, then she steamed some jars and set a table full of green with nowhere to put a plate. I laughed. Then I scrolled, again, all of her backstories.
To her first ever post.
Years ago.
The Proposal:
How to Make a Man Fall in Love AND Stay in Love with you:

1. Ask a question first always in conversation this moves the conversation on but never make it threatening or personal: Something concerning him. 2. Wear fresh and bright colours. Avoid Black. 3. Avoid complaining. Use your mother for this instead. 4. Never mention menstruation. 5. It is more than OK to date, but sex should be reserved for special occasions, or even, I know, old fashioned Kelly, Marriage. 6. Make space in your life for God, and make space in his life for God, you know you must. 7. Children are a blessing, choose some names together so you know you are on the same page. 8. Be Bright and Alive and use eye contact when he speaks to you. 9. Allow him his manners, opening doors, walking into rooms before you (and remember he must walk in before you, this is not rude, this is to make sure that no threat lurks inside that restaurant). 10. Watch how he talks of his mom – he will speak similar of you sweetie. Good Luck, You Are Amazing, and We ARE BLESSED to be ALIVE.

I threw the phone across the room, irate, and tossed and turned, and yes, Johanna had greatly pissed me off, and I am nothing if not competitive when I am risen to it. I thought back to a date-night in London, a little Italian place down by the Cut. The waiter swerved me a glass of Prosecco with a strawberry. I hate strawberries, and Tom had looked at me, stared into my eyes, and I was sure he would propose for the second time and I was ready to accept now, but instead, he asked if I wanted him to eat the strawberry.

Soon, I would ask him to move in, fuck Johanna.

18

I spent a long time at my desk staring out the vast window onto the river – thinking about the shift in my life from no talk to too much talk to no talk again. I sent my brothers a picture of the river. A quick yellow thumbs-up from Conor and a heart emoticon from Brian, with a follow-up:

Hope to see you over the Christmas, Claire. Ah that place brings back some great memories. Loved bushing by the river. Hashtag Buckfast.

Brian had taken his masters in Human Rights. I returned a hug. We hadn't all texted since we commented on Josh as fat pumpkin.

I called Tom. I wanted to take him to an Irish language film in the Pálás. We agreed to meet beforehand in a little Indian restaurant right by the cinema.

'Wait,' he said, just as we were about to hang up, 'there will be subtitles, right?'

We shared poppadoms, cracking them greedily about the little basket, then dipping into mint yoghurt and a sweet red-onion chutney. I hadn't eaten all day. We ordered a bottle of red.

'Are you gone veggie?' he said, alarmed when I chose saag aloo.

'No, no, just being more conscious about it.'

Tom chatted about his parents' holiday in Vegas. He said that Sharon needed to use a mobility scooter now and his father had suggested he open an outlet as an adjunct business to the car sales. His mother seemed unhappy about ageing. I said it must be very difficult to be strong of mind and weak of body, for a woman with such a lust for life. I knew Father had raged against his cancer at the start, like a madman, but after a while grew docile and compliant, the most compliant I had seen him my whole life. It was a terrifying compliance. Even to his last breath I thought he would rise up in the bed to scare me, that he would come back to life as fit and ferocious as he had been in his forties. I kept this to myself.

'They were asking for you.'

'Were they?' I said, and for some reason this made me feel content.

'Yes, yes, they seem happy we are at least – civil. Sarah is over the moon, though she keeps on about the book and how that should be my priority. I reassured her that seeing you is helping the book fall into place.'

'How so?' I asked, alarmed.

'I write better when I'm happy.'

'Are you happy?' I said.

'Yes.'

He didn't return the question. 'They think it's time I settled down,' he said.

'And what do you think?'

'I think I'm trying to,' he said and held my hands at the table over the end of the chutney and a flame of the small foil nightlight that was fading.

The film was about a lonely, ireful man who had been institutionalised as a child, adopted out, and now lived alone on an island. His rage had made him turn against everyone in the area and he was often found wandering the beach late at night, roaring out to sea. He fell out with his sisters and brothers and a kind nun he used to like, one who had helped with the adoption, who was once his teacher, and she still called for tea once a week to his cottage by the sea. The more dramatic his actions, the less everyone seemed to care.

Afterwards we took a taxi to mine, giddy after some impulsive negronis in the cinema. I invited Tom in. I had imagined this scenario so many times in my life, Tom in my family home.

'But wouldn't you hate to end up your life like him? Angry and lonely,' Tom said as I rattled keys in the front door.

'I think he brought it on himself,' I said.

'But he had such a hard life.'

I didn't reply as I opened in the door. Though I had played it all out in my head, Tom in my home, it was not like this – so random, unplanned – and that made it more exhilarating. Inside, I set about the bungalow like a mad woman, turning on low lamps and lighting candles. I picked up things here and there and thrust them into presses. Tom was chatty and natural as he went rummaging about the place, dipping his head into the small, dark rooms. He remarked on all the oddities, on the eighties stone fireplace, the pine wardrobes, laughed at my old armchair, the yellowed doilies on the tables with plants on them that I had never taken much attention of. He asked about the next house over – Máire and Joe's – and if the dog ever quietened.

'Sadly no,' I said, 'I don't know what's wrong with that dog to be honest, he's an odd sort, so unsettled. He was grand before lockdown, I often think that maybe he got Dog-Covid?'

'Is that a thing?'

'I don't think so.'

Tom laughed. I uncorked a bottle of red wine in the kitchen and poured.

'Whoa, nice,' he said, calling out from a cupboard. 'And look at this, my God, Claire – have you actually lost it?

'I just like order a little more,' I said. 'I find the chaos, all too—'

'Too?' he said, picking labelled boxes out of my larder. 'Plain flour, wheat germ, oats, rolled oats, quinoa, holy shit, Claire, this is Michelin prep standards. Where's my girl gone?'

The word *girl* unnerved me so I said: 'Won't Johanna mind you staying over?'

'Johanna's in West Cork. She's rarely ever at the house, Claire, that night was a one-off, she had called unexpectedly.'

I imagined the stupid bitch coming all the way from West Cork with the lobsters scraping in the boot of her Tesla. I hoped they clawed through the leather seats.

'Johanna's a friend,' he said. 'I promise. She is just a friend.'

I sipped from my glass and nodded as though I cared less.

'This place is pristine, I can't help thinking that maybe I was the messy one when we were together,' he said, and stopped abruptly with his head in the larder, his shoulders tense.

'You weren't, not really,' I said. I slipped my arms around him, kissed his back. He turned about to face me and kissed my mouth, then broke away gently and continued opening laundry presses and the fridge and the wine press and with each one, he howled in delighted panic.

'I mean, it's kind of spectacular,' he said.

'Enough about the fucking presses,' I said.

'Presses?'

'Cupboards. Enough.'

And then he spotted the mad picture of the Sacred Heart with the light underneath him. 'Jesus, Claire, it's like a bulb you'd find in a whorehouse.'

'That's blasphemy,' I said. 'And how would you know what kind of bulbs are to be found in a whorehouse?'

He punched me playfully and pulled me to him, and I kissed him for a long time, and when we gently broke free, he said: 'Well, it'll have to go,' and I took his hand and led him down the narrow hall to my bedroom. The dog had stopped barking over the fields. Tom tapped the wall for a switch. 'No lights,' I said as I took his full wine glass from him, sipped from it, and placed it by feel onto the locker beside my bed. I pushed him gently to the edge, where he sat, and in the blackness I kneeled, taking him hard from inside his jeans, ran my hand along the inside of his thigh, bit down on his lips, and then I held his hardness before I put him full into my mouth, so full up now, and now, until the pleasure of after when I slept soundly and did not dream.

19

The weeks flew by after Tom and I decided to try over and by December he was spending most of his evenings in the bungalow. He liked to write during the daytime in Johanna's place, or go out interviewing in bars and coffee shops, and then come back to mine.

'I swear to God, Claire – every time I think I'm done someone else comes out of the woodwork. I'll never finish it.'

'You will,' I said.

'I've been thinking about what you've been saying – that maybe I am more interested in their psychology, and the selfish piece about their personalities. Now the why of it all doesn't seem entirely clear to me, I'm a little confused to tell you the truth. It's changed my perspective.'

He ate in mine and fucked in mine and I liked it. I cooked for us every evening and on Thursday mornings I cleaned the house from top to bottom, and restocked the presses, and changed the sheets. He offered to help, but I told him I wanted things this way.

'You know I can cook too,' he said, but I insisted. I enjoyed long Saturdays making love. I cooked new recipes, most of them successfully, taking tips from a Galway chef that was into foraging and local produce, beef with kale and silver-skin onions, lemon roast chicken, colcannon, and many more kinds of potatoes. Triple-cooked roasters, Dauphinoise, Hasselback roasters, pierogi, fondant. I followed more people on Instagram, chefs, fashion tips for size 14, and I took to doing some somatic workouts – but always in my office and never in front of Tom.

'I now see the Irish obsession with potatoes,' Tom said one evening.

I grinned. It felt like a relief, cooking for someone else.

'Tom,' I said, one lazy Sunday afternoon as he sat by the Christmas tree lit with bright white lights in the living room.

'Yup,' he said looking over his laptop, he had a pen in his mouth and his reading glasses on. I loved watching him in his glasses, a new Tom emerged when he wore them, one I had started to trust. I left a hot whiskey beside him.

'Oh, thanks,' he said, 'drinks for tea. Nice.' He picked out a piece of dried orange that was floating on top of the amber liquid. 'This is beautiful,' he said.

This pleased me. 'I cut them and dry them in the oven.'

'All this attention to detail, maybe it's a way of telling you that it's time to start to write again?'

I shrugged. 'Teaching is draining enough,' I said.

'I know,' Tom said, 'but you've always taught before and managed—'

He stopped suddenly. Another writer would never mention the word block, and perhaps he also held back in order not to jinx himself. My rejections had all come so suddenly, a slew of short stories turned down, and then Mother's death which felt like a massive rejection of its own. I felt terrified to even go back there. I reminded myself that London had been busy, I was busy, it was normal for a woman to be busy. Mother should have been busy as I was, if it wasn't all so fucked up. But she wasn't, she was rattling around the bungalow, unloading a dishwasher, putting a light wash out on the line, attending Father. Ultimately, Tom had rejected me, too, though I never framed it like this. And in the flurry of all these thoughts, I suddenly felt so alone in the world, and on an impulse, I said: 'Would you consider moving in for good?' without a tone, just breezily so that another rejection would be a non-issue.

'I would,' he said, and kissed me. 'I would love that.'

One evening, Tom met Doll and Prof for drinks in the Bierhaus. We got quite drunk on chilli margaritas. Conversation moved to the war. Doll said Ukraine was a whore of the US, and Prof took great umbrage at this and they rowed ferociously. Doll said that Trump would get back in because young people didn't care any more about mainstream politics, they didn't trust politicians, they didn't trust their parents as their parents had been posting them on the internet since they changed their first nappy.

'But you're online, right?' Prof said to Doll. 'Remember

you were showing us the crazy conservative wives a little while ago.'

'Trad wives,' Doll said.

'That's right. Crazy bitches,' Prof said.

'In your opinion,' Doll said.

'Trad what?' Tom asked, confused.

'Trad wives,' I said. He looked puzzled.

Doll continued: 'Typically refers to women who believe in traditional sex roles and marriages. They make a sacrifice for their husbands by making homemaking their priority.'

'Seems like a real dream,' he joked.

I didn't reply. They wouldn't listen to me if I tried a defence of Kelly Purchase, not now. Not with all the alcohol and the bravado of opinions that come late in the evening, when no one was actually listening to each other, though Tom was bright and fun and articulate.

Prof hit him on the arm, and Doll said: 'Good whole-some values, g'wan, Tom, ya absolute devil. You'll have Claire barefoot and pregnant yet. Claire, I'm not sure we can allow you proceed with this dalliance.'

We all laughed, and then I kissed Tom on the mouth and he kissed me back and neither of us closed our eyes.

As we waited outside for taxis, I suggested: 'Let's throw a party, Tom, a welcome-Tom party.'

He looked at me in shock. 'Claire, don't go making any rash decisions tonight,' he said, and pinched me gently, but Doll and Prof jumped at the idea.

'I've never been out to the sticks,' Doll said blowing some pink bubblegum.

'It'll be like a faculty tour,' Prof said, excited. 'To rural Ireland. Research maybe.'

'Oh, fuck you both,' I said laughing.

The next morning I woke with a dry mouth and banging headache and lying in bed, in a panic, I turned to Tom. He reminded me of the party. I lied and said that I was quite happy about it. I hadn't thrown a party in the longest time, and never in Athenry. It would be a lovely affair, the four of us – a mini Christmas. Tom got up, his head heavy with his own hangover, and went out for a long walk.

I was up about the kitchen when he came in a couple of hours later.

'I saw Joe next door,' he said.

'Oh,' I said. 'How was he?'

'Yeah, he's well. I invited them both to the party.'

'Oh no. Shit,' I said. 'Fuck. Fuck. Shit, Tom, what have you done?' I couldn't conceal my panic.

'The party!'

'I heard you the first time, but not with Doll and Prof, please tell me.'

'Why not?' he said.

'Why not?' I said. 'Why not? You have *met* all of these people.'

'So?'

'Well, because they don't know each other. They're not the same kind of—' I stopped.

'Sorry,' he said, 'have I put my foot in it?'

'Yes.'

'But I thought Máire and Joe were like your best friends? And now everyone can get to know each other.'

'They are, kind of – well, like they're my oldest friends.'

'Then it will be nice, no?'

My head spun. I couldn't conceive of us pulling Christmas crackers together in any harmony, and I felt weak and panicked all of a moment. Safety in numbers, I would invite my brothers. They might bridge the conversation. Maybe.

Kelly Purchase was throwing a late Thanksgiving dinner for all of their friends who had been away serving overseas and had missed the date itself. 'There is nothing wrong with wanting what ten-year-old you wanted. Always, make it all perfect. You got this.'

Mountain Ellen, Athenry

2022

I

'It's so good to see you,' Brian said, arriving in to the bungalow just moments after Conor and kissing his sister warmly on the cheek. Shaking hands with Tom, he walked on into the kitchen, unwinding a chequered neck scarf and placing it on the counter. Claire followed him and picked it up and put it away, chatting about the drive, the roads, the rain, the irritating Christmas music on the radio. Brian sat himself down at the counter.

'This is new,' he said, touching the white marble top with the palms of his hands. He traced his long narrow fingers along the dark marbling: 'Very nice. And new floors too – are they walnut?' He didn't wait for a reply. 'I feel like I should remove my shoes?'

'Don't be daft,' Claire said, coming up behind him and hugging him tight again, 'but I have considered shoe coverings, or even a workman's entrance. Opinions?' Brian widened his eyes as she handed him a beer. 'Only joking,' she said, and ruffled his hair.

'Right, let's begin!' he said as he pulled the cap off with a bottle opener attached to his keys. He took a gulp.

His father would have noticed the keys if he were still alive. He would have asked how the car is going. If he had dipped it for oil recently. He would have widened his eyes at the beer and looked at his watch. 'Fuck, it's always so strange to be back here,' he said.

'I dunno – it's Christmas and it feels somehow that there's so much more of Mam about the place. Yet the whole place is so different. Weird.'

'You're just in the door,' Claire said.

'I know, I know, but still.'

'She really loved Christmas,' Claire said, as she swept the bottle cap up and put it in the bin under the sink.

'Is it Mam's old room? Is that where you'd like us?' Conor shouted up the hall as his daughter, Leah, toddled about coming into the kitchen where Claire and Brian fussed over her.

'Yeah, yeah,' Claire shouted down, 'I have a little pull-out bed set up for Josh.'

'Great, thank you for all of this,' Lara said, sweeping elegantly into the kitchen, flicking a cashmere shawl about her shoulders, and popping her long feet into pumps with perfect balance. She filled a bottle of juice by the sink for one of the children.

'It's no problem at all,' Claire said, 'it's just so lovely to see you.' Claire placed red bowls with deep-fried parcels of vegetables and some dips on the counter. Tom made funny faces at the toddler.

'It is lovely, unexpected but lovely,' Lara said. 'Can I help?'

'No, no, thanks though. All under control,' Claire said.

Lara eyed the kitchen table and scanned each of the nine settings before asking: 'So what time are the guests arriving?'

'Eight for eight-thirty,' Claire said, lifting a roasting tin from the oven.

'Never understood the Irish and their sense of time,' Tom said. 'Since living here, I think I understand it less.'

'True,' Brian said smiling, 'it's often eight-thirty for ten. Or for not turning up at all. I'm shocked this kitchen takes such a large table, Claire. It all seems bigger somehow?'

'Less clutter,' Claire said.

The table was dressed in a white linen tablecloth with narrow brass candelabra evenly spaced down the middle, and draped with ivy and holly sprayed delicately in gold. Claire had tied red ribbon about the centre of the candlesticks. Two dark bottles of Beaujolais with cream labels and gilded writing were open to breathe, their corks neatly turned up and placed beside them. Miniature pottery jars with delicate lids concealed condiments, and a large plain wine glass and a slim water glass were placed to the right of each setting. Nine place settings in total, with two squashed at one end of the table with a leg either side. This made Claire glance over and panic a little. At first she thought she would put herself there right by Tom, but she decided to put Tom alone at the top and herself and Lara at the other end. Lara would not complain about the table leg being in her way as she ate her meal, and it was likely anyway that she would need to move about for the children should they not settle.

Brian got up holding his beer in his fist against his chest: 'Anything I can do?'

'Yes. Just relax,' Tom said, kindly.

Brian crossed the kitchen and stood looking out the patio door, down to the Old House. The windows were blackened and the oak tree was bare, and he sipped on the beer as he watched a wren dip down into a little birdbath. It was on an old statue of a cheruby thing, he had painted it often as a child. Some of that paint was decades old. There were bird feeders placed all about the yard now. 'You'll need to treat the roof of the Old House, Claire. The rust will destroy it. Already has a job done on it.'

'I was thinking of knocking it,' Claire said.

Brian turned about to her in panic: 'Surely not? No, but you can't.'

'Why not?'

'Dad said that . . . he said not to. Like the fairy tree in the far field.'

'Dad's not here,' Claire said.

Brian considered this a moment. 'Fair,' he said, softly, and turned back to the house again. 'But I dunno, between the house and the fairy tree, I would be afraid of the wrath it could bring down on us all.'

'Oh, don't say that, that's only silly talk,' Claire said, 'mostly it's pisreogs.' She felt a panic rising in her voice. 'Don't jinx it . . . Surely you don't mean that.'

'Have you cut down the fairy tree?' Brian asked.

'No,' she said. 'I won't either, but Joe looks after all of that because I don't go near the fields and with him using them for grazing, it's been great, he's fixed all the fencing, and there's pumped water now, below the hazel.'

'Fair play, Joe,' Brian said.

'I hope he's paying you,' Conor said walking into the kitchen and placing some of the children's foods into the fridge.

'What?' Claire said, startled.

'Joe – for the grazing. He should be paying us some rent. Always a tight cunt, Joe.'

'No, he doesn't, why don't you ask him?' Claire snapped. 'He'll be here any minute.' She looked out the back window. Máire and Joe would arrive in the back door, as was local custom.

'Ah, look, the place looks lovely, Claire, fair play,' Brian said, distracting his siblings. 'I never thought you'd stick it here, I really didn't.' In the short time since he had arrived, his sister's calmness had taken him aback a little, and the house's organisation also – though he was happy to see it. She had never thrown a dinner party in all the years he could remember. 'Suits you, you know, having Tom about.'

'Watch it, you,' Claire said, poking her brother. 'I can manage quite well without anyone. But yes, it's been nice. Very nice.'

'It's been great,' Tom said kissing her softly on the cheek.

Brian was always fond of Tom – though Brian was fond of everyone. He had visited Claire often when she moved to London first, crashed on their couch, gone to the pub with Tom, and they always had good time for each other.

'So did you get work here, Tom?' Brian asked.

'Or are you a kept man?' Conor added, watching Claire collect the side plates up and fuss about the sink.

'I'm working,' Tom said. 'Writing.' He grabbed a beer from the fridge, opened it and sat by Brian.

'Oh, great,' Brian said.

'What are you writing about?' Conor asked.

'I'm working on a book about men in extreme sports, Irish men. I'm getting no further. Every time I think I have an angle, someone more remarkable comes along.'

'Sounds like Grinder,' Brian said.

'Why just Irish men?' Conor said.

'Oh, please, don't start him. Here, please, put the caps in the bin,' Claire said as she washed some mint leaves by the sink. She checked the piece of paper by her, crossing things off, a pen neatly on top of it, things left to do, timings for meats. The ducklings and a ham were already baking in the oven.

'I considered roasting a goose,' she said, as Brian eyed the amber door of the oven, 'but decided not to, so much work.'

'Very little meat on a goose,' Conor and Claire said together. Claire smiled at her older brother as he jerked open the patio door.

The door often came undone from its runner when Conor was a little boy and he was terrified of it, the sound it made, the sound that signalled John O'Connor was in from the farm and one of them was in for it. The sound of it coming out from its hinges and smashing out on the concrete yard once when he was in a rage. Conor tipped the toddler's nappy into a wheelie bin, threw an eye to the Old House, and stepped back inside.

Claire had planned everything meticulously and Tom had agreed to all of it. He had collected items. Shopped. Helped decorate the tree. Got the last-minutes. He had filled up the crate with logs. Collected the wine.

They would start with dressed crabmeat and a fresh Chablis to accompany and that would be followed by the crisp roast ducklings stuffed with plums, dried basil, parsley, bread, pecan nuts and raisins. She would serve the baked ham with collard greens, a variety of differ- ent potatoes, mustards, chutneys and some honey glazed carrots dipped in poppy seeds from Joe's garden, some Beaujolais. Plum pudding for dessert, and it was to be lit at the table in honour of her mother, who loved plum pudding. An assortment of cheeses to follow, Young Buck, Ardrahan, Camembert, a soft sweet goat's cheese from the Burren, accompanied by figs, honey and some apricots. A crémant from Luxembourg.

Conor was quiet and set about the sink making him- self and Lara a cup of tea, he squeezed honey into hers, stirred. 'Jesus fucking Christ, Claire, it's like *The Great British Bake Off* in this larder. Are you a secret chef also?'

'That's my effect,' Tom said.

Conor had met Tom Morton once or twice briefly

and had no recollection if Tom had ever had a real job. It upset Tom that Conor remembered so little about him. Once he had met him in The Swan when they were both very drunk, and another time at a birthday party of a friend he shared with Claire since childhood, who had then lived in Shepherd's Bush but had gone on to take his own life shortly after the party.

Tom went outside to load up on wood for the living room fire, which was his only instruction for the night, that and to refill everyone's drinks. Claire had hoped he would curtail his conversations about his book but so far this was looking unlikely. Conor mooched about the place, picking things up and setting them down. Asking questions like: 'Is this new?' Or: 'Was this Mam's?'

Claire grew weary. 'Where's Lara?' she asked.

'Breastfeeding Leah.'

No one commented on the fact that Leah was walking with a full set of teeth and sounds. Their own mother had never breastfed any of them, though they were used to ewes and lambs, mares and foals – but all animals would have weaned by now. Leah was proficient in life as a toddler, so the breastfeeding seemed unusual, when the child was more than capable of chastising everyone and had taken to dismantling the house with glares on her arrival. Lara had said not to pay any heed, and Leah had proclaimed: 'No, no,' to almost everything Claire had to offer.

'Don't worry,' Josh said, careful and slow, 'she likes nonly her own toys not mine.' Josh was built like his father, wiry. Like his father he took up very little conversation space, but much of the atmosphere when he entered a room.

'Don't judge,' Conor said looking at his sister and brother.

'No one is judging,' Claire said.

'Inclusion,' Brian said, 'always about opening space.' And he burst out laughing.

'Lara is doing what's best for the kids, and I'm watching you two flutes – judging my wife.'

'I'm not judging anyone,' Brian said. Conor bristled and said he was taking a walk before dinner.

It was dark now, and everyone seemed more relaxed when Conor left and headed off in the direction of Máire and Joe's with a high-vis jacket and a head torch. Claire watched him from the back of the house going up the fields. She turned on Christmas music and popped the first cork from a cold bottle of crémant as the kids came in and played and ate their tea, and Lara toasted the night, and everyone was relaxed and happy waving Josh and Leah to bed. Claire selfishly hoped they would sleep through the evening.

II

'Let me take your coat,' Tom said, as he welcomed Doll and Prof at the front door.

'Merriest of the holiday season to you, Tom,' Prof said, kissing him twice. They handed him bags with wine and cheeses, chocolates and some pale ales. Large church candles were lit in glass lanterns by the front door.

'The place is so lovely – very homely,' Prof said, looking about her as she handed over a beige trench coat, and fixing the belt in place before letting it go. Claire came from the kitchen to hug the two new arrivals.

'Happy Christmas.'

'You're literally only standing in the hall, we've just arrived,' Doll quipped at Prof. 'Settle. What kind of a road was that we came up, Tom? The taxi driver nearly cried with the state of it.'

Claire laughed and kissed Doll twice – once on each cheek. Conor stepped in behind them, his high-vis in one hand, and on hearing his voice Leah jumped out of bed and ran up the hall into his arms.

'Hi,' he said, 'I'm Conor, Claire's older brother.'

'Hi,' both women replied, cooing about the child as Tom set about the introductions. Leah charmingly shook her fat left hand with both women.

'She doesn't do hugs,' Lara called out, making excuses

for her toddler, whom she felt was far more formal than her other child had ever been.

'Quite right too,' Doll said to the little girl. 'Quite right. Nice rags, kiddo,' she said, admiring the child's unicorn hairband. Leah dipped her head down and put a fist in her small mouth, smiling coyly and telling the women that Conor was Daddy.

In the kitchen Claire filled glasses of crémant and handed them to the guests.

Doll drank it down in two gulps.

'Lordy, you were thirsty,' Prof remarked.

'I've brought beers, Claire, I drink fast. I think Tom put them in the fridge. I might just grab one,' said Doll, and she pulled a can from the fridge, offered one to Brian as Claire snuck right behind her, ready to catch a spill or a fall. 'So Claire, this is your family home, huh, it's nice! You weren't previous, Prof, in your admiration. Apols. So spill, does that mean you're mortgage free?' She glanced at Tom and Claire in turn. Brian took a can.

'Doll!' Prof said, tapping her on her free hand, and coughing gently. She set to fixing her glasses on her nose. 'That's so rude, you can't ask a question like that.'

'What?' Doll said.

'You never ask people about their money.'

Doll said: 'It's not about money, it's about housing.'

'Same thing,' Prof replied.

'It's fine,' Claire replied. 'Yes, you're correct, it's mortgage free,' and she folded a tea towel by the hob.

'So you were the favourite child then – was there land with this or just the house?' Doll pressed.

'Doll!' Prof said, loudly now.

Conor, Brian and Claire all eyed each other and laughed. 'She wasn't the favourite, it's left to the three of us. Claire just lives here. And there's a few acres, mostly rock, but some OK grazing,' Conor said.

'Right, right,' Doll said, 'so technically you could evict her then? You know, if it all goes tits up.'

'No, no, not at all,' Brian said. 'We would never do that, Claire's our sister. This house is, well, it's for everyone. It's for anyone, who wants it. I don't, I couldn't – ever live here,' he said, and he hesitated, tore at the label on his beer. He glanced at Conor, and his brother's narrow lips were tight and paler now.

'Like a commune?' Doll said with devilment.

'No,' the siblings said together.

'Well, I guess,' Conor said, looking down at his shoes, for fear they had dragged in dirt from his walk to Joe's, 'we could. I mean if we really wanted to, we *could* evict her.'

'Ha.' Claire laughed breezily. 'Funny.'

'But we never would, never,' Brian said.

'But it's a possibility. Like, as she said, *technically*,' Conor said.

'But we *never* would,' Brian said.

'It's not the argument I'm making,' Conor said.

'No one is arguing, and indeed,' Claire said kindly to her two brothers, 'if you wanted to evict me, I guess technically you could, but you'd have to get past Máire's Labrador first.'

But the talk of eviction stabbed the air and Prof, sensing the discomfort, interjected eloquently and spoke about the British imposition of primogeniture on their colonised, about inheritance rights and men, and about many instances of inheritance issues in literature.

'Where there's a will there's a—' Tom said.

'Relative,' Doll said.   'Row,' Conor said, simultaneously.

Prof said that such ructions were the mainstay of the Victorian novel, and everyone agreed that the rooms of nineteenth-century novels were vaster and so perhaps everyone had more to lose, though inheritance and property were still arguably some of the most contentious issues in any domestic and political space.

'Well, at least you haven't inherited a deranged housekeeper,' Lara said, coming into the kitchen. The women understood and smiled.

'Our granny lived with her mother-in-law for years. Our grandfather's mother. They all lived in that house,' Claire said.

'What house?' Prof said.

'The one outside.'

They all moved to the patio door, and peered out.

'She had seven sons,' Conor said, 'and they were the first to be given the land from the Land Commission. Forty acres almost, give or take.'

'From who?' Doll said.

'The landlord – like from an estate.'

'Really?' Doll remarked. 'I never realised.'

Conor nodded.

'So like a king?' Doll continued. 'Sorry, I'm half Serb, my mother's a Gaeilgeoir from Carraroe, but I'm afraid my dad is the more forceful historian. Mam's family just make up stories, ghosts, banshees, that kind of thing.'

'Think of the landlord as the whore of the king,' Conor said.

'Conor!' Claire cried out. 'What in the name of God did you get in Joe's?'

'Poitín.'

Everyone laughed, except Claire. 'Oh, shit. Tell me Joe Grealish didn't drink any.'

'I can't promise,' Conor said, smirking.

'Or Lear,' Brian said, circling back to the landlords. 'That was a shitshow of an inheritance.'

They all set to chatting about the idea of Lear's Love Test, and half the room agreed they would sing for their supper, and do what was needed, words were only words after all, Lara said, but the three O'Connor children were certain and absolute that they would not dare ever sing for any supper. Off anyone. Not ever – even if it meant going destitute. Not if it meant grass stains on the sides of their mouths while they died in the ditches.

'You're all hard-ass,' Doll said, smiling. Her diamonds seemed duller in the low light, like four cavities on her front teeth. Brian looked closely at her. 'You see, I often wonder who knew the kind of shit Goneril and Regan had to put up with? For all we know, Lear could have been a nonce, and they knew how to play him.'

'Because he was a nonce? But how does that make

any sense?' Prof said, taking a high seat by Brian at the counter. She was unsure what had come over her younger colleague. 'Surely we would know this, if that was the case?'

'I didn't mean it – I mean, OK. No, no, sorry, that was flippant, but I just mean, Shakespeare slices us into all drama. We don't know the first thing about what kind of a father Lear was, everyone expects filial loyalty as though it's a given.'

'I can categorically say that the father was drunk. Wait, wait, no, blind,' Conor said.

'I think we can all agree that kings might not make great fathers,' Tom said.

'I don't remember enough about Shakespeare,' said Brian. 'I have selective amnesia around the Leaving Cert.'

'And we know less about kings or power,' Conor added. 'So, do you teach also?' he asked Doll.

'No, no, I'm an administrator in the university.'

'Sort of like a secretary?' Conor said.

'If that's the word that helps you understand,' Doll said, wryly. 'But no, not a secretary.'

'That's an incredibly responsible job, long hours I'd say,' Lara interjected, placating the nonsense from her husband as she set to pulling a pyjama top with a little dog-policeman on Josh's wriggly body for the second time that night. 'Sorry,' she said, nodding at her son, 'he is relentless, he likes to get out of bed and run about naked – he's a free spirit.' She smiled at Josh as he squashed her face in between his hands.

'Takes after his dad,' Conor said. Tom laughed.

'I don't understand the idea of giving all your inheritance to one person though,' Claire said. 'It seems so unfair.'

'Well, it makes it all easier, I guess.' Tom was taking more beers from the fridge. 'Better for lineage too.'

'Easier for whom?' Prof added. 'Men? It's sexist and it's actually dangerous.'

'Not all men,' Brian jested. 'You can blame him for the primogeniture, before—' and then he stopped, realising what he was about to say, and he was suddenly stuck for a suitable word in the company of the Englishman. Claire knew in ordinary circumstances someone would have said something derogatory. Her father would have. Brian said: 'Before the laws changed –' by which he meant the Penal Laws – 'any holdings were divided into smaller parcels between the children.'

'That would have meant very little though,' Tom said.

'Of course,' Prof said. 'This goes without saying, and that was also a problem, but it's slightly more "democratic".'

'Nothing from nothing leaves nothing eventually,' Conor said.

Tom looked at him, uncertain of his temper.

'There was no land ownership, not by the native Irish,' Conor said.

'Yes, of course,' Tom said, nodding as he passed the bowl of fried vegetables to Conor, who waved them onwards.

'Right,' Claire said, moving about the room as she filled the flutes with more crémant.

'Well, it's all the same to me,' Doll said, ignoring

Claire's easy tone change. 'I'll never own a house, so it is all academic.'

'You might,' Brian said, encouragingly.

'Yeah, if I do the Lotto.'

'Do you?' Prof said, looking at Doll as though she had met her for the first time.

'No.'

'You should,' Prof said.

Doll threw her hands into the air, and her top rose about her pierced navel. 'And so that's the answer, in a room full of seemingly smart people, for me to do the Lotto. I have as much chance as being hit by a runaway Arab stallion.'

'Why Arab?' Brian said.

'Walter Farley,' Doll said.

III

Joe Grealish's plaid shirt was tight about his chest and his skin red at the collar where his neck was sore from a very recent shaving. He stepped into the full kitchen of the bungalow, followed by Máire, who pulled shut the patio door quietly in her wake. Joe smiled widely at all the faces in the kitchen, some he knew, some he did not, as did Máire. She was wearing a faux fur jacket and a heavy wine-coloured lipstick. Her hair was set and blow-dried and she seemed self-conscious and awkward behind Joe for some moments.

'Jesus, I thought you were roadkill coming across the yard,' Brian said.

'Don't mind your insults, Brian O'Connor, I remember changing your nappy,' she said, swatting him gently. 'Happy Christmas everyone.'

Claire came to them both, and hugged each warmly in turn.

'Here, just something for you,' Joe said, handing Claire a seasonal bag.

'I hope you haven't overdone this, Máire Grealish, or I'll kill you. I really will. But thank you both,' Claire said. They had a habit of using a second name when they were serious, about to berate someone, or if about to announce a piece of gossip about a person.

'The place looks really great, Claire,' Joe said, looking about and off into the living room. 'Tom, nice to see you again, and you, Brian, Christ, I hardly recognise you.' He was stiff and awkward, a little conscious of the poitín on his breath and the clothes tight on his body.

Lara, arriving back from putting Josh in bed, hugged both of the neighbours.

'My God, Lara O'Connor, but didn't you get thin?' Máire exclaimed.

'I did not, Máire,' Lara said, coyly, 'well, maybe a little bit, sure you know yourself, running about after two would keep anyone trim.' Lara immediately regretted it for she was conscious that Joe and Máire had never had children.

'That's for sure,' Máire said, breezily. Máire Grealish was a woman who was very happy with exactly how her life had worked out. Doll stood about listening, fascinated by the women's comfort with discussing body shapes, something she and her friends would never dream of mentioning.

After a while, Doll went to stand with Prof and the men. Joe asked everyone in turn how their jobs were going, like a quiz-show host, and was corrected twice on Doll's name, and then he was puzzled as to why anyone would go as Prof.

'Like as a Christian name, isn't it a bit, I dunno, bizarre. What's your actual name?'

'Suzanne.'

'Well, Prof Suzanne, you see, I think it's a bit like being at a party and being called, Mechanic, or Tiler, or here, Butcher, catch this here, you chicken.' Máire glared at him and the ridiculous nonsense coming from him while Conor found it very entertaining and laughed hysterically.

'Joe, what on earth has come over you?' Máire said across the room to him.

Prof was used to men like Conor from university who allowed others do their bidding, loaded guns, but rarely fired them. 'I suppose,' Prof said, 'but it's kind of just stuck since grad school. I will answer to either name,' she said diplomatically. 'And I love Leonard Cohen, so in a way, that makes my name more special.'

'Where was school?' Máire asked, attempting to override any more mad moments Joe might have until everyone became a little more comfortable with one another. Jim Reeves seemed loud in the background singing 'White Christmas'. Tom passed by and crouched down, stacking some more wood on the burning stove in the living room.

'Undergrad in Yale and postgrad in Harvard, but I hail from Rhode Island – Cranston actually. I'm a blue-collar girl at heart.'

'Impressive,' Máire said.

'Rhode Island?' Joe said. 'City or a state?'

'Yeah, it's a state actually, but a very tiny one. We are right by Boston, not everyone's heard of us, Rhode Island, so we keep it a secret.' She knew Irish people liked a Boston comparative.

'I have cousins in Boston,' Joe said. 'Brighton mostly,

but some in Quincy. And older ones, second, some in Southie.'

'Third and fourth generation in Southie,' Máire said.

'Right,' Prof said, 'so many Irish in Boston. It's almost like going to Clare.'

'Yeah,' Brian said, 'though Clare is a little wilder. Grandad's brothers all emigrated though most went to England. All except him. One to the US, Boston too. At least I think it was that way, or maybe it was the other way around?'

'So many Irish in London as well,' Tom said.

'Are you Irish?' Joe said, checking Tom's height.

'No,' Tom said as he threw an eye to the flames in the stove.

'I mean your people, are your people Irish?' Joe said.

'They're not, as far as I know, I'm fifth generation East End, I'm afraid, and then, I think for the most part, I'm German.' Everyone nodded politely as people tend to do when they have no reference or relative for the country.

'Oh, Máire likes *EastEnders*,' Joe said, 'don't you?'

'Not everyone wants to be Irish, Joe,' Máire said back to him.

'They seem to,' Joe said. 'A third of Irish now, are not Irish at all. Imagine that?'

Máire swatted him: 'That sounds wildly incorrect, where did you pull that from?'

'I heard it on the radio.'

'Did you now?' she said.

'Sounds like an opinion and not a fact,' Brian said kindly. 'Or propaganda.'

'Maybe,' Joe said.

'Stonecutters,' Tom said, 'my family, a lot of stonecutters on my father's side from Idar-Oberstein. As far as I know. Came from Germany to the East End to work on cathedrals. A few came here in the nineteenth century, but not many stayed.'

The women broke away and gathered around the sink. It was almost time to eat and the children had settled again. Lara was having a glass of bubbles, but still seemed anxious as anyone might feel with children tucked up in a strange place. They chatted about Máire's most recent work fiasco where a patient had snuck a bottle of Chardonnay in her hospital bag and drunk it before having her appendix removed, lying to them about fasting.

'She vomited for days after,' Máire said. 'Stupid cow, she could have died on her own vomit when she was under.'

'How did you not smell it off her breath?' Claire asked.

'You'd wonder, but everything moves so fast in theatre. And do you know what she said when she was leaving?'

'What?' Lara said, intrigued.

'At least I won't have to diet this week.'

All the women laughed, except Doll, who had no idea what they meant, so she walked into the living room to the men who were sat about the television watching a darts competition from Alexandra Palace in London. Doll liked to add up the three throws.

'We'll keep you,' Joe said to Doll as she quickly calculated the score for every participant, and she found this comment weird, but she liked Joe, and Brian handed her another beer. They all watched the screen intensely now, leaning forward with their elbows on their knees, and Doll felt relaxed for the first time in the evening.

IV

Claire lifted the heavy Nicholas Mosse platter of dressed crab towards the crowd and placed it in the middle of the kitchen table. The crab was set on a bed of baby gem lettuce, dressed with some hard shell, samphire, cracked black pepper and fresh parsley. Lemon wedges were perfectly set about the plate beside a basket of brown bread, warm and covered with roasted almonds. Ramekins of yellow butter were dotted about the table, crusted with flakes of Aran Island sea salt. Lara went into the living room and turned off the television at which, the darts fanatics all sighed and expressed their discontent, but they soon got over it, refilling drinks and making their way to the table where they were distracted by the spread, heaping their plates with the crabmeat and pulling Christmas crackers. Joe was the only guest who placed the delicate paper hat from the cracker on his head and it split down the middle to make two large purple fangs. They chatted on about the darts, and a short but energetic argument erupted as to whether darts was a sport or a game.

'I don't think we'll settle this tonight,' Tom said, sensing Claire's unease.

'It's *absolutely* a sport,' Joe said. 'Of course it is.'

'I really think you're pushing it by calling it a sport,' Brian replied.

'See the size of some of those players – wouldn't want them to do a stress test,' Conor said. 'Fucking well unfit if you ask me.'

'What about chess?' Tom said.

'What about it?' Conor said.

'Definitely a sport,' Brian said.

'It is not,' Joe said, 'that's crazy talk, at least in darts they have to fling a thing.'

'Ah, that's a little crude,' Tom said. 'Chess is definitely a sport, not sure about darts,' he said clearing away the cracker innards from the table, little plastic die, a nail clippers, some puzzle that would remain unsolved deep into January, when real winter set in.

'That's just class snobbery,' Doll said to Tom and so Tom moved on and picked up his glass by the narrow stem and raised it to Claire, and said: 'To the beautiful host!' Everyone clinked and thanked them both, this way and that across the busy table. Sláinte.

'Don't thank me,' Tom said, pushing some crab into his mouth, 'I only had to lift my feet now and then for the hoover to pass underneath me.'

'Lucky man,' Joe said.

'Joe Grealish, what are you like tonight? Tom, he wouldn't know where to find the hoover,' Máire said reproachfully. Joe grumbled an apology to his wife, something he had grown used to doing in public settings over their many years of marriage, but tonight she saw that he grew red in the face and it would never be her intention to upset him, or worse, embarrass him in front of strangers. She winked at him, and he winked back.

Tom read from a slim piece of cracker insert, a joke: 'What do you call a boomerang that doesn't come back?'

'A stick,' Brian said.

'Touché.'

'A stick,' Doll said, repeating Brian and she began laughing: 'That's good, so much you can do with a stick,' and she mock threw a cracker once or twice, with one eye shut but didn't release it.

'I only had to drive to the market,' Claire reassured everyone, 'I didn't catch it myself. The fish.' Her comment about the market and the fish, though untimed and out of place, brought the conversation around to sea-swimming. Tom began by telling everyone how invigorating it is – the sea, so good for just about every ailment one can have from over-heating to impotence to death. Prof agreed. Doll said she loved to jump off the tower in Blackrock every day before work and liked it best to jump feet first from the high board, though only if the tide is in, of course. 'It's exhilarating,' she said. 'I am truly addicted and it is legit the very best thing for a hangover.'

'That must be why you have great skin,' Prof said, turning about to her.

Doll dabbed her face and smiled widely. The compliment was out of the blue.

'The thing about sea-swimmers—' Conor said, and Joe interrupted: 'Just call it fucking swimming, when did everyone start to say sea-swimming?' His curse was ill-timed. 'I remember going out to Blackrock for a swim once a year when I was a child. It was just swimming then and it was fucking cold and miserable. It always rained. Don't know what the big fuss is. Give me green fields or the dark woods around here any day over the bloody sea. I get seasick just looking at it, and who knows what sort of creatures are underneath you when you're thrashing about in it. We were made for land.'

'But it is only a short trip in the car from here, why so scant, your visits? Even if just to walk by it,' Prof said.

'Long time to be away from a farm,' Joe said. 'A full day. Besides, all that bloody sand. Definitely put the sand in sandwich.'

'A day?' Prof said. 'Just one day.'

'An hour is a long time to leave a farm unattended,' he said. 'Anything could happen. You could lose your livelihood if you just took off to the beach for a long day of laziness.'

'Leisure,' Máire said. 'People don't go because they are lazy, Joe, they go for leisure.'

'Very little difference between leisure and laziness,' Tom said.

'Are you dairy farmers?' Doll asked.

'No—' Joe began.

Conor interrupted: 'Thing about sea-swimmers, no, no, wait – let me get this right –' he slurred a little as he took a large gulp of his Chablis – 'wait, wait,' and he motioned about the table at everyone with his finger.

'Everyone *is* waiting, darling,' Lara said and flashed

her husband a concerned look. She watched him place his empty glass down and was nervous as Doll filled it to the top again. Then he said: 'Got it. How do you know a sea-swimmer?'

'Their skin?' Doll said.

Claire and Prof laughed and said: 'Their smile?'

'They'll tell you,' Conor said.

Máire and Joe laughed. 'Damn fucking right they will,' Joe said in delight.

Doll considered it a moment, adding: 'Fair.' And everyone nodded.

'So what do you do?' Prof asked Conor across the table, realising he had slipped the occupations net earlier. She was sure Claire had mentioned that Brian worked for the Refugee Council, but she couldn't quite remember what Conor had said. Conor coughed for a moment, lifted his napkin to dab his mouth and glanced down at his plate. Along the sides of the table three men were squarely facing three women, and Claire was regretting the accidental confrontation of it. Tom sat oblivious at one head, finishing a crab claw as Lara and Claire, squished at the other, had been polite and nimble with their elbows. 'Hasn't Claire said?' Conor asked, as he scooped a crab claw with his thumb and finger and placed it between his teeth.

'No, no, I don't think she has,' Prof said.

He pulled on the black claw gently, and slowly, bringing it forward in his mouth, as though he was smiling, and nibbled about the cartilage for a little while. 'These are really delicious, Claire,' he said and left the naked claw down, picking at his teeth. 'I drive for a company,' he said.

'Really?' Prof pressed.

'What company?' Doll said.

'Doubt you'd have heard of it.'

'Try me.'

'It's a horse stud, I drive the owners around. Mostly Sheikhs.'

'Right,' Prof said.

Everyone aside from Doll and Prof were familiar with Conor's work – his long hours on the road, with rich men from the Middle East who came to visit their horse stud farms in Tipperary and Kildare. Lara was aware of the kind of men that Conor minded, but she never complained. The money was incredible, and she reassured herself by considering it like a taxi service. Taxi drivers must drive every fare. A stall seller at Moore Street. A runaway. The Taoiseach. Drunk people on nights out. Patients from hospital. It is not a time or a job for morals. You pick them up, drop them off.

'Do you like it?' Doll asked.

Conor nodded.

'I often thought I'd like a job on the road, keep me moving, I like to keep moving, the office can be stifling,' Doll went on.

'I can see that,' Tom said, 'from all the extreme sports guys I'm talking to – all of them have that in common. They don't like to stay still. And failure is the by-product of success, you can't have one without the other. Hard to live like that.'

'Need to do it as a writer,' Claire said. 'Hours of stillness, and bad backs.'

'And rejection,' Tom said.

'I pick up when I'm told, I drive where I'm told, I speak when spoken to and I am silent the rest of the time. I ask nothing of them, and though I know a great deal about horses, I like to forget I do, so I pretend I am ignorant of all things equine. It's perfect,' Conor said. 'No one knowing my business. I don't know theirs. For now it is what it is.' Lara knew how this would hurt him and that he was ashamed that his career as an actuary had not worked out, that he had taken a long time out after his mother died, that he had had a breakdown during the slow days after the crash, a breakdown he never admitted, like his sister. Lara was the only one who knew about his breakdown. At the time he claimed to everyone that he had had a bone infection in his arm, osteomyelitis, and it took a long time to heal, so the doctor had advised him he needed to move about more, and long hours at a computer would no longer suit. The truth was, he'd been let go and it was only through a friend of a close friend of Lara's, and an exemplary knack of never saying much to anyone, that he had landed this job. Lara dabbed her napkin at the corners of her mouth. She was proud Conor had found something he could cope with, that didn't mean a huge financial step down for her or the children, but it had taken its toll on his pride, his status, and for that, she was concerned.

'Bet the tips are amazing,' Máire said, 'rich men and their horses, are they fun?'

'Sometimes, but mostly it's all business. Great tips, yes,' Conor said.

'Do you work at home with the children?' Doll said to Lara.

'I do, yes,' Lara replied, enthusiastically, grateful of a segue. 'It's great to be able to. A real privilege.'

Prof didn't comment as the table mostly made approving noises.

'We have similar jobs,' Joe said.

'Husbandry of some kind,' Máire said and Joe looked confused.

As they finished the starters, Máire said to Claire: 'Did you see the new bakery that has opened beside Lauren's hairdresser?'

'I did,' Claire said. 'Looks great.'

'They're Polish,' Máire said.

'Well, that's great,' Joe said.

'Joe?' Tom said.

'That they have started a business. I mean it,' Joe said, 'it's really great.'

'Yes, yes,' Máire said, a wave of relief coming over her.

'How did your father manage when he came to Ireland?' Joe asked Doll.

'Yeah, hard at the start, but he got a job doing furniture removal, my father, has been at it all his life now – as far as I know. But he's quiet about himself, I don't know if it's a male thing, or an immigrant habit.'

Joe was quiet for a moment, and Prof feeling defensive of her friend said:

'You could ask me the same question.'

'About?' Joe looked confused.

'About if I have a job, as an immigrant.'

'But sure you told me you had a job. You work with Claire. I know this.'

'What Joe means, is, it's different,' Conor said, apologetically, to both.

'How so?' Doll asked.

'Prof had been to Harvard,' Conor added bluntly. 'But you know this is different,' he said, squarely to Prof. 'You're just badgering him.'

'More bread?' Claire said, loudly, and lifted the basket high about, to a resounding no around the table.

'No, no,' Joe said, 'just it's all OK when you work, right? But we can't sustain it, you know all the people coming in and not working, it's no life to be living in a tent on the street in Dublin or Galway. Shop Street is littered with them, God help us, having to lie there all night, every night, on the wet ground.'

'How do you mean, sustain it?' Brian asked.

'You know what I mean,' Joe said, avoiding Brian's eyes.

Máire smiled at Brian across the table, and he knew she wanted him to step down a little. He respected Máire. She had nursed his parents, minded him, and always been like a big sister, he nodded a little at her to denote compliance. 'So what does your mam do?' Máire said to Doll.

'She works in the hospital.'

'Ah, so do I! What department?'

'Catering,' Doll said.

Máire realised she knew Doll's mother, and she liked her greatly, commenting on what a wonderful soul she was. New conversations branched off about the table and Máire and Doll discussed the patients they had both known, that Doll's mother had talked about, all the sadness and exhaustion her mother had felt on late nights after coming off a shift.

Claire was relieved that everyone had soon forgotten about immigration and employment and seemed happy again.

As she cleared plates there was a swift table change to talk of a TV show some of them had binged about a man who locked his wife away for years in a cellar with only a bed and a toilet, turned her into a kind of robot for him, and eventually convinced her that the world was in free-fall, wars were looming and she was better off staying put in the room he had locked her into, and in effect he was minding her and she was so grateful.

'He's not wrong about the state of the world,' Conor said, 'but what I don't get is how she bought it and believed him – it all seemed unlikely.'

'I haven't watched it,' Tom said, 'but it sounds unusual.' He looked at Claire a moment.

'Women are their own worst enemies, sometimes,' Lara said. 'I say this as a feminist, but a feminist who doesn't like all the women I meet. And save me from the kindergarten parent zealots I'm meeting at the gate dropping off Josh. They can be so gullible, and idiotic,' she went on, 'it's as though they are all waiting to be rescued or something.' She sipped some water.

Doll pulled the ring off another grapefruit beer. 'Weren't you in research before the kids?' she said to Lara.

'I was.'

'Sounded fascinating.'

'It did?' Lara looked bewildered. It felt like another lifetime ago.

'Yes, your project. Grey matter – Claire was telling us about it one night. Pharma, right?'

'Right, yeah, it was great, grey matter, fascinating on memory and so much other important stuff like tissue development.' She stopped abruptly. 'I was married to the lab and it was so time-consuming. What I noticed when I stepped aside when I was having Josh, was that I was so easily replaced.'

'I doubt that,' Claire said. Lara had been lead on the research project.

'Oh no, she's right,' Conor said. 'Look, truth is, everyone's replaceable.'

'I really don't think so,' Tom said, 'at least not on an interpersonal level.'

'But you have a PhD?' Doll said.

'I did,' Lara said. 'Yes, I do,' she corrected herself, bringing her qualification into the present.

'So why not use it?' Doll said.

'Doll!' Prof said. 'Not your business.'

'I'm only wondering,' Doll said.

'Because it's about choice,' Prof said, 'and Lara does not have to reassure you of her choices.'

'I'm not asking her to do that,' Doll said.

'What are you asking?' Conor interjected.

'Just seems like an awful waste to me, especially if it was funded.'

'Raising my children is not a waste,' Lara said, flatly.

'That's not what I meant,' Doll conceded, 'but fair,' as Prof pinched her leg beneath the white tablecloth.

'Máire is definitely not replaceable,' Joe said, dabbing the bread around the serving dish to finish off the end of the crab.

'Returning to that Netflix series,' Prof said, 'just for a sec. I think what you're talking about is that sometimes there is a conditioning of women from the patriarchy, and it means that we compete for attention, and this attention that the protagonist was getting in the show, maybe it was better than no attention.'

'A bird in the hand—' Tom said.

'Yes, yes,' Prof said, turning to Tom, 'exactly this. It's about fear, and that fear stems from feeling as though they are dependent on a man for their finances, in effect, survival.'

'I don't think that women are down on other women because of men, I think that's such a lazy way of looking at it, and frankly reductive. Maybe women can be mean to women, because, women, and only women,' Conor said.

'Disagree,' Doll said. 'Politely. Women are collectively excluded from political, social and economic positions of power.'

'Right,' Prof said.

'They are less well paid for work of equal value as done by men. Women are more likely to experience poverty and unequal access to resources, and services—'

'And,' Brian said, 'it's not equal, women in other countries are far more vulnerable than anyone around this table. But so are some men.'

'That's not what we're saying,' Prof said.

'I know,' Brian said, 'but at work we are trying to house single men from tents to hostels – it's all relative.'

'I think it's all nature,' Joe said, suddenly buoyed up by the fact that he might have something to offer. 'Take a cow abroad in the field with a calf, she'll mind it far better than the bull. She's the mother. The bull is a sire.'

Doll began laughing.

'No, no,' Máire said sternly and quickly. 'Stop, Joe. Just stop.'

'Nothing like a bit of gender essentialism at Christmas,' Doll said. 'What a fucking hoot.'

'No, no,' Máire said looking firmly at Joe and Doll in turn. 'We are not reducing all the centuries of progress that women have made with your cows, Joe Grealish, so stop it, no cow talk, thank you very much. Humans are not cattle. And yes, yes, Brian, all things considered, I agree.'

Joe smiled widely at his wife, she made such sense, and he was so grateful for her. Having conversations around a dinner table was his idea of hell in all truth.

'So do I,' Claire said, 'I agree. But I hear you, Brian,

too, and we can't completely negate structural issues, these are hard facts.'

Everyone went quiet at this and nodded, and Claire turned to Tom and said: 'Let's move on with the mains,' and Tom chatted easily to everyone about carving duck breasts.

V

Claire carved the crisp ducklings on wooden boards beside Tom who sliced the ham, the aniseed of the cloves filling the room, the glaze sticky between his fingers. Together with Lara, carrying platters, they served the table. Then Tom took a seat, and as requested by Claire, he made a toast to everyone's good health.

'Mam would love to see this, Claire,' Brian said.

'Not that she would touch a morsel of food,' Conor said.

Doll looked at Prof awkwardly as Máire dropped her cutlery down gently and dabbed her face a minute with her serviette, before excusing herself from the table to use the bathroom.

The conversation turned to Christmas Day – who would do what, where everyone would be – and most people agreed that Christmas Day was much to do about very little, and even caused a lot of pain.

Doll told a story about how her father had often kept a carp in the bath on Christmas Eve, though it was a Polish tradition and he was Serbian, from a little village outside Belgrade. Her grandfather was Polish, she said, and he had started the tradition, and her father had first killed a carp with a heavy stone to the head when he was six. Her father had asked Doll to do it, shouting at her in the bathroom: 'Smash it, smash it, come on, do it.' She refused. It was all so disconcerting as a young child, she said – when everyone else in school was awaiting the arrival of Santa, Doll was awaiting the murder in the morning of the fish she had made her friend. Her father would gut it, because her mother, despite being from Connemara and the daughter of a fisherman, wanted no hand in the murder of a fish. Doll said eating it later in the day made her gag and cry. When everyone was drinking, she scraped it into the bin before heading upstairs to bed, and for the most part no one noticed. After Doll had told the story, Prof was crying softly and she put her hand on Doll's knee next to her.

'It's OK', said Doll, 'I like to go unnoticed, you should know this. Also, it's hardly that bad, it was a silly fish, we are eating the underside of a pig and a family of ducklings.' She suddenly felt defensive of her father. But still there was something about a child being forced to kill a fish at Christmas that had upset the table, even Joe, who said that Christmas was about happiness and joy for children, but everyone there also knew this to be a fallacy.

'My father drowned pups in barrels by the side of the Old House,' Conor said suddenly.

'No,' Lara said, 'stop it, please. Just don't.'

'What?' Conor said. 'It's life. I had to do it too. Claire was never asked.'

'It's not everyone's life,' Prof said, 'with respect.'

'Oh, respect noted,' Conor said petulantly, lifting some duck meat on to the tines of his fork, and he smiled, oddly. 'Respect noted.' He looked around the rest of the table, landing his focus on Lara: 'Lara, it was the only way to cull them. Little groups in hessian sacks and lowered—'

'Just leave it, Conor,' Lara said. 'Stop it. Please.' But he didn't. He went on talking about it, about the hessian sack, the bitch sad and her tits hanging, dragging after her, and then weeks moping by the back door.

Brian was upset and he too asked his brother to stop.

'I'm checking on the children,' Lara said scraping her chair from the table, and eyeing her husband. She rose to move. Máire had not returned from the toilet. 'I'll check on Máire too.'

'You do you, darling,' Conor said.

'What do you call a boomerang that doesn't return?' Doll asked.

'Lucky,' Conor said.

With the plates cleared away, everyone agreed that air was needed, or a smoke, a vape, or even a short walk before dessert.

'Don't know where you'd walk to,' Prof said, peering out through a window at the dark. She took her wine glass and headed into the living room, filled the stove and turned up some music. 'I'm going nowhere.'

'Do you want help, Claire?' Doll asked.

'No, no, thanks but it's easier if I clear by myself, with Lara,' Claire said. 'She knows where everything goes.'

'Fair,' Doll said, following after Prof with another can of beer. 'Thanks again, it was really something.' And everyone agreed about the loveliness of it all, before filing out and leaving Lara and Claire together in the kitchen.

The men headed outside. Though Conor didn't smoke, he took a bottle of Chablis with him by the neck, and Tom helped Claire with some clearing, kissing her softly on the mouth by the sink, and Claire was happy and relieved with the way of the night. 'No, go out to the men,' she said to him, when she broke from his lips, like her mother would have said.

'Why?' Tom asked.

'I dunno,' she said. 'It would be rude not to. Please,' she said, dropping her head to the side. 'For me.'

'OK,' he said, unsure of what he'd have to say to them. He took a bottle of spirits from the draining board, mocked a stagger, and Claire laughed as he kissed her gently. 'Man talk.'

Lara and Claire swept the floor, turned on the dishwasher, washed the glassware by hand and dried each piece carefully. They placed items back in the fridge, cut up the rest of the meats and wrapped them in foil, lit some new candles, placed more wine in the fridge, cut fresh wedges of limes for drinks, prepped the plum puddings and put a pot of coffee on the stove to percolate. Máire had not returned to the kitchen, and when the coffee pot whistled, Claire lifted it from the stove and went to check on her. Lara went to check on the children, and soon she fell asleep, Josh tucked under her arm, Leah wormed up and flat out at the end of the bed.

'Máire, Máire,' Claire said, gently tapping on the door, 'open up. Are you OK?'

The key turned in the bathroom door. Máire's face was red and swollen, she was crying gently, sitting back on the edge of the bath with a facecloth in her hands.

VI

Joe said: 'A grand clear night,' as Brian lifted the huge bolt to the Old House and dragged it across until it was free of its holder. Inside, Brian tapped about on the whitewashed wall and turned on a switch. A bare bulb hanging from the rafters gave him enough light to seat himself on a small pony trap set in the middle of the floor, where he set to fixing a joint. The other men looked about them: old bicycles were hanging by the back wall, a well-worn Belfast sink was cracked right through the centre, a wheelbarrow had a flat tyre, the remnants of some type of plough lay about beside the neck brace of a carthorse. There were some old engine parts, horseshoes hung up and down, luck and no luck, some were huge, bigger than a human head, rusted and out of use for decades now. The place stank of cat's piss and earthen clay.

The old kitchen where they stood, by far the largest space in the house, had a concrete floor, uneven, and some cats scarpered from the loft, where a long ladder hung down. The loft was an open space just above the kitchen with no railing or guard to catch a child that might stray from sleep. Tom walked to the back door, it was a half-door, and he inspected it.

'That used to be the front of the house,' Joe said. 'So we just came in the back door.'

'I never knew that,' Brian said.

'Yes, it looked out to the field, see. So it was more useful.'

'Hurry up, Brian, for fuck's sake, or we'll catch our death,' Conor said, going to sit on an old water barrel.

Brian licked the joint, sealed it, then sparked it. Joe stood with his hands in his pockets, refused the smoke. 'Never interested me,' he said, shaking his head and pursing his lips. 'Máire said I'm calm enough without adding to it. Horizontal may have been the exact phrase.' The men laughed. Joe sipped from a bottle of whiskey instead. They spoke about bicycles, front brakes that were lethal when they were kids and caused many a stitch on a chin from flinging over the handlebars. They showed each other war wounds and cuts. Conor told a funny story about fixing a chain on a long ride up the Alps once, and Tom chatted on about the kind of intense cycling he liked to do, and after some while, Brian asked him what it was like to be back, and then corrected himself realising that Tom Morton wasn't back, he was arrived, and for all intents and purposes, he was new.

'We haven't seen much of you about the place,' Joe said. Joe was used to neighbours working on farms. It was hard to understand what a man like Tom could be doing cooped up at a computer all day, writing words about the more extraordinary lives of other people.

'You would be surprised how fast a day can go by,' Tom said.

Brian took a long inhale, held the smoke in for a few

moments. Conor refused any more, he shook his head, and folded his arms.

'You can make time do strange things when you sit looking out a window, trying to find the right words in the right order and all of that.'

'It's nice to see Claire in such good form,' Joe said, introducing the topic.

'It is,' Brian said. 'It was hard, you know – I think it was hard on her when Mam died.'

'It was hard on us all,' Conor said.

'Yes,' Tom said, as he walked about, 'it did seem to really—' and then he stopped for a minute. 'Badly affect her. Might be a daughter thing.'

'How do you mean?' Conor said. The men sensed tension. He had known more than either of his siblings of his mother's demise. His father had leaned on him, in a way, in muttered phone calls, and Conor had confronted him on one occasion about Anne's treatment at the hands of her husband, his father, and that didn't end well. Eventually, like Claire, he had taken some distance, but not as much.

'Oh, just, she wasn't herself for a while in London, hardly got out of bed, not cooking, not washing, drinking—' Tom interjected.

'Washing?' Brian said, taken aback by the comment.

'Herself. Mostly neglecting herself,' he said.

The three men grew quiet now. Joe glanced at the ground.

'I was surprised she made the move home,' Joe said, 'but I'm glad for Máire.'

259

Brian nodded.

'I dunno,' Conor said, hands folded, as he eyed Tom now who took a swig from a bottle. He was sat on a narrow racer bike. 'I dunno, she just seems, it's not together as such, I can't quite get to grips with it, but she seems . . . different—'

'Happy?' Tom said. 'She seems so happy at the moment, and so – capable.'

'Yes, capable,' Brian said, impressed by his sister's spread, by her phone calls of late and her sudden and welcome interest in his life. In his boyfriends, or lack of. His social life. Work.

'No, no,' Conor said, pensive now, 'it's not that, it's not that at all, she seems, you know, all this cooking tonight, I mean, what was that all about?'

'It was delicious,' Joe said, missing the point.

'Yes, yes, it certainly was,' Conor said, 'certainly fucking delicious,' his hyper-articulation on his consonants now.

'Aye, aye, a grand feed indeed,' Joe said.

Tom cycled a little forward and back on the bike, the wheel ticked.

'No, it's more, I wouldn't say she seemed nervous, but she seems to have lost something. Don't get me wrong – I always thought Claire was missing something, but it was Claire, and I liked her for it – it made her who she was. You know?'

'We've all lost something,' Tom said. 'Age maybe, or time.'

Conor felt Tom was making excuses.

He stood up. 'She was fun, more fun at least, even

when she was irritated. Or irritating. Nothing ever came together quite right.'

'Ah, sure, we all grow up,' Joe said.

'Do we?' Conor said, watching Tom closely, dragging his shoes along the dusty ground. 'But do we change?'

'You've been here less than twenty-four hours, Conor.' Brian defended his sister.

'Change?' Joe said. 'Maybe I mean changed, you're right.'

'She seems to pay such close attention to everything now,' Tom said, as though it were entirely unremarkable. 'I only have to feel hungry and there's food, or she has decorated the entire lower bedrooms.'

'I noticed,' Brian said. 'Every room has a manifest-ation of hope.'

'What now?' Joe said.

'Tat,' Conor said, 'tat, every room has some rubbish to tell you to keep going to fuck.'

'I think it's nice,' Brian said. 'So, she's changed. Maybe it's good. We've all changed.'

'She's Mother,' Conor said flatly.

'No,' Brian said, 'that's unfair.'

'On who?' Conor said.

No one answered him.

'She's hyper-vigilant,' Conor said.

Everyone eyed the floor. Conor's temper seemed ill-placed. Tom noticed an old sack that had been nailed to a low rafter, hopped off the bike a moment, and tugged at it, lifting it off to distract them. Conor watched him closely.

'Look,' Tom said, tracing his finger along some words.
'What is it?' Joe said, moving closer to look.

'It's nothing,' Brian said, 'throw the sack back over it.'

'No, no, look,' Tom said, tracing along the beam
again. 'There's something carved here, wait.' He ran a
slim finger over and back of it, then turned his head
to the side, to read almost upside down. 'Wait, wait, it
says –' and he laughed – 'what the actual fuck, it says,
I killed the pig of the pigs. Yeah, that's right, that's what it
says.' He shook his head. 'What's with the subterfuge,
what the fuck does that mean? Is it about cops?' he said
looking around at the faces.

Joe put down the bottle of whiskey. Brian deadened
his smoke as Conor rose from his feet.

'No, no, Conor,' Joe said, moving across the floor.
'Fuck, no. Don't, settle, he doesn't mean it, he has no
idea about this. He doesn't know.'

'He knows damn fucking well what he's saying,' Conor
said, and bounded the few feet towards him.

'He doesn't.'

'Stop,' Brian says, 'he has no idea.'

Tom stood still and moved only to lift his hands, as
though to signal retreat, or nothing-to-see, as though to
say something. The bicycle he had propped now, top-
pled and the others waited a moment. But Conor was
full of spirit.

'Sit fucking down, Conor,' Brian said.

'What the fuck did you just say?' Conor said, squarely
to Tom.

'Tom, go!' Joe urged, but Conor was face-to-face with him now. Tom didn't concede an inch.

'Say it again,' Conor said. 'G'wan, I fucking dare you, Tom Morton, read it, g'wan. Out loud, nice and slowly, fucking dare ya—'

'Look, I'm sorry, I have no idea what—'

'Conor, Conor, stop,' Brian said. 'He *has* no idea, this is absolutely crazy, you've had a lot to drink.' Tom didn't take his eyes off Conor, and Conor swept fast behind him and lifted his right hand and went to catch Tom's neck.

'Sit back fucking down,' Joe roared, 'you lunatic, or you'll regret this, Conor. It has absolutely nothing to do with Tom.'

'So here, this, this is what it fucking says. You want to know? I'll fucking tell you—' Conor said. 'There was a knock, Morton, a knock on this door here . . .'

Mountain Ellen, Athenry

1920

Knock
Knock
Knock
Knock
Knock

Let us in let us in by the hair of your chinny chin chins,
'you Fenian bastards, you'll let us in, do you hear us?'
   and in they came,
   breaking the door off its hinge and Paddy rose fast to
come between the men and his son Pat who on hearing
the banging was making sounds and had his head in his
hands. Lily dropped the kettle into the fire, the blackandtan men stood about them, smaller than the Irish men,
   with their noses up against them,
   'I smell pig shit of these Fenian bastards,' one said.
'You can do the search, Andrew, wouldn't get too close,
can never tell what you'd catch.'
   But the man did come close to Lily, sniffing her, and
she could feel his breath on her. He moved closer again
to her, and he ran his fingers along her lips and down to
the curve of her breasts. The boys stood and looked at

the stone flag of the ground, it was too late to run. Jack stood, eyes down too. Pat couldn't make it to the flour bin, he was on his feet now, and shouted and came to him, to the man, and lifted his hands and shoved him from his mother.

Lily cried out, and the blackandtan lifted his rifle butt and struck Pat in the temple by his wide eyes that never looked in the same direction. The boy turned white and fell to the ground, a foam from his mouth, pinkish, where he lay to experience his first moments of dying – which would take a little while, but he would die quiet and silent, watchful of his mother.

Yes, in they came into the house and into the kitchen, one took a fistful of raisins and stuffed them into his mouth.

Lily beside herself now, sobbing.

Paddy said: 'God is good, God is good, wife, hold yer whisht, lad,' and Lily went and stood by her son – the young man that would become the grandfather, Jack, and go on to raise good sons, save for one, his youngest John who he said had a bad kink of the violence, who he said seemed to remember the atmosphere, and who he would grow afraid of, and no one could make reason of it – and Jack froze for those moments, and dreamed about it for the rest of his life.

Jack stood still and Lily stood by him and by Thomas while the blackandtans were pointing and shouting, looking for guns, and roaring about the O'Shaughnessys and they mocked the crockery set on the shabby table, and there were some out abroad at the log-house and calling out.

Lily was feeling weak, but held her nerve, for she had the younger boys up in the loft all silent under the hessian sack, and she was afraid of her life if the youngest would sneeze or call out.

The men, well, they looked around at the bread on the table as they finished the raisins. Thomas was hungry in his belly and felt the hot stream of piss between his narrow legs flood the stone floor, and wondered how he managed to make a stream so large.

'Fucking dirty Fenians, where are you hiding him, eh?' one man shouted into his ear, and then he demanded that the two boys take their pants off and Lily screamed but was slapped hard in her face.

'Trousers off, right now. What are you all hiding, eh?'

Lily closed her eyes to pray while they stripped her sons and their penises were startlingly among the thicket of black hair on both their groins. She had not seen the boys naked since they grew to men-boys. They stood with shirts loose and naked arses over their brother convulsing on the stone flag of the simple kitchen.

'Out, out, ye two fucking cunts, out,' the men roared at Jack and Thomas, and were angry they had not recovered a gun by now, and out into the garden they were brought with their hands over their heads, the bigger man of the blackandtans, who was missing a front tooth and all the rest rotted in his head, strung rope around their narrow ankles and hung them up on the horse-pole beside the barrels of rainwater, and flogged them until they both passed out. Neither roared. Not once.

And to Lily then.

It went like this:

'Come out come out whoever you are and give me a key, you Fenian fucks, and come out come out and show me your Fenian guns,' they kept shouting about the place and then—

Fee-fi-fo-fum – 'You have a gun, mother?' they said, their twisted-up faces in her hair, and then, quiet a moment, suddenly speech took her over, and she spoke with courage: 'I do not, go home, go home, we have no want for you here, we are simple people, we are simple to our souls – go back to where ye came from,' she howled.

'Or else?'

'Or else, God will judge you all,' she screamed now at them, manically, pointing her fingers and her face curled up in pain.

Paddy said: 'Shh, shh, woman. Whisht now, for the love of God. Bí cúramach, ná habair faic.'

'The fucking Irish, and their prayers.'

'I don't know what we ever did to the Irish but try to help them,' one said to the other.

'Savages,' another said, and took the heel of his boot to Paddy's bicycle by the gable of the house.

'There's no helping the Irish. Too thick.' They all laughed.

Then one pulled the woman out of the cottage by

her hair, and out with her into the yard where Jack hung from the pole and was writhing.

Lily blessed herself and then the four or five soldiers, for they called themselves soldiers to each other, reached up and said you have a gun and she did, for she had held it in her drawers.

'She has it in her whore drawers,' said one to the other.

'I have it in my chemise,' she said, 'you might mistake us for bogtrotters –' and she articulated perfectly now, for she knew what was coming, and would at least be articulate in this moment and give herself some dignity – 'but we are good people.' She patted his head as he yanked up her skirts and pulled the gun from her. 'And you are not. Pat O'Connor is an innocent boy now, may God have mercy on your soul. I am older than your mother,' she said to him and he struck her hard on the face until it bled. 'I am, and you know this and she would be ashamed of you.' Lily was fired up and felt she had nothing more to give to God, all her kindest children were gone now. And she cared less what happened to her.

The chamber of the gun they took from her was empty. He threw it to the wet ground, unzipped his fly and turned her to the wall, where he stuck her face to the cold of the whitewash and put his hand over her mouth – it tasted of raisins. He entered her roughly and penetrated her for a short time, before he passed her over, on and on – she didn't keep count, and now she didn't make a sound at all, for she did nothing to distract Paddy down on the floor inside next to Pat.

Lily was hopeful he was giving him his last rites. Paddy rubbed the dead eyes of his son, and patting the gentle boy's fat face, cried into him. As Lily out the yard kept her eyes closed tightly, she thought how Pat had gone to the girls, for it was too cruel a world for the likes of him. She was happy when she heard Paddy shout the prayers, that maybe her son was still alive long enough to be absolved of all sin and he would leave her in a state of grace.

Then she prayed mad in her head, her face against the cold wall, her body on fire, to her deceased mother and father to watch over her and not make her carry a child for these devil men – if they could intercede in any way at this moment, it was to do this for her, and to take Pat to them quickly and without pain.

The blackandtans zipped up their trousers and took to walking on up the narrow country road as a blackbird was making a rumbling, and up the road they walked, when one turned and came back to the house, the toothless one, and took his knife from his inside pocket, and went into the shed and slit the throat of the cow, and next the pig. He took his knife and went back inside and into the rafters he scraped and scraped there for what felt to them like an eternity.

Jack hung with his eyes wide open now and watched the gossamer unfold as a spider spun a web and kept the ordeal to himself his whole life, never breathed a word to anyone.

*

The woman howled and howled as the men took final leave, drowning out the blackbird, and the neighbours came to look after the sons' injuries, and she tried to catch the blood of the pig in her hands to make something with it to eat.

Mountain Ellen, Athenry

2022

VII

'You're crying for a reason,' Claire said to Máire in the claustrophobic confines of the bathroom. 'It's not like you, was it something someone said?'

'It's just, it's being in the house, it's a lot.'

Máire had so much love for Claire's mother. Claire herself found it hard to fathom and wondered if it was because Máire had lost her own mother when she was young.

'I know,' Claire said, kindly, passing some tissues and rubbing her back.

'I just, I feel sometimes, you know, that I could have, maybe I could have done something. It was all so—'

'Fast,' Claire said.

Máire nodded, blowing her nose hard.

'I could never get my head around it all,' Claire said. 'It was so fast—'

'Around what?' Máire stopped crying, and was serious, low and formal in her tone, and cautious too, she'd been drinking, she shared bad news with people every day as a nurse, sometimes she was unsure of who had said what to whom. She stared at Claire who was kneeling down by the bath looking into her eyes. She ran her hands through Claire's hair, she remembered plaiting it when they were young. She would knot long daisies into it.

'Here, let me,' Claire said, 'your mascara is running.' She dabbed wet tissue under her friend's eye, gently.

Máire held her wrists. 'Around what?' Máire said again.

'Her dying, so young, Mother, and she wasn't sick.'

'Oh, Claire,' Máire said, and then she blurted out: 'She refused to eat, for a long time. I can't let you go on like this. Not knowing.'

Claire froze. She widened her eyes. For a minute her whole body felt like it had doubled in size, blood whooshed about, mostly to her heart, and then her face. She reddened as Máire looked at her with an intense and unnerving focus and let her wrists go. She stood back from her friend as though to take her all in.

'I am so sorry. Nothing anyone could say would make her change her mind. She had refused to eat for months.'

Claire stood absolutely still. Máire reached for her again. 'She didn't want to . . .'

'What?' Claire said.

'Nurse him. Nurse John. She didn't want to be left with him,' Maire said.

The Black Mare and I

I didn't move, not at first: the mare was blowing out softly, her nostrils dripping with warm mucus. I wondered if horses could cry like I did. Shep had come to life and was sat by the mare's hind legs in solidarity, yes, the dog had survived, which was a small mercy now that the future of the bungalow was ruined. Then again, it was a brittle future in any case if it was destined by the whims of these English men.

I stood by the fence, still, waiting in front of the Old House as I pressed my shaking hands to the mare's neck to curb the bleeding. It was crusting over, but I could feel the smooth texture of her gut beneath my skin, pulsating. I panicked that the mare would die, if not of bleeding out, then of shock. So I knew somewhere in me that if I didn't move in some direction, or someone take some action, the results would be final. That said, taking independent action was rarely rewarded on the farm but often punished. There would, no doubt, be retaliation, but it was impossible to read Father now. He was ranting. Any move could have ended everything. Myself. Mother. The Mare.

'You have to call the vet,' I said eventually, shaking now, and cold, sure I would pass out. My throat was tight.

Father put his head in his hands, but after a little while

he lifted it slowly, as though he would have made the whole bad situation disappear. Or worse, he looked at me like he had never seen me before in his whole life. Lips chalk pale now, dried spittle on the sides of his mouth.

I considered quickly who might be to blame. For blame would be attributed as always.

Me?

I wasn't my best observational self. I was doing a job that I had never done before. I was sick and distracted. I was unable to hold the rope.

The mare?

She was skittish and uncertain. Though in her favour she was a brave horse and she was tired after her great hunt. Poor bitch. Unwittingly, she had worked for her freedom and now here she was, ruined. She might be destroyed.

Father?

Father had not checked the box. Father was Father. He destroyed people. And animals. The nail came from somewhere. How do you have a horsebox with an exposed nail?

It was futile running questions in my head: he darted about the place like a lunatic, on fire, and dancing as though every moment were a threat, that the sky would fall in, or had fallen in, as though we were all threats, all of his children.

'Is it bad?' he said.

'Yes. It's very bad,' I said. I will never be sure where

the courage to say this came from. I have not considered it often until now.

'They'll never want her now, fuck, sure they won't, they'll never take her from me now. Who wants a ruined mare? Can't show a horse off in Buckingham fucking Palace with its throat slit.'

I didn't respond.

So he did what he always did when I didn't respond, he said it louder, and louder again, until soon, as I stood there with her guts throbbing in my hands, he did exactly as I predicted – he shouted and ranted on about something else, someone's inadequacy, likely it was me, and it attracted attention from the house, and predictably, Mother came to us, her face a sheet of worry.

'Is everything OK?' she said as she waited at the back door.

Silence.

'Claire, what's going on? You are all making a terrible racket.' I hadn't uttered a sound at all. But we knew what she meant, simpler to challenge me.

'Oh, Jesus,' she said, 'the mare, is the mare OK?' As she walked to the scene, she eyed Shep furtively, and my shaking, bloodied hands.

Silence again. The silence must have overwhelmed Father as he took off roaring at her, chasing her, and in the short distance that lay between them, roaring at her as though she had intentionally slit the mare's throat, and she ran and ran fast now, and ran past me to the Old House where the large door was open, the simple bulb bright.

'Don't you say another fucking word. You have me

277

cursed, you stupid bitch,' he said as he went on and roared at Mother. 'You and your fucking spells, and your bad energy.'

And then he drifted to noise, incomprehensible, and then to the worst insult you can call a woman according to Mother. But it wasn't. There are far worse.

I knew I needed to follow her to save her. I also needed to go to the toilet, the pressure was intense. I was halfway between the bungalow and the Old House, and I looked at the right eye of the horse, her black puffy eyelid was closing on her deep brown eye, and she was about to give in.

'No, no, don't do that, good girl, don't,' I said. 'No, wait a while, come on, we'll get you help,' whispering softly into her ear as her head dropped to me and her coat on her neck was hard and crusted, warm, and the daylight was all gone. I wanted to rub her coat all across her body and over the rump of her hindquarters as she stood there shivering but I could not let her neck free for fear of what would fall from it. She could tangle herself on her own insides. I held the heel of my left hand against her neck hard as I looped her lead rope around the tarred fence with my right, and tried to pull my pullover with one arm and my teeth off my body. I was too warm in any case. Eventually it came free.

I waited in the cold of the night now in my shirt, as I wrapped the blue woollen jumper tight around the mare's neck and pulled the two sleeves until they held around her like a neckerchief.

'Now,' I said. I think I was crying. 'Now, good girl.'

I was,

my face was wet,

I remember, perhaps I was sweating now, the pressure making me faint: 'Now, look,' I whispered, 'you're just like a cowboy.'

On both sides of my tight knot in the soft jumper a great bulging could be seen as I bolted to the doors of the Old House, pulling it open to me. The shadow of the horse loomed large on the ground from where she stood outside, the little window at the front letting in light, was it the moon? I was opening it so gently so as not to make a sound, I was sure I would find them by the sound of his voice, berating her over and over. But not a word. Just a gasp, was it a gasp? and another gasp, were they dancing? a waltz? and in the dim light, the beams to the loft, the smell of burned tar and the piss smell of feral cats, where were they now, I wondered, where had the cats gone? A teapot had fallen over, and was cracked in two, some paint cans were upended, and one spilled apricot paint across the grey flagstone.

At first it looked indeed like they were dancing, so grace-ful on the large shadow of the horse, her feet like a ballerina, but lifted up from the stone flag, at first, yes, he looked like he had lifted her in a waltz. Or maybe he was helping her up to the loft, and soon my arms were on his back, clawing at him, and I was climbing up along him, and pulling myself up the strong hair of his forearms from behind. I remember him giving me a piggyback across the beach once, and the dog bounding ahead, we had raced Conor carrying Brian and they had fallen over, and we won.

I hooked my hands onto his and dragged, and was pulling his fingers free, one by one, until I pulled the last one, his little finger, a baby finger, that was twisted from a break and had not reset correctly. It sat over the rest of his hand like a mourner. The fingers were damp and pliant and they unhooked from her thin pale neck easily, like I was opening the action figure belonging to one of the boys, something they had gotten for Christmas, the kind of thing that they would attach to something, a parachute, or a bridge.

'Stop,' I said, 'the mare. She's not— Please, stop, stop.'

Like a puppet cut from strings, she slipped to the flaggy stone floor of the house, a wallop on the ground, and cried out a little and she lay curled in a ball, her hand on her head, holding it, until I went to her.

'It's OK, it's OK,' I whispered. 'He's gone.'

He was gone, yes, yes, he went to the phone, to the vet to see if he could reclaim any of the fortune that escaped him.

I went to bed soon after I knew Mother was OK.

I slept on for days in a haze of fever and dreams. Looking back, I never wanted to leave the bed. For days I couldn't feel my legs. I wanted to take to it, like they did then, women, with an ailment of the mind, or so the men said. Take to it and never get out. But like thoughts of death, I cleared it from my mind, I unlearned the scene bit by bit. After some weeks, I visited the mare in her shed, rubbed oil on her scar, a thin long ropey thing, that didn't stop her being who she was but stopped her being who she could perhaps have been, and got on with things.

I forgave him in the bedroom before he died. I didn't tell him, he wasn't looking for forgiveness. He burned on until the end, no one was enough for him. I reasoned that I didn't know what it was like to raise a family on a few acres of stone and rock, I didn't fully know what kind of wage package a postman got, or what he had been through, what had set such an unquenchable anger in him, fear, was it fear of not having enough to cover the basics. Mother never spoke of that night. Though she showed flashes of resolve, his rage still and often got the better of him, and he would land a punch or a kick on us. Until eventually I saw nothing but resignation in Mother, and a clipped tone, that she often used to tell me: 'You don't know how good you have it, Claire O'Connor,' she used to say, 'swanning around London town with your fancy degrees and not a care in the world. Not to mind coming home the odd time to see us.'

'I'll be home for Christmas,' I said.

'You will,' she said, 'but you won't be home for good, never.'

'The man who made work, made plenty of it, Claire,' Father would say for years after to me, as though it was a way of telling me he had been up against it, and what would I know of the ways of a man who left school at fourteen. All different now, all different. He demeaned books, my learning, and my head stuck in them, striking me a few more times as I entered adulthood, like he had when I was a child, striking me for learning, for not learning, for being a woman, for not being a man, striking me for bleeding on the flagstone of the Old House, finally for the last time beating me because Brian didn't want a woman and we all knew this, and it was my fault, because Brian had told me, arrah, we had all cursed him, it was us, he said, something had cursed his existence until he died to the whirring of a fan and a grandchild who was placed into a cot in the next room for a long sleep after suckling on the breast of a woman.

Mother brought me medicine for days after, things to help me, sanitary pads, big bulky things that never stayed in place, old cups of water, and rubbed my face, crying now and then as she brushed my hair. I watched the bruises on her neck, at first so angry and purple and unwanted, but they faded day by day to a sunshine yellow, and soon they were gone, and I was relieved at this, that after some days they faded to the track of a love mark, the kind of mark someone leaves on you in passion, in a moment of orgasm, or a moment of ownership. How close both sensations feel.

Mountain Ellen, Athenry

2022

VIII

At first Máire thought she imagined it, that maybe it was the graceless cry of a bird awakened, or a fox caught up in some wire. But then Claire heard it too, and they waited to listen again. Claire lifted her eyes up and to the left to concentrate on the sound. Then she bolted to the door with Máire behind her and pulled back the patio doors, and ran fast across the yard.

The doors were ajar.

Inside the large old kitchen, Tom Morton was stood deathly still, his eyes were numb in his head and Claire and Máire stopped running and lay their hands down by their sides. Máire flashed her eyes to Joe, who widened them as if to say he was as surprised as the women. But best not to move. Or interfere.

'Conor,' Máire said softly now, 'Conor, what happened? There's no need for this – whatever it is. Is there a row?'

Her eyes met Tom's and he was quiet. She looked at Joe.

'He's mocking us, Máire,' Conor said, 'he's fucking

mocking us,' and shook his head. 'He made a joke about us, about us, and you, and Joe.'

'Jesus Christ,' Brian said, 'stop this. No one mocked anyone.'

'Look,' Conor said, 'look at this, you see, my sister, well, she has turned into some kind of – I don't know, some kind of fucking freak.'

'Conor,' Claire said, crying, 'stop it.'

'Crying, Claire?' he said. 'That's not like you, and this, this guy,' he said, pointing at Tom. 'Like, what's with all the perfection, I can see what's going on here, I have watched you all night, terrified of him. Lara even remarked on it. It's weird, Claire, you're weird now.'

'What?' Claire said in shock.

'You heard me, and you've turned into Mam, and look how that fucking ended,' he said. He was crying now too, and spitting hard. 'One minute you're living it up in London, all relaxed, and the next you're serving little bites of food on fucking doilies. What happened to you?' He stared at his sister squarely, then turned to Tom: 'No one fucking wants you here, Tom.'

'I do,' Claire said. Picking herself up a little, she rubbed her nose, raised her voice: 'I want him here.'

'Yet another fucking interloper,' Conor said. 'Haven't we had enough of them already?'

'Stop that,' Máire said, 'stop it, too much bloody shouting in this house for many lifetimes!' Máire shocked Conor. She had never berated any of them.

'It's nothing to do with, it's not . . . I am certainly not

284

terrified of Tom,' Claire said, and she ran to him. 'It's nothing to do with him. I'll bloody well do as I please, and all your anger, Conor, well, it's your own fucking business to deal with, surely you can get a big therapist above in Dublin? And for what it's worth, though its none of your business, I am nothing like my mother. Maybe it's you – maybe you're just like your father, but that's for you to decide.'

She pushed her brother hard now and he hung his arms by his side, defeated, and took to panic, saying over and over how sorry he was, and how sorry he was. Claire turned away from Conor and went back to Tom and hugged him, Tom who hugged her back, saying: 'I'm fine, I'm OK. It's OK. I didn't know. I had no idea of that story.'

'How would you?' she said. 'What did you need to know? Nothing.' She turned to tell Conor to pack now and leave. Josh was waiting at the door, his pyjama top hanging limply from his hand, his bare chest, and with Lara behind him, as he had crept from his bed to follow the sounds of his daddy.

IX

Lara packed her children into the car, and drove away back to Dublin at three a.m., the time for dead souls and catastrophe. Doll and Prof were in an embrace asleep in the living room as a film about space played out loudly. It would have been an event to cause great ruptures in the ordinary life of Claire O'Connor and her colleagues, but now Claire was very glad of the distraction of someone else's tryst. Doll's top was fully undone, and Prof was lying beside her. Claire rang them both a taxi, that arrived shortly after.

'Where's everyone gone?' Prof asked. 'Shit, sorry,' she said, confused, and then drunkenly thanked Claire over and over, and walked into the bathroom instead of out the front door, but Doll dragged her along. Claire waved at them without a word, but with relief that at least her family were hidden from them.

'Do you need us to stay?' Máire asked Claire in the kitchen.

'No, but can you take Conor?' Claire said. 'Please.'

'We will if he'll come with us,' Joe said and went to the bedroom where Conor was sat on his bed with his head in his hands crying hard now.

'Conor, Conor,' Joe whispered, 'come on, good man, we'll head over to ours.'

Conor was compliant. 'I didn't mean it,' he said, a number of times, he said he was sorry, in the pathetic way people do when the adrenaline wears off, and he hugged Joe, and cried. For this reprieve, Joe was grateful. 'I just, I find it so . . .'

'Shh, good man, no need for words now.'

After everyone left, Brian and Tom and Claire sat around the kitchen table.

'I'm so sorry,' Claire said. 'I don't know, I have no idea what came over him.'

Tom was quiet as Brian made some tea, and Brian was pale now also, and didn't seem to offer much in terms of psychoanalysis but more in the way of immediate soothing. Tea mostly.

A tap came soon after to the patio door and Johanna stood outside shivering in a wax coat. Tom jumped up when he saw her and turned and said: 'I'm heading off.'

Claire felt like she had been wounded. 'Oh,' she said, 'I didn't know, I hadn't known, you called Johanna.'

'I think it's for the best now, given the night we've had,' Tom said, gently.

'Please, don't,' Claire said.

'I think I should,' he said.

Brian consoled his sister. Eventually the exhausted conversation came around to what Máire had disclosed in the bathroom.

'Claire, I tried to tell you, we all did, Máire even wanted to go to London, but you wouldn't hear of it. It broke Conor. He just still can't get his head around it. I'm not excusing him, but he's not well.'

'Why would she do it? It's such an awful way—'

'We all know why she did it,' Brian said, flatly. 'Why would she not do it?'

Claire winced.

'Who could go on living with that man? No one – but there was no talking to him, and cleaning and cooking for him, and he was getting worse, his patience with her, and temper, it was no way for any woman to live.'

'But she was always so, abrupt – on the phone, when I came home, she never wanted to talk.'

'What's the point in talking?' Brian said. 'And she was hurt, she saw us leaving as abandoning her.'

'We didn't abandon her – that's crazy talk.'

'We did, Claire, we really did, sure there was no point in talking to us then, we were young and living our own lives. I could rarely come home without the remarks about men, or a wife, or a lack of, it was stifling. You didn't want to know, Claire. I remember ringing you in London over and over just after Mam had passed. You stopped me, so I was sure you knew, I was sure you had been told.'

Claire shook her head.

'It's so hard,' he said, 'being here, in this house, without her, and you have –' he eyed her – 'you have turned into a version of her, just a little, and I think it terrified Conor.'

'I think you're wrong, I have no idea—'

'No idea of what?' Brian said.

'How to be,' she said, flatly.

'How to be?'

'Yes, how to be, how to keep Tom. How to live without being terrified all the fucking time. Just how. I'm so exhausted.'

'How to *keep* Tom?'

'I was so, so—'

'He's here,' Brian said. 'Tom. Isn't that enough? He wouldn't be here if he didn't want to be, trust me. Showing up. It's all there is. Tom's going nowhere.'

'He's not here now,' Claire said.

'Ah, to be fair, he'd had drink, she's his only friend around here. If he wanted Johanna wouldn't he be with her?'

'I don't know.'

'Do you love him?'

'Yes.'

'That's enough then. You can't *keep* someone no matter how many fucking puddings you make them. Come on, you're so much smarter than this.'

Claire laughed softly. 'Is love enough though? We have no way of knowing—'

'Knowing what?'

'If I can love?'

'Of course you can love, you're full of daft love, Claire O'Connor – and that's both to your credit and your madness.'

*

Brian O'Connor knew everything about his sister. He knew also how hard it was to love in the aftermath of all they had witnessed. He had lived his life trying to trust men, a man, find one, love one. He had spent long nights worrying about his brother and his sister, and mostly he was ravaged with a huge sadness at the waste of a life his mother had endured. As the night went on, Claire told him about trying to copy wives on the internet, chefs, anyone who might put order on her.

'You've lost your nerve,' he said. 'That's all, and you need to relax, I don't mean this in a glib way, you really do, you have a lot to say, you always had when we were young, but it seems, for whatever reason, that you have lost it, Claire. Something. You. Maybe it's the house, but if you can, look for yourself, a little at least, Jesus, do it, before it's too late.'

'What about Conor and Lara?' she asked.

'There's no talking to him. He is demented with anger. We both know that. But she's well, Lara – she is nothing if not patient.'

It was strange to be alone without Tom that night. A strangeness that was a loneliness – and Claire realised this was loneliness – and how sorry she was to be without him, and how desperately sorry she was for Anne, for her mother, both her lack of opportunity and choice. Worst of all was how she could never tell her.

Mountain Ellen, Athenry

May 2023

Claire looked out the back window of the bungalow. It was May and some red tulips had come up in the yard and over the fields. Joe Grealish was spreading slurry. The miniature bulldozer started with the roof of the Old House, pinching away layer by layer, and the other machine clawed into the guts of the building as the driver idly moved levers in the cab, swivelling every now and then to place loads into a large articulated lorry back in across the yard, beep beep it went and startled Claire. The oxidised roof crumbled fast and was followed by the teasing out of the gangrened beams, pulling them like old incisors, and by the afternoon, stone by stone, the walls of the house were dismantled. In parts, it was weakened limestone and daub, held together by twigs and clay, and some horsehair. A patch of salmon paint splashed on some wall in the front room reminded the three O'Connors, again, about the people that had peopled them. The windows were pulled out now and smashed into the back of the truck. The floor was final, and was then cracked open, dug up, darkened flag of stone by flag. There were no foundations, Claire noticed, just clay and earth and worms opened in the soil to early summer's promise.

Conor said: 'And not before time.'

'It's good to see you looking, well, a little better, brother,' Brian said.

'Thanks,' Conor said, but he was quietly reticent about his long journey, kept it with Lara, and with himself.

'We've done the right thing, right?' Claire said all of a sudden, worried that her whole world was being tipped. 'Right?'

'We've done a thing,' Brian said. 'Who knows what the right thing is. But a decision is better than no decision at all.'

'I agree,' Conor said, his eyes full of water, and his guts alarmed with it all.

Claire packed the last of the boxes erratically, and Tom filled a skip out the front on days when she was at uni, or away at a conference. He knew she would not let go, maybe she would never let it go, if she held an object in her hand, even something benign like the little jar her mother used for cotton wool balls in the bathroom. Tom dumping all of their past seemed like the only way forward, and she was grateful for it.

'I hear they're English,' Brian said, 'the buyers.'

'Is that a joke?' Tom said, concerned, looking up from kneeling as he sealed a box with a large tape dispenser.

'No, no, it's not,' Conor said, laughing, 'and good luck to them.'

*

'Claire,' Conor said later in the evening as he set about wrestling a large tea set into a box, 'I liked you better when you were doing all the mad organising.'

'No,' Tom said, 'no, we'll do just fine now, better not to mention the Organisation Period.' It made her feel like a mad artist. 'I like her with her crockery and shit falling out of all the cracks. Thank you very much.' And then he held her in a warm embrace.

They sowed some wild flowers on the site, and left Anne's photo, the one at the zoo when the pandas came where Conor is smiling, and he has his arm around his mother's neck. They left it buried on the site in a freezer bag, and Claire left a note.

When the new family of four moved in, two young boys about the yard, large daisies bloomed where they ran.

Epilogue

The sky was blue and vast and cloudless. I walked down Fifth Avenue to the park, onwards, following pace with those on the sidewalk. People were busy at the crossings, checking mobile phones, slipping things into cross-body bags, a couple were seated at Claudette's window – a queue was forming for brunch. Kids went by on scooters, backs straight like young trees, and old men with tartan rugs on their knees and large sunglasses wrapped on their faces were hunched forward, being pushed from grand apartments, out through large doors in wheelchairs along the pavement.

A couple of kids vaped by Glucksman House at NYU where I would teach a class on Irish poetry at two o'clock. I had some time to myself.

I walked on through Washington Square Garden where an excited child was having a pirate-themed birthday party just inside the arch, and a man in a sharp suit played piano by the fountain. By the right wall, some lay sleeping on benches, knees to their chests and hands in their pockets. Nearby, spoons and needles were scattered, and some tinfoil by their feet. Some trees had started to turn, and I thought of the trees in Galway down by the canal, how they changed from green to orange overnight. After a couple of blocks I ordered an Americano and sat outside a hipster café in Greenwich Village. Refuse trucks were noisily emptying bins nearby. On one corner, men in lycra played paddle tennis. I watched them, focused on the ease with which their bodies cupped over the bat, almost like a claw or a hook, and how energetic they were, and smiling. It was quietly competitive, one or two voices expressed a need to return, or score. How the body can sometimes so comfortably know what it needs.

I read over my notes on Eavan Boland. Domesticity. Imagery. Technique. A woman in a world made by men, how a woman at home was as political as a man at war. Note: Mothers alone in kitchens all day with the battle cry of babies. Notes for Myself: The domestic is political. Note: A heavy horse from a nearby camp destroying a suburban Dublin garden, plundering through it as the world around slept. Note: A couple dying at the end of a famine road, like one of the roads near Mountain Ellen. I thought about the grassy roads we had walked on as kids, one in particular that stopped abruptly for no reason in the middle of a field of heather. Rem: The road by the railway line near the bungalow that ended in the middle of a field, stopped at a dead end after being dug out, as hungry people worked for months – until the bitter end of their lives – for the promise of getting some meagre relief. Note: Working considered better than letting someone have food for no labour.

It is safe to assume that they all had died, maybe on one day, likely in the grey rain. Were they full of love or loneliness? The road had grown over fully by the time I left.

I considered how I was close by so many thoughts and ideas stuffed in books in grand libraries in this city. Close to all the abundance of art near our apartment, Van Gogh's *Starry Night*, or Leonora Carrington's *And Then We Saw the Daughter of the Minotaur*, or Kandinsky's *Blue Mountain* – I considered how they once reasoned their lives, and now I reason, and I come up so short again. I wondered what became of the people that ended up here from some provincial scene. And what of the people who peopled them who had stayed put?

'Hi,' Tom said, pulling up a seat. His canvas tote was full of paper.

'Oh, hey,' I said, leaning in to him, kissing his lips, soft and full, and then his forehead. He had a warm glow from the sun, glasses on his face and he smiled at me. I had written a couple of hundred words by the time he sat, but I wasn't going to divulge this to anyone, not until it was finished. Secrets are not always a poison, sometimes they're a tonic.

'How was the interview?'

'Good,' he said. 'It was great. He's third generation, and had a lot to tell me.'

'Great,' I said.

'He has some stories from his family, and he firmly believes it, the second-hand retelling, and so I'll record those at the very least. To be honest, I think he really wanted company and someone to listen.'

Tom's latest book was called *Tans*. He had abandoned the one he was writing, called it an eye-opening experience, but decided that he had more interest in the circumstances that lead people to where they must go, rather than those who can choose to go wherever they wish. It added a tension, he said, a juxtaposition, and was intriguing on everything from choice to opportunity.

'Where were his people from?'

'His mother was from North Tipperary, and his father's people were Connemara – but left many decades ago.'

The waiter brought an espresso outside for Tom and left it down in a neat white cup on a saucer. He tore a sugar pipe so very carefully at the top, neatly folded it, placed the contents on a tiny teaspoon and stirred it.

'Food menus?' the waiter asked.

'Yes, yes,' Tom said, smiling. 'We always eat out.'

'We've no kitchen,' Claire said, laughing.

'Well, lucky you two,' the waiter said, turning on his heel, he walked away.

Acknowledgements

I am very grateful to Dr Sarah Anne Buckley and Dr John Cunningham for their advice on this book, and for their support and collegiality over our years working together. To all my colleagues at Ollscoil na Gaillimhe/ University of Galway – thank you.

I wish to acknowledge Sophocles' *Electra* translated by Anne Carson as inspiration for the title.

Much gratitude to my mother, Catherine, for close-reading every draft – as difficult as that was. I'm very grateful to Emily Stokes for publishing an early extract of Claire and Tom's life in *The Paris Review*. To family and friends who keep me going, especially Sinéad, Rita Ann, Claire-Louise, Lisa, Róisín, John, Mike, Douglas, Amy, Edel and Alan. Thank you to Ellie Steel and Anouska Levy at Harvill Secker/Vintage for all your work on this book. Much admiration to Owen Gent and Yeti Lambregts for the cover illustration and design. Thanks, as always, to my wonderful publicity team: Mia, Sam and Hannah at Vintage; and to Gray at Penguin Studios. And thanks to the brilliant team at Penguin Random House, Ireland – Leonor, Kate, Sophie and Michael – for all their support.

To readers, book-borrowers, event organisers, librarians, teachers, booksellers, printers, box-fillers, typesetters, translators, agitators, rebels, artists, creatives, chapbook-makers, journalists, dreamers, poets, editors, protestors, students and book people everywhere – keep going!

To Ray, Jack and Finn – you are the very best.

Love and gratitude to Peter Straus – I would never have written this book without your encouragement and advice. And to all at RCW Literary Agency, especially Emer.

And, finally, to Kate Harvey, the most considered, intelligent and brave of editors – *grá mór*.

About the Author

Elaine Feeney is an acclaimed novelist and poet from the west of Ireland. Her debut novel, *As You Were*, was shortlisted for the Rathbones Folio Prize and the Irish Novel of the Year Award, and won the Kate O'Brien Award, the McKitterick Prize and the Dalkey Festival Emerging Writer Award. *How to Build a Boat* was also shortlisted for Irish Novel of the Year, longlisted for the Booker Prize, and was a *New Yorker* Best Book of the Year. Feeney has published the poetry collections *Where's Katie?*, *The Radio Was Gospel*, *Rise* and *All the Good Things You Deserve*, and lectures at the University of Galway.